THE TATE HOLLOWAY SERIES

VENGEANCE IS NOW

BY
SCOTT D. ROBERTS

Copyright © 2013 by 3L Publishing. All rights reserved. No part of this book may be reproduced or transmitted in any form or by any means, electronic or mechanical, including photocopying, recording or by any information storage and retrieval system, without the written permission of the publisher except in the case of brief quotations or except where permitted by law.

Library of Congress Control Number: 2013934937
ISBN-13: 9780989136006
Vengeance is Now Softcover Edition 2013
Printed in the United States of America

For more information about special discounts for bulk purchases, please contact 3L Publishing at 916.300.8012 or log onto our website at www.3LPublishing.com.

Book design by Erin Pace-Molina
Cover image from Shutterstock.com

ACKNOWLEDGEMENTS

I wanted to thank my sweet Rae for rekindling and jumping into the commitment pool together. It's going to be a great swim.

To my daughter Eliana and my son Dylan — you both inspire me emotionally and creatively.

To my fantastic parents, Carl and Dorothy, who have supported me in all that I do.

To Ashley, Kassi and Tony — thanks for keeping me grounded and making me laugh.

To 3L Publishing for their support and guidance throughout the entire creative process. Michelle, Bo and Erin rock! Thanks to Michelle Gamble for giving me the opportunity to go from writing screenplays to writing my first novel. Thanks to Erin Pace-Molina for your extraordinary cover art.

To my high school English teacher, Megan Boyle, for allowing me to push the envelope with creative writing without reporting me to the authorities.

1

You've never really lived until you've seen the life leave another human being. That's what I wish I would have told my narcissistic aunt and uncle whenever they came by my mother's apartment in the 'Loin. "Slumming in the 'Loin" is what I'd called it. They'd only come by to brag about their latest extravagant vacation. *You've never really lived until you've seen the Eifel Tower. You've never really lived until you've taken a helicopter ride along the coast of Hawaii.* I was only 10 at the time, though. My mother was ill most of my childhood. Not ill as in cancer or a debilitating disease like multiple sclerosis. She was sick in the head. She did the best she could for my sister and me while dealing with her bi-polar outbursts and her schizophrenia. My father had left us the year prior. Not that he was a stabilizing force in our lives. His idea of being a father meant thanking us for fetching him the glass pipe. And her pompous fuck of a brother and his whore wife had the audacity to rub their good fortune in our faces. Almost dangling the hint of a happy childhood in front of us — and then snatching it away at the last second. If I only knew at 10 years old what I know now.

Mother always told us to relish in their stories and use our imaginations to fly away and pretend we were actually there. It must have been easier for her considering the amount of medications she would ingest on a daily basis. My sister, Libby, who was eight at the time, took great pride in knowing when to distribute her pills. She wanted to make sure and have them ready before the alarm went off and reminded Mother it was time for her medication.

Libby was such a sweet girl until she was raped. One of Mother's doped-up boyfriends, Doug, felt he wasn't receiving enough attention from Mother so he forced the attention from Libby. I witnessed most of the assaults from Libby's closet and burned with rage — a rage I didn't know how to manage. I'll never forget the blank expression on her face when he would pull her panties down. Her eyes became vacant as if she purposely left her body to escape the realization of what was happening. Her vacant stare. If I only knew then what I know now. The closet is the only place I feel I can collect my thoughts and pretend the life I was forced into wasn't real. I stole grease paint from a construction site and painted a giant eye in the back of the closet. It was the only time I could feel noticed and appreciated. I had to figure out a better way for that attention. National attention. *You've never really lived until you've seen the sunset in Spain.*

They weren't so pompous with their hands and feet tied up. They weren't so eager to brag about their lives while being stripped naked. I always knew my aunt had a great set of tits. Her nipples were inviting and my mouth watered, but this wasn't about that.

"Why are y-you do-doing this?" she asked with a frightened stutter.

Uncle James was coming out of the baseball-bat-induced daze I gave him when I knocked him to the ground. I placed the plastic bag over his head and watched him struggle. Aunt Melanie panicked when she fully realized they were going to meet their maker; whoever that was. His eyes fluttered and his chest released the last gasp of air.

"Open your eyes, fucker!" I yelled.

He convulsed before the gurgling sounds ended. Yes! No more vacations for you! Why didn't I do it eight years ago when I was 10? Then I could have seen the joy in Mother when I told her they were dead. My buddy Meyers would have loved it!

I turned my attention to my aunt who sobbed uncontrollably or as best she could with a gag in her mouth. The adrenaline in my body was intoxicating. Unlike her pussy of a husband who closed his eyes, this bitch was going to see me kill her. I saw the small box-cutter sitting on the table and grabbed it. She had lost consciousness from the shock. This should wake her up.

I pulled the skin from her eyelid down and placed the razor just below her eyebrow and began the incision. How much pressure will it take to slice off an eyelid? My inexperience made for an uneven slice. I'm so much better at it now. The sting from the carving woke her up, but she was still powerless. A very carnal moan permeated from deep inside her. After the second eyelid was intricately sliced off, I wiped the blood away with her blouse. I chuckled at the fact that the elasticity of her skin reminded me of peeling off one of those fruit roll-ups. Mother used to give those to us as treats when Libby and I first started school.

I placed the plastic bag over her face and squeezed at the base of her neck. She was resigned to her fate. You could almost hear the fear in her eyes. She took her last labored breath and her chest was still. Oh, the vacant stare. Yes, *you've never really lived until you've seen the life leave another human being...*

It usually didn't rain this hard in San Diego, but the sound of raindrops on his windshield always reminded Tate Holloway of being on a stakeout. He missed stakeouts. For being 42 years old, Tate kept himself in really good physical condition. Not many people his age were lucky enough to have a full head of blond hair and a thirty-two inch waist. He attributed his abs and his tan to surfing five mornings a week at Sunset Cliffs at Ocean Beach. He was told being six-foot-three made it more difficult to balance on the board, which resulted in constant core training. That's not why he surfed, though. It was a chance to collect his thoughts and clear his mind. Surfing was one of three things that relieved him of the stress he had endured over the last few years — weed and tequila were the other two.

It had been seven years since he left the force as a homicide detective — and he missed the actual police work of the job. The business of investigating, interviewing, deciphering evidence, and especially sharing the camaraderie with his partner, Jack. He missed Jack. It was eight years to the day their partnership ended. The anniversary had always been a somber reminder of how life could change in the blink of an eye. But he didn't miss the bullshit of the job: the bullshit from upper management or the hypocrisy of his superiors. Those assholes were more concerned with their future status as politicians or city officials rather than catching the bad guys at any cost.

Being a private investigator allowed him to be his own boss and fed his appetite for investigating. He liked it that way. He opened his P.I. firm four years ago with the majority of his cases dealing with infidelity. How ironic, he once thought, he couldn't stay faithful to any of his three wives and now he paid the bills catching wealthy husbands or bored housewives with the same problem.

Most of his clients were wealthier San Diegans who watched the sunset from their multi-million dollar homes in La Jolla. He thought he would feel sorry for the victimized clients when he sat them down for the photo and video reveals. Yes, their spouses were in fact cheating and here is the hard evidence to prove it — no pun intended. However, most of the time it was a race to see who would catch each other in the act first. These people wanted the perfect documentation for their divorce cases to ensure the most lucrative settlements. What's more perfect than having photos and video of a spouse banging someone else? There were never any emotional outbursts or the hurt feelings that he expected. Not that he could talk when it came to marriages.

The difference between homicide suspects in the affluent neighborhood of La Jolla and the dilapidated section of Logan Heights were the clothes they wore during their interrogations. The rich also seemed much more desperate for their freedom. They had so much more to lose.

When he nailed someone wealthy they felt they should get a "this-doesn't-happen-to-me" get-out-of-jail-free card. As if they could utilize the card from the Monopoly game. Tate admitted it was always a little more fun busting the rich. He also loved using his trademark phrase, "You thought people like you don't go to jail."

What was the one thing that pissed him off the most? If the suspect had political connections downtown or their family was a heavy donor to the mayor's campaign. He'd get the courtesy meeting with Captain Steward to let him know that he'd be losing the bust.

"Are you fuckin' kidding me, Captain?" pleaded Tate.

"It's coming from upstairs," conceded Steward.

"So this asshole gets a pass 'cause his daddy has drinks with the Mayor?" asked a bewildered Tate.

"I don't make the damn rules, Holloway," added Steward.

This conversation usually took place as the silver-spooned jackass walked by the office window and smiled. It's one of the reasons he didn't miss the job. Well, one of the many reasons.

Tate checked his watch.

"Come on, lady," grumbled Tate.

He glanced at the address Rita wrote down to make sure he was parked in front of the correct house on Briarwood. He thanked God every day for being so lucky to have Rita Jones on his team. She was a redheaded spitfire from Alabama whose personality seemed too large to fit into her five-foot-tall frame. She spent many clandestine years in the military before she worked as a dispatcher with the police department. He always referred to her military career as clandestine because she never spoke about it and he never asked. Tate always loved the way she spoke her mind. She held nothing back — and he loved her for it.

He remembered the first time he met her at the precinct and his girlfriend at the time brought him lunch. He walked by her desk and introduced himself.

"Welcome aboard, I'm Detective Holloway," offered Tate.

"Well, howdy, Detective," she said. "Don't y'all ever sleep around here? You look like shit." Rita continued, "And that was so nice n' all of your daughter to bring you lunch."

Looking back on that introduction put a smile on Tate's face. He did look like shit and his girlfriend was much too young for him. Her honesty is why he trusted her impeccably, and she knew every secret there was to know about him. No skeletons would fall out of his closet that would shock Rita. He couldn't say the same about her skeletons, but he was working on that. She also worked hard to keep her accent and not turn into one of those fake San Diegans where every question ended with "man" or "dude". Tate made sure to include those endearments in his questions just to watch her tilt her head in disgust and ignore him.

When he opened his P.I. office, she was the first person he called. She had no problem leaving the job for a little less money. It allowed her to focus on her other "job" and the reason Tate sat out in front of this house.

The instructions were very specific: Park in front of the house on Briarwood and turn your engine and headlights off. At 8:15 p.m., look for a light to be turned on in a second-story window. Wait five minutes and then enter through the side gate and continue to the sliding glass door, which will be unlocked.

He had interesting requests and instructions in the past, but this one took the cake. Rita warned him that this was a brand new client who seemed nervous and flustered during their phone conversation. He could have declined the meeting, but in this economy it was difficult to turn away paying customers.

He saw the light illuminating through the curtains of the second-story window. He looked down at his watch — 8:25 p.m. She was 10 minutes behind the schedule she laid out for him. He took a swig from his Rock Star energy drink and ran his fingers through his dirty blond locks.

It's time to go to work.

VENGEANCE IS NOW

Tate felt like an intruder as he covertly entered through the side gate of the home. He had a difficult time adjusting his eyes to the darkness so he leaned against the wall and waited for them to focus. The patio and sidelights were off, but the light from his iPhone illuminated ominous shadows onto the ivy-covered stucco walls. He didn't realize he would need a flashlight for the job.

The side walkway ran a good 40 yards before he spotted the sliding glass door mentioned in his instructions. Thank God they had their patio furniture stacked and covered or the neighbors might have heard him yell after he crashed over them.

The home was beautiful and located in an upscale neighborhood. He wondered if this was his new client's primary residence or one of the many homes she owned. Either way he felt assured she would be able to pay his bill. As Jack used to say, "The only people in San Diego who couldn't afford it were military grunts and cops." Jack would be laughing his ass off if he could see Tate right now — or knew why he was there.

The 12-foot high fencing around the property kept the residence and backyard extremely secluded. He placed his hands over the sliding glass door and cupped his face so he could see any activity inside. All of the furniture in the house was covered with sheets or blankets. "What the fuck?" thought Tate. Something felt very off about this situation. Tate gripped the handle to the sliding glass door and gave it a little tug. It was unlocked just as the instructions stated it would be.

He caught a reflection in the window from the house next door that sent his heart racing. He quickly crouched and turned to see the curtain move in the neighbor's window. In his haste to hide, his foot clipped the side of a huge terracotta flowerpot, and he went down hard.

"Son of a bitch! Did they see me?" he thought.

He felt the rip in his slacks and felt the trickle of blood roll down his ankle.

"Shit, just what I fuckin' need; a nosy neighbor calling the cops on me," he thought.

He figured he couldn't blame them. He was creeping around the side of a dark house.

"I'm gonna kill Rita," he whispered to himself.

The thought of being popped by any of his former colleagues from the precinct made his head spin. If the department found out why he was there it would be bulletin board material for the Captain and the Chief. Tate didn't exactly leave the job on good terms. In fact it was brutal. There were a lot of issues left unsettled and memories Tate preferred to keep buried. Nonetheless, his arrest would be the water-cooler topic of discussion for weeks. And Rita? She'd be arrested for being a madam.

It was a couple of years ago that Rita asked if he was interested in accompanying a "client" to the San Diego Opera while she was in town on a business trip.

"It's a friend who likes to have company is all," Rita explained as she nervously fidgeted with her scheduling book.

"Company?" Tate asked. "That sounds pretty vague."

"She's in town on business," Rita said as she looked up at him with her puppy-dog eyes. Her accent always had more twang when she wanted something.

"Just going to the opera?" Tate continued.

It didn't take his years as a detective to recognize she wasn't telling him the whole story. She was definitely spoon-feeding him information.

"Well sugar," she continued cautiously. "I know you've been strugglin' with money and the boat payment n'all. I just thought I would help out."

"How is that?" he asked inquisitively.

He thought he knew what she alluded to but didn't want to come out and say it in case there was a slim chance he was mistaken.

"It pays five bills, honey," she admitted. "Or more if the evening goes ... well."

Very few things shocked him in life. While on the job he witnessed horrific crimes scenes and arrested the most unexpected people for murder every day. He thought he was prepared for anything — except for this request. Rita was asking him to be a *male escort. A gigolo. A man-whore.*

She wanted him to go out with women, on their dimes, and be compensated to have sex with them. He'd already done that for years only he was the one at the end of the night with the empty wallet. He didn't qualify for his full pension and his abrupt exit from the force left him deep in debt. He had to take out a loan on the sailboat he lived on just to get by for a while. The sailboat was his grandfather's passion, and he left it to Tate when he passed. If you combined the money that was already owed on the sailboat coupled with Tate's loan — he was in jeopardy of being on the hook for $75,000. The bulk of the loan was coming due soon, and he didn't have the extra cash lying around. No nest egg and three ex-wives later; he just wished this was a job opportunity back in the day. What young man wouldn't accept that challenge?

It brought him back to high school when they had a career day in the gym. The tables were set up and representatives from various professions would attend to recruit or answer any questions students might have. They had the police department, fire department, local utility company and various branches of the military. Could you imagine if there was a table set up with a sign that read: *Sign up here to get paid to have sex with wealthy women*? That line would've curled around the gym three times, and the people that operated the other career tables would've been twiddling their thumbs — and then getting in line themselves. Not to mention, Tate had a couple of close friends on the girls' softball team who would have cut in that line.

Of course not everyone would qualify for the gig. Tate was lucky enough to have his parent's good genes. He never had any trouble getting dates or having a multitude of sexual experiences and partners. Despite his stress over the years, he maintained his physique and he always had a full head of hair. A trim waste and great hair at his age basically separated him from 80 percent of the guys who pranced around trying to score pussy. The other 20 percent who weren't getting laid? They had money. Those guys didn't know it yet, but in a few years, Tate would be fucking their wives and being greased with the cash they provided. He didn't necessarily feel good about it. That's not how he was raised; but again, who wouldn't want that job?

The added income allowed him the freedom to continue his P.I. gigs even when times were rough. It was obviously an important secret to keep, but other than Rita and his select list of wealthy clients, no one knew. Not even the women he dated over the last couple of years. Not even Nicole, the girl he was currently dating.

They were extremely cautious and selective when it came to clients so when Rita booked someone new; it always made him feel à little uncomfortable. Just like now. He'd been involved in sting operations before where the person they would catch had the most pitiful look on his face. He didn't want to be *that* guy.

His *roster*, as Rita eloquently referred to it, was mostly out-of-towners although he did have a few local regulars. They were wealthy upscale San Diegans who married much older men in the 1980's and now desired more than a credit card to get them off. He tried not to think of the husbands but hey, they got what they wanted out of the deal by marrying much younger, beautiful women. Now they were too old to handle the physical aspects of their unions — that was Tate's job now.

He slid the sliding glass door open and stepped inside. The living room was completely empty. No furniture. No decorations. This house was either for sale or was going to have some remodeling done soon.

"Hello?" said Tate hesitantly.

There was no answer. The "creepy-factor" radar went off in his chest and the hairs stuck up on the back of his neck.

Something wasn't right. He started to feel like he was on an episode of *Ghost Adventures* and was waiting for a ghost to communicate with him through the spirit box. He was just about to leave and give Rita a call when he heard them — sirens. The neighbors must have seen him.

"Fuck me," panicked Tate.

This neighborhood was way too high profile for the 9-1-1 call to be bumped down the priority list. The closest black-and-white must have decided to respond immediately. You never knew what political donors lived in the vicinity, and God forbid the police department got reamed for taking too long to respond.

Tate closed the sliding glass door behind him, and he urgently headed for the side gate. There was nothing he wanted more than to get back to his car and get the hell out of there.

"Shit!" he thought.

He turned around and ran back to the sliding glass door. He used the sleeve on his overpriced shirt from Barney's and wiped down the handle and the glass to eliminate any prints he might have left behind. The sirens were getting closer. He looked up and saw two silhouettes leaning down to get a better look from the neighbor's upstairs window. He thought this might be the best time to run. He bolted out the gate and hustled to his Jeep — just another day in the life of a man-whore.

Grace Harper hadn't realized how tough her schedule was as she blended her hours of volunteer work with her college studies. She hadn't anticipated the dual workload. She volunteered at two different homeless shelters and also delivered food to people living with AIDS and HIV. Her work with the less fortunate had been a passion of hers since she was a little girl. She understood that growing up with extremely wealthy parents would be a double-edged sword. She had made it a mission of hers to utilize her great fortune and was always passionate about the programs that enabled her to give back to the community.

She admired the late Princess Diana after writing a school report on her and promised herself that she would also use her parent's money and fame to help the less fortunate.

She respected her parents and the fact that her father had become one of the most influential people in the city. However, she wasn't that excited about how he accomplished it. She always introduced worthwhile investments in social programs for him to consider and to his credit, her father had financed one of them. Nevertheless, she realized he didn't share the same enthusiasm.

Grace could have got into an elite sorority but that just wasn't her thing. She couldn't stand the rich bitches who felt entitled because of who their parents were. She felt fortunate to be allowed to live in her parents' multi-million dollar home as long as she went to college and received exemplary grades. She felt that was a fair tradeoff.

She basically had the house to herself because her parents utilized their empty nest time and traveled throughout Europe. Empty nest? She didn't really find their vacations and business trips any different than when she was growing up. They seemed to be gone just as much. It didn't bother her at all though. She felt fortunate to have her own bedroom and beautiful bathroom. No loud roommates or sloppy people in the house.

She had heard horror stories about dorm life and the sorority houses that had crazy parties and naked people running around. She had bigger plans than finding out how much she could drink or how many people she could sleep with. It also allowed her the time to focus on her goal of becoming an elementary teacher and educating kids at an inner-city school. She was compelled to give them the best education they could possibly receive.

She knew one thing; she loved her family but there was no way she would join the corporation just to make six figures a year. There was more to life than money. She wanted to be fulfilled and help others. Of course, one day, if she reached her goals, she wouldn't mind having a few cocktails and a lover. She chuckled at the thought.

Grace walked into her bedroom and tossed her book bag on the messy bed. She kicked off her flip-flops and yawned as she raised her arms in the air for a long stretch.

She walked over to her closet and pushed the door wide enough to reach in for her bathrobe. She kept reaching without success. She pushed it open a little further to get a better look. She flicked the light switch on and off, but there was no light.

She took two steps into her closet to get a better look. The light from her bedroom spilled into the closet enough that she recognized her bathrobe lying next to the shoe rack on the floor. As she bent down to grab it, she noticed that her laundry hamper has been knocked over. She wondered if her two Yorkies, Antony and Cleopatra, had gotten into her closet. As she turned to leave the closet, she didn't bother to close the door.

"Antony and Cleopatra?" she muttered. "Little fuckers."

She pulled off her blouse and tossed it toward the hamper in the closet. She slid her jeans down her silky legs and stepped out of them. She kicked them in the direction of the closet doorway. She stood in front of the mirror and admired her tattoos. Those didn't exactly make her parents happy, but it was her body. She looked beautiful in her matching violet panties and bra. She might not be the stereotypical "girly-girl," but she enjoyed buying matching panties and bras with the best of them. Wearing them made her feel better. She cupped her breasts and squeezed them together giving her more cleavage. Her boobs were the perfect size for her, she thought. She wondered why so many young women destroyed their bodies just to satisfy someone else's idea of a "perfect body".

She walked into her huge bathroom and turned the water nozzles to fill her built-in tub. The floors were a beautiful cream marble, which became very slippery when wet. She laid down a giant bath rug and then glanced outside the window behind the tub. She didn't want old-man Reynolds pretending to attend to his lemon tree while attempting to catch a glimpse of her in her birthday suit.

"Don't wanna give old-man Reynolds a heart attack," she said to no one in particular.

She walked over and turned on the iHome that sat on a long vanity table that occupied the far wall. Led Zeppelin's *Black Dog* blared through the speakers as she stripped off her panties and bra. She danced around naked to the beat of the song. She was definitely not shy about her body, and why should she be?

Grace opened the towel cabinet only to find it empty. She walked naked across the bedroom and back into the closet. She always had a difficult time seeing in the dark. She wished her closet wasn't so huge. People always called her a diva because she had so many clothes and shoes. She realized those people didn't really know her. They never knew that she cleared her closet of clothes and shoes once every three months and sold everything on eBay. She donated the money to a homeless shelter that used the funds to stock their kitchen. Her parents never questioned her spending habits so she continued the tradition for the last two years.

She remembered she kept a small lamp on a shelf in the back of her closet. Using the row of clothes as her guide, she felt her way through the dark. This reminded her of one of her favorite books as a child, *The Lion, the Witch, and the Wardrobe*. She wondered if she would emerge in the snow and smiled at the thought.

As she reached in the dark, her hand stopped on something solid that startled her. Her heart raced as her imagination got the best of her and crazy thoughts rushed through her head. What was that? As quickly as she touched it she couldn't find it anymore. The hair on her arms stood up as a chill traveled down her spine. Her lethargic attempt to find the lamp had now turned into a frantic search. Using her hands, she desperately felt for a shelf. She heard a loud thud coming from inside the closet. She quickly turned and swore she saw a silhouette of something or someone.

She was too focused to scream as her shaking hands found the lamp and searched for the switch. She looked over her shoulder in terror. The fact that she was alone in the house had just entered her consciousness. The lamp flicked on to reveal Grace hunkered down naked in the closet. She chuckled to herself when she noticed the mannequin lying on the ground. The same mannequin she took home last week when she wanted to design T-shirts for an afterschool youth program.

"Holy shit, Batman," she sighed and felt relieved.

She picked up her hamper and stood the mannequin back upright. She grabbed a towel and headed back to the bathroom to slide into the tub. As she crossed in front of her bed, two hands reached from underneath and grabbed both of her ankles and yanked hard. The force of the heave lifted Grace off the ground and backward onto the Berber-carpeted floor. Her lower back hit first, taking her breath away. The back of her head slammed down on the floor with a disgusting thud. She was shocked and stunned as she lay there and attempted to alleviate the fog in her head and the ringing in her eardrums.

A man dressed in a dark sweat suit emerged from underneath the bed and straddled her limp body.

"Weren't expecting company, princess?" he asked condescendingly.

She didn't have the wherewithal to answer, but he wasn't expecting a response.

"Can't use daddy's influence to get out of this one," he continued angrily.

Her senses slowly came back to her as she focused on the shadowy figure on top of her.

"Is this really happening?" she thought.

His arms pressed her shoulders down, and she could smell his awful breath and the latex gloves as he leaned closer to her. He stuck his long tongue out and gently licked her nipples. She unleashed a blood-curdling scream.

"Help!" she cried out. "Please, no!"

He laughed at her.

"No one's gonna hear you, bitch. Scream louder!" he encouraged.

She squirmed to get away, but he was too strong. He placed his wrist over her face and showed her his watch.

"Look at the time," he ordered. "What is it?"

Her sobs made her answer inaudible.

"It's 8:15," he snapped. "How does it feel to know you won't be alive to watch the clock strike 8:30?"

He reached into his pocket and pulled out an orange box-cutter. He slid it open with his thumb to reveal the sharp blade. Her body convulsed for one last attempt to get free. She used all her strength and freed herself enough to knee him in the crotch. He felt the pain shoot up to his stomach, and his body weight shifted as she slithered out of his grasp.

"Fuckin' whore!" he yelled as he reached for her hair and missed.

She began crawling for the door, but he pounced on her like a cheetah attacking his prey. He wrestled her to the ground and grabbed the front of her hair and smashed her head into the base of the wall. The force of her skull hitting the wall vibrated a lamp off the dresser and it shattered. She continued kicking and screaming as her body flailed doing anything possible to free herself from this madman. He placed his hands on each side of her head and positioned his knees on her shoulders.

"I can show you the safe," she whimpered just before passing out from the shock.

He checked her pulse making sure she didn't leave this world prematurely. He smiled knowing it was time. He picked up the box-cutter from the floor and used his index finger and thumb to delicately pull her eyelid away from her eyeball. He didn't want to accidently injure her eye so he placed the blade just below her eyebrow and made the incision. He could feel her heart rate increase as he pulled away the severed eyelid. Blood trickled down her temple and pooled next to her ear.

"Yep, just like riding a bike," he thought.

He repeated the steps for the other eye and now had both eyelids removed. He pulled out a small capsule from his pocket and cracked it open to release the ammonia in the smelling salt. He held it under her nose. She instantly jolted back to Earth with a long, guttural moan. Her eyes were now wide open and full of fear. She couldn't close her eyes. He placed his hands around her neck and squeezed. He leaned down close and put his face three inches from hers. She struggled for air and finally the last gasp escaped her lungs. Her eyes were staring vacant of any life right through him — and he became emotional and euphoric.

"Oh, the vacant stare," he thought and reveled in the feeling.

"I'm back!" he exclaimed aloud.

I had Grace Harper's schedule down to perfection. I probably knew it better than the granola bitch herself — except for the part where she dies. That was my entry into her schedule. Just like riding a bike I kept telling myself. The adrenaline was flowing through my body like hormones through a 13-year-old boy. I've never ended the life of a young boy before — that might be fun. I don't think Meyers did either. Maybe another day.

Her closet was comfortable and large. A walk-in closet? I grew up in fuckin' walk-in apartments. The biggest place I ever lived had nine people living there. It was my fourth foster family, and Meyers and I had to share the floor. It was one of the better homes I was ever in, and it's where I met my best friend. I fuckin' miss him.

I'll never forget when we realized we were connected. It was electric. There is nothing like growing up isolated and feeling like an outcast in society. I knew that too well. I know what society believes is the difference between right and wrong. I understand it. I'm forced to live it. Even though, deep down, I had my own set of rules. Dark rules. I was never so happy to find someone who not only lived by the same rules but also enthusiastically celebrated them. It was fun to meet another player.

I had to move into a new foster home because I had frightened the previous family I was assigned to live with. They were one of those "do-gooders" who pretended to house me because they wanted to give back to an "unfortunate kid" and give him or her a chance in life. What a fuckin' joke. They never mentioned how much they got paid for this "do-gooder" service. If the checks stopped coming, I would have been on the street faster than a chick trying to avoid getting fucked by her step-dad. They caught me sneaking into their daughter's room. They thought I was going to sexually assault her. If they only knew my true intentions. A rape wasn't on my agenda, and I had the razor blade to prove it.

The county shifted me to another "do-gooder" family. At least they were honest and upfront. They told me if I was looking for a mommy or daddy, I went to the wrong house. They informed me if I shut the fuck up and didn't get arrested; I'd get to eat and have a bed — or floor. I could see the cocaine residue on my new "foster dad's" nose when he told me that. Fuckin' jack-ass. Meyers was in one of the bedrooms when we met.

I walked into the small bedroom after being told I had to introduce myself to my new foster brother. I noticed that he turned around quickly and shut the drawer to his small dresser. It was the only thing he owned, and he took the damn dresser with him to every new house.

"Hey, you like Deep Purple?" I asked after noticing the poster on the wall.

"This ain't my room," he said as he looked at the dresser drawer. "It's another kid that lives here. I'm more into Alice Cooper, man."

"I'm more of a Cooper fan, myself," I agreed.

"If you touch my stuff," he warned, "I'll fuckin' kill you in your sleep."

I liked him from the very beginning. If he touched my stuff I wouldn't have waited to kill him when he slept. I would have slit his throat while he watched me.

"Far-out, glad to be here, too," I said trying to get him to smile and break through his wall. It worked. That's when I heard it. It sounded like a small whimpering or whine. Then some scratches. It was coming from his dresser drawer. He appeared nervous.

"What's that noise?" I asked as I noticed he held a few straight pins in his hand.

Seeing him with the straight pins sent a chill up my spine. Not a bad chill — an exhilarating chill. I gave him a knowing stare that was immediately understood. I could see our connection in his eyes — and it wasn't from a similar taste in music. I walked over to the dresser and opened the drawer. I saw a guinea pig that had straight pins inserted up and down his tiny legs. The bottom of the drawer was blood-soaked. Not fresh blood from the guinea pig but dull brown stains that had painted the wooden drawer and seeped into the grain of the wood. This wasn't his first rodeo.

"It's going to die soon," I told him. "You've got to limit the torture so they build up a tolerance, man."

"What do you mean?" he asked as his eyes darted at the bedroom door. This truly was his secret.

"If you build up their tolerance for pain," I explained to him, "you can keep them alive longer and savor the kill. Snap a leg off but stop the blood. A week later, snap off another leg."

"Yeah, far-out," he said.

The look in his eyes was priceless. Like a proud parent who just realized his or her child had a special talent. It was an acceptance that I know he'd never felt in his life — I know I hadn't. For almost a year-and-a-half, we went on to rid our shitty neighborhood of all rodents, stray cats, and almost anything that had a pulse and could feel pain. Not people. Not yet.

We left that house when our "foster-daddy" offered us dope to suck his dick. He got his, though. Meyers switched out his cocaine with dishwashing detergent, and he died from a brain aneurysm. We watched the whole thing happen. It wasn't as funny as the new episode of *All in the Family* that was on TV, but it was pretty close.

Focus! The scent of Grace's perfume lingered in the air from her clothes, and it was making me hard. Bitches like this only buy the expensive shit. No Wal-Mart fragrances or shitty-smelling sauce hocked by celebrity endorsers for this chick. She was a hot piece of ass. I was still not sure if I was going to fuck her before I end her existence. There was a method to my madness. I'll just allow the rage to overcome me and go from there. I have to stick to the ultimate plan. No mistakes. Meyers would be so proud. Eight years between the smell of fear and the vacant stare of dead eyes has made me thirsty again. A thirst that hasn't been quenched since Meyers left me. Tonight I will quench it. I didn't even realize I had this much self-control. I miss it. The finality of a kill. Knowing I am the last human to see them alive. I hope she can't hear my heart pounding.

I've never seen a 19-year-old with such an incredible body. Smooth tan skin. A sweet tight ass. Completely shaved pussy. Beautiful body art. This bitch took care of herself. I wonder how Libby would have looked if she lived to be 19?

Oh, sweet Libby. I'm the one who found her curled up in a puddle of her own vomit. The needle had got the best of her. I knew she'd get hooked because she confessed that heroin was the only drug that could numb her of the pain. I witnessed her absorb that agony so I understood where she was coming from. Heroin was the sickle to her Grim Reaper. Maybe I should have killed her earlier so she wouldn't have suffered. Should I have? Would that have been the act of kindness from a loving brother? If I did, I wouldn't need to see the life leave her eyes. I already saw it the night she was first raped.

I wanted to grab Grace when she came into the closet, but I was mesmerized by her movements. I couldn't tell the difference between a fuckin' DaVinci and a Picasso, but I know what moves me. She was like staring at a piece of art. My own creation before the world sees it as a masterpiece.

This bitch scares herself with a mannequin? I'm no mannequin, Batman.

I have to be clean, but how do I not fuck that? I'm not sure what makes me rock hard; her body or knowing she has no idea what's about to happen to her. My concentration isn't what it used to be. Living life on the straight and narrow has weakened my predatory nature.

Time to crawl under the bed. Focus! Fuck yes! Vengeance begins now, Meyers!

Tate blazed down the highway back to his boat in Marina Village when Rita finally called him back. He couldn't believe he cut his ankle on that damn flowerpot, and it was throbbing badly. He just bought those pants and was pissed they had blood on them.

"What was that all about?" he asked Rita through his Bluetooth.

"Y'know how some new clients are, sugar," she explained. "They get paranoid the hubby's will catch 'em."

"Did you vet her?" he asked.

"This ain't my first time," she quipped.

Tate knew they conducted background checks on all new clients, and if there were any possible red flags, they wouldn't take them on.

Rita explained, "Nothing unusual, honey. She didn't have much of a history n'all. She married a much older man when she was young and he's kept her like a prisoner. She's still pretty young."

"The neighbors called the cops," he said. "I ran down the fuckin' sidewalk, limping, my slacks were ripped. Sirens were blaring ... Wait, how young? No, never mind!"

He was a little curious about her age. He usually didn't get many clients younger than he was albeit they were in terrific shape. Money and loneliness usually equaled gym time and salon treatments. Rita knew that Tate rarely complained so she'd have to make it up to him.

"I'm sorry, sugar," apologized Rita. "I'll make sure you get some new britches n'all. And I'll toss you some green for your trouble."

"Have you tried to call her?" asked Tate. "Was that even her house?"

"She's not answering and probably won't 'cause she's embarrassed," responded Rita. "Maybe she saw the enormous bulge in your pants n'all — and she knew she couldn't handle your manhood."

"Yeah right," he laughed. "Chicks *hate* big dicks. They'd much rather sit on a Vienna sausage."

Rita always tried to put a smile on everything and always made sure he was taken care of. He often wondered why she couldn't be 15 years younger — or maybe even 20. He wasn't sure due to the fact she never offered to reveal her age. He felt sure it was one of the many secrets she kept. He felt she was his kindred spirit in many ways. Maybe he'd get married to someone like her one day. It might be difficult to find a woman who allowed him to sleep with other chicks for money.

"Women are so picky," he thought as he chuckled.

The only good part about getting stood up was having the evening free to spend some time with Nicole. She was a registered nurse at Scripps Mercy Hospital in San Diego. She was 27, tall, tan and beautiful. He thought the best part of the package was she didn't even realize it. To him, there was nothing sexier than an athletic woman who could throw her hair in a ponytail and look better than most women who spent hours prepping for a night out. He preferred dating younger women, and the age difference never bothered him. This time, however, Nicole's Dad was a huge *Magnum, P.I.* fan. Tate sometimes felt uncomfortable when she gave him shit about his job. She asked about Higgins' Doberman Pinschers and T.C.'s helicopter and wondered what he did with his red Ferrari. Tate laughed most of it off and felt it was a small price to pay to crawl between the sheets with such a hot piece of ass. He knew her shift was over so he thought he'd give her a call.

"No stakeout tonight?" asked Nicole.

Tate hated the fact that he had to lie about his life. It was one of those situations where he didn't realize he would enjoy her company so much. After a few months together, he felt he reached the point of no return with the secret. He honestly thought he'd be hanging out with her for a while and then would move on; like he did with every other girlfriend in his life. This was much different. She surfed.

"Nope," he lied. "The husband stayed home with the 'wifey' tonight."

"How thoughtful of him to spend the evening with his wife and kids," she quipped.

"Wasn't it?" said Tate hoping to change the subject. "How 'bout I grill up some steaks and pop a good merlot?"

"Will we be naked?" she asked.

"I wouldn't have it any other way," responded Tate.

"I'll be there in half 'n hour," she said.

Tate felt very lucky that his grandfather left him a 35-foot Columbia sailboat; complete with a lifetime slip in one of San Diego's premium marinas. His grandfather was a huge part of his life, and he missed him daily. Making sure he didn't default on the boat was the main reason he "hooked". Or at least that's what he told himself when he jumped into the shower after a gig to wash off the guilt. He couldn't stand to lose the boat.

He couldn't believe his grandfather had been gone four years already. If it wasn't for him, Tate would have never entered the Academy and been a cop. He more than likely would have continued to hustle pot, surf, and accomplish little in life. That was the positive outcome. On the flipside, if he wasn't a detective he wouldn't have suffered the agony of his crumbled career, the loss of a partner, and his rebutted quest for the truth. If it weren't for the intense therapy that helped him digest the past and move forward, he'd always said people would have found his body on that boat.

Curt Munson, 38, quietly tip-toed up the stairs in his two-story Spanish-style home for fear of waking his sleeping kids. They had school tomorrow and he didn't want his wife, Melissa, to get on his case about being too noisy. He also knew that the odds of seducing his wife were much higher if they didn't wake up. He did have his priorities straight.

He peeked in on both Kara, 7, and Johnny 5, and recognized that they were in a deep sleep and wouldn't be startled if he kissed them on their foreheads. He loved how peaceful they both appeared and how fresh they smelled when they slept. The scent of innocence.

He wondered if they had a good day at school. He hoped so considering how much they spent to send them to such a prestigious private academy. Melissa made sure their uniform logo was visible on their school pictures when she sent them as a Christmas card last year. He was pretty sure she did that so relatives believed they had a lot of money. "That wasn't his thing," he thought.

He wished he would have gotten home in time for dinner but duty called. It's the first late meeting he'd had in a while so Melissa was very understanding. She always understood when there was a chance of increasing their income. He could still smell the remnants of his wife's special garlic spaghetti sauce, but he wasn't that hungry — at least not for food.

"How was it?" she asked while pulling the sheets back on their massive canopy bed.

She wore a long white t-shirt that was so thin he could see the pink of her nipples and the outline of her thong.

"It was productive," Curt answered while placing his briefcase next to the dresser. He took his suit jacket off and hung it in the closet.

"Did you make a deal?" she quizzed.

He always hated how she would interrogate him after a meeting or anytime he had to go out of town for business. He was a sales representative for a pharmaceutical company based out of Chicago and had covered the Southern California territory for the last seven years. Curt met Melissa when she was a surgical assistant for a surgeon he supplied. It was love at first sight for Curt. They became emotionally and physically attached after their first date and had been together ever since.

"It was just dinner with a client," he said, "and you got to keep them happy so they stay clients."

"Where'd you take him?" she asked.

"A snooty little sushi place you would've loved," he joked.

"Figures," she said with a pouty face.

She sat on the bed and watched while Curt continued to get undressed in the closet and threw on his nightly uniform — boxers and a T-shirt.

"I would have honestly preferred your spaghetti," he complimented. "You can still smell it in the house."

"I can heat some up," she offered.

He stopped what he was doing and stood there staring at her for what seemed like a minute.

"What?" she snapped.

"I'd rather eat something else," he remarked as he glanced at her thighs.

He had an ornery smirk on his face that Melissa had recognized many times over the years.

"Kids asleep?" she asked almost as a statement rather than a question.

"I drugged them myself," he teased.

She saw that his manhood was pushing his boxers out like a tent and realized he was already turned on.

"Going camping?" she asked.

Curt emerged from the closet, quickly stripping away his nightly uniform and was naked and on top of her before she could react. He ripped her nightshirt completely off her body and began sucking on her nipples.

"Babe!" she giggled. "What the hell?"

He grabbed her hand and wrapped it around his hard cock so she could feel how excited he was. He couldn't wait. He slid down and began tasting her. He maneuvered his hips in her direction and she fully reciprocated the 69, and took him into her mouth. They were both pleasuring each other when Curt pushed her off him. She looked at him confused. He couldn't wait. He grabbed her by the hair and spun her around.

"Hey, easy," she whispered.

She'd never felt him so forceful but was surprised how much she was aroused. He turned her over and entered her from behind with authority. He gripped each side of her ass and pulled tight. He fucked her mercilessly as sweat ran down his face and dripped on her lower back. She seemed to be into the pounding until she reached down to pleasure herself and he grabbed her wrist and held her down. He ignored her pleas to go easier until he finally released with an unprecedented orgasm.

He fell onto the bed exhausted and covered in sweat. There was an awkward silence as Melissa clutched her torn nightshirt and wiped the perspiration from her brow. Her hair was disheveled, and her eyeliner had smeared across her face. She covered her body with pieces of her nightshirt as she slithered off the bed and slowly walked into the bathroom.

She had never experienced vigorous sex with him before — and he had never acted that way. She was always open to experimenting but was extremely disturbed by that episode. She gathered herself together as much as possible without Curt being alarmed by her uneasiness. She slipped on her robe and looked at Curt. He hadn't said a word to her at all. He just stared at the ceiling and appeared to avoid eye contact.

"I'll warm up the spaghetti," she said as she crossed in front of the bed and headed for the doorway.

"That'd be great," he responded as if everything were normal.

He hopped up from the bed and grabbed his clothes from the floor. She leaned back into the bedroom and pointed at his briefcase.

"Don't forget to lock up your drugs," she reminded.

"Gotta take the trashcans out, too," he said. "I love you."

"Love you too," she answered from the hallway.

She leaned on the stairwell railing for a second and took a deep breath. Maybe she was making a big deal out of nothing, she thought.

VENGEANCE IS NOW

Steve Pelletti, 44, had been a cop for over 20 years. He started in a patrol car dealing with petty drug dealers and prostitutes before being upgraded to homicide detective about 14 years ago. He'd seen a lot of partners come and go in his tenure, but it was the first time in his career that he began feeling like the "old guy". There were so many new faces at the precinct he often wondered if he was going to get the early retirement pink slip. A *"Thanks for your service, now get the fuck out"* letter he had seen given out a couple of times over the years.

He knew his hairline had receded and his hair had thinned so much he could see his own scalp; but he felt he had a few more years left in him. He still bought jeans with a 33-inch waist and felt he was in better shape than most of the new kids on the block; including his newest partner, Detective Ramon Aguilar.

Ramon, 29, sat next to Steve in their Ford Crown Victoria during their dinner break. They were parked in the lot next to the taco truck. Steve had realized in the four months he had been partnered with him that he had a reputation for being a hot head around the precinct. Ramon had confessed that people were just jealous because of his very high self-esteem. Steve knew his colleagues thought his partner was an arrogant prick, but he never cared as long as they felt he was a good detective — they did and he was a great detective. He was very good. He assumed Ramon's six years undercover with the gang task force and two stints in Afghanistan with the marines shaped his arrogance and occasional overzealousness. The only thing that annoyed Steve was how Ramon referred to everyone as "bro".

"A definite generation gap," he thought.

Steve had torn apart the aluminum foil that was wrapped around his sandwich and sniffed it to identify the contents.

"Shit," he said. "I think she tried to hide some'a that wheat germ again."

He placed the sandwich back into his lunch bag and settled for an apple. He wondered if the taco truck would have been a better choice after he smelled Ramon's burrito. Ramon held up his massive steak burrito and placed it under his nose. He took a long, deep inhale as he sniffed his lunch.

"None'a that shit in here, bro," said Ramon. "All good shit." He laughed as he took an enormous bite. "Why don't you just buy your own dinner shit?" he asked with his mouth full.

Steve always chuckled at the way Ramon used the word "shit" to describe anything and everything he talked about. It was yet another reminder of the age gap between them.

"Marcy enjoys packing my food," said Steve. "I would've eaten that crap 10 years ago, but now I try to keep lean."

"You're married, dude," quipped Ramon. "Who gives a fuck how you look, bro?"

"Just wait 'til you turn 40," lectured Steve. "You'll understand what I'm talking about."

"We'll be flying around in spaceships and shit by then," laughed Ramon.

"Fuck off," joked Steve.

"Don't worry bro," chuckled Ramon. "You'll have that Alzheimer's shit and won't remember any of this."

That comment wasn't lost on Steve, and he wondered if it might be better having the years of violence, death and sorrow magically wiped from his memory. He often wished he could use the "neuralyzer" Will Smith used in *Men in Black* to erase all the memories he had accumulated over the years. He had seen the ugliness of humans and the heartache of parents knowing their loved ones were never coming home. He had known cops who retired but could never put away an unsolved case they had worked. They carried the files and crime photos with them until their deaths. He never wanted to be that guy although he had some cases that still haunted him.

He remembered the time a mother insisted on seeing her deceased daughter's severed leg. It was the only part of her daughter that was found, and she wanted to connect to any part of her baby that was recovered. She had needed the closure. He understood that. He had a case that he felt needed closure in his mind, but he hadn't spoken about it in a few years. He often wondered if other cops had "perps" who were convicted and sentenced when they thought it could be the wrong guy. He was sure he wasn't alone.

"And that tofu shit you eat," said Ramon, "looks like cum Jell-O, bro."

"No one asked you to eat it," answered Steve after taking a crisp bite from his apple. "And you'll change your mind when you go for angioplasty before you're 35."

"Fuck that shit, bro," joked Ramon. "I'm a machine."

Steve stifled his comeback to that statement when he heard his cell phone ring. Ramon was still running his mouth when he answered, "This is Pelletti."

Steve was told about a situation in a mansion in La Jolla. He knew by the sound of the dispatcher's voice and the fact he was informed it was a "10-3 for open carriers" that this wasn't your normal status quo. It meant they wanted radio silence from anyone working off a radio and that all inquiries or callbacks be done on a cell phone. He knew that meant the powers that be didn't want the press involved until absolutely necessary.

"We have a body?" asked Steve.

Steve had a strange look on his face that caught Ramon's full attention.

"I'm not at liberty to discuss," informed the dispatcher. "I was only told to get you guys there and maintain radio silence. It's an APE situation."

Steve knew that APE was an acronym for Acute Political Event, which meant someone of political importance to City Hall or Police Headquarters was in trouble. If it had been a DUI or someone getting popped for picking up a prostitute, the call wouldn't have come to homicide. This had to be big. He was told he would receive the address via text and was advised not to speak to anyone regarding his destination.

"Has to be a body and shit," said Ramon. "Why would they call us, bro?"

"We'll find out soon enough," answered Steve.

They flew down the streets of San Diego headed for their mysterious location in complete radio silence and without their portable siren. They had to remain dark.

"Never been on an APE and shit, bro," confessed Ramon.

Steve was lost in thought as he watched the buildings soar by his passenger window while Ramon drove their vehicle up I-5 to La Jolla.

"I have," admitted Steve. "Do yourself a favor and use your ears instead of your mouth."

"C'mon, bro," pleaded Ramon. "Seriously?"

"Shit slides down from the top," he lectured. "You don't want to be standing still while it hits you in the face."

"This shit could be that fucked up?" quizzed Ramon.

Steve chuckled to himself, "Get ready to see the underbelly of the job's political bullshit."

VENGEANCE IS NOW

Nicole Stafford, 27, was wearing a turquoise sundress with matching flip-flops and toenail polish. The color of the dress accentuated her perfect tan and brought out the crystal blue eyes that always melted Tate. If he looked up the definition of "stereotypical blond beach babe" — her picture would be displayed.

He watched her as she gathered up the dirty plates from dinner and placed them in the sink. He grabbed the bottle of merlot from the table and freshened up their wine glasses.

"Now that we're done eating," she said with a mischievous grin.

"I'm game for blood and gore, baby," Tate said as he chuckled at her enthusiasm for her work.

"So, a guy gets brought in who can't breathe. No response to the oxygen or the intravenous line. Nothing," she explained. "The only thing to do was 'trach' him."

"No," he begged. "That's so nasty."

"The ER doc looks at me like I'm supposed to make the incision," she said with disdain as she picked up a steak knife. "I'm like, whatever."

"You don't do that, right?" he asked.

"No, that's his gig," she said. "He's kind of a dumbass, anyway. He's got really tiny hands and feet."

Tate always laughed at how she could tell a story and then drop in the most random information that never pertained to anything she was talking about.

"Is it the 'por-shay,' guy?" asked Tate.

Nicole laughed at the fact that Tate remembered that a doctor tried to bang her by asking if she wanted a ride in his Porsche. Only he pronounced it, "Por-shay."

"Yes!" she said as she hopped up and down. "It's totally that guy."

"Figures. So?" he prodded.

"So he cuts'im here," she said with her head tilted back and holding the steak knife underneath where her Adam's apple would be. "And a yellowy, gross liquid spurted up and literally went up his nose."

"You mean his 'nos-ay'?" joked Tate.

"It was like a milky snot," she said laughing at Tate's puckered facial expression. "It smelled so sour, too."

"What'd he do?" he quizzed.

"What can he do?" she asked.

"Wash the shit off!" he exclaimed.

"He had to get the tube in or the guy dies," she explained.

"That's why I could never be a nurse or doctor," he said. "I'd barf all over the fuckin' place."

"Shut up, Tate," she said. "You worked homicide for Chris 'sakes."

"Twenty-seven-year-old women don't say 'Chris 'sakes'," teased Tate. "You sound like a grandma."

Nicole was standing at the sink and looked over her shoulder at him very seductively. She raised her sundress above the back of her thigh and exposed the bottom of her beautiful ass cheek. No tan lines.

"Do I look like a grandma?" she asked.

"I know grandmas, I'm friends with grandmas, and you dear are no grandma," Tate joked as he referenced Lloyd Bentsen's famous line about Jack Kennedy in his 1988 political debate with Dan Quayle.

Nicole laughed but Tate was pretty sure it was out of courtesy and not because she understood the reference. It was another subtle reminder of their age difference.

"Dead bodies are dead," he said.

"That is *so* profound, *dude*," Nicole mocked.

"Yes it is, smart-ass," said Tate. "I didn't have to see them die. They were just dead. Totally different."

"Like you've never seen someone die," replied Nicole.

Tate wasn't comfortable responding to Nicole's comment. He didn't want his response to open the door for any more questioning. He watched as she wiped off the table and grabbed her glass of wine. She held her glass up for a toast and Tate reached over and obliged.

"To not watching people die," she toasted.

"Amen," he agreed.

The two took a long swig of their "vino". Tate took their glasses and placed them on the table as he pulled Nicole close to him. Tate was seated and she was standing as they wrapped their arms around one another. He buried his head into her stomach and inhaled her smell. He loved the body spray she used throughout the day.

"Dinner was amazing," she complimented while running her fingers through his blond mane.

"Did'ya get enough?" he asked.

"I still have room for dessert," she said.

Tate looked up at her with a devilish grin as he reached over and grabbed a can of whip cream from the gulley counter.

"You can't have dessert without the whip cream," he said.

"No, it's not wise," she playfully replied.

Tate grabbed one of the spaghetti straps of her sundress top and gently slid it down her shoulder and past her arm. He did the same with the other strap, which left her top barely covering her perfect breasts. He leaned up and gripped the hanging top between his lips and pulled it down exposing her naked tear-drop shaped D-cups. Her tiny pink nipples were perfect. He could hear Nicole lose her breath when he lightly blew his warm breath on her nipples and used the tip of his index finger to softly massage them until they were completely hard.

"You like that?" he gently asked.

"Uh-hmm," purred Nicole.

Tate grabbed the can of whip cream and touched the cold cylinder against her skin. He could feel the goose bumps form on her body. He placed the nozzle tip right next to her nipple and squirted a dollop of cream that covered it. He did the same to her other nipple. He took it into his mouth and lightly sucked and licked until the whip cream was gone.

Nicole moaned softly as he licked and kissed his way over to the other nipple. As he nibbled on her breasts and chest, he slowly ran his hand up her calf and under her dress. He gently followed her leg until he was almost tickling her inner thigh. He continued on his journey until he felt the lace of her panties and could feel the warmth and moisture building in her pussy. Nicole leaned her head back and enjoyed the exploration of her body.

He used his fingers to lightly caress her through her wet panties until her hips were into the motion of his fingers. He slid her panties to the side and used three fingers to gently rub her clit and labia in a circular motion. He could feel her juice drip into his hand as his rhythm increased. Nicole slapped her hands down on the table as she lavished in the tingles that were screaming through her body. She could feel Tate swell as her leg pressed against his lap.

Tate had two of his fingers inside her as he slowly slid them in and out while taking turns sucking on each nipple. He used his free hand to pull her dress down to her ankles. She instinctively stepped out of the dress, leaving her standing in her turquoise lace panties with Tate's hand still maneuvering in and around her pussy. Her breathing escalated and the tingling sensations were building to the point where she was either going to cum or Tate was going to have to fuck her right on the spot.

"I want you to cum, baby," he said softly.

"I need you inside me," she breathed.

"I need to taste you," he said.

He pulled his fingers out of her and placed each of them in his mouth and sucked on each one as he stared up at her. Sweat had gathered like tiny raindrops on her nose. He went ahead and pulled her panties down with his teeth until she was completely naked in the gulley. She reached down and unzipped his pants. She pulled out his hard cock and stroked the chord right under his mushroom. He grabbed her hand away and stood up. He gently kissed behind her ear and took her earlobe into his mouth.

"This is about you," he whispered.

He picked her up and carried her down into his cabin as they kissed passionately. He used his lips to pull and nibble on her lower lip, which drove her crazy.

Tate loved how the moonlight peeked through the windows of his boat and perfectly illuminated his bed. It was almost as if he had a blue-hued spotlight that showcased his encounters with Nicole. Of course, he never needed special lighting for her to look edible.

He laid her down on his bed, but she popped up on her knees so she could pull off his shirt and help get him naked. Once accomplished he gently pressed her down on the bed.

"You have me so wet," she confessed. "I'm dripping."

He used the whip-cream can and slowly rolled it up her thighs, over her stomach, and back down again. He started from her anklebone and squirted whip cream all the way up her legs, behind her knees, up her middle thighs, and covered her beautiful pussy. He loved that she was shaved so he could taste all of her without worrying about anything getting in the way.

He grabbed her face and gave her a strong kiss before working his way down her chest with tiny nibble kisses that resulted in taking her nipples into his mouth. He used his tongue and lightly outlined her areola, which sent shivers down her spine.

Nicole loved his strong body and the fact that he was in better shape than most guys her own age. She wasn't afraid to admit that Tate was the best lover she ever had.

She thought he had the sexiest cock she'd ever seen and his size was perfect for her. She loved how he took his time and made sure she was always satisfied.

Tate licked the whip cream from her ankle and followed the trail behind her knee. He spent a little extra time nibbling the sensitive skin on the back of her knee. He continued upward and inch by inch licked the inside of her thigh. Nicole squirmed with every touch of his tongue on her skin.

"You're killin' me," she said impatiently.

Tate chuckled as he placed his tongue on the outside of her pussy and lightly ran the tip of his tongue along her clit. He traced the outline of all of her nooks and crannies. He could taste how wet she was when he sucked up the rest of the whip-cream that covered her warm spot. He slid his index finger inside of her and pressed on the inside of her sugar walls to find her G-spot. Nicole responded with a long moan. Once he found where to tickle and press, he took her clit into his mouth and softly sucked on it. His tongue and lips were licking and nibbling on her in a rhythm with his finger inside her. Nicole barely contained herself as she moaned and breathed in unison with him tasting her.

"Oh shit, oh shit," she whispered.

Her body tingled from head to toe as she exploded with a deep, long orgasm. Her legs quivered as her hips rose off the bed and locked Tate's face between her legs. She collapsed back onto the bed and exhaled. Tate rested his head on her stomach, and she ran her hand through his damp hair.

"You taste so good," said Tate.

"Come here," she ordered.

Nicole took Tate by the shoulders and pushed him down on the bed. She was pleased to see that he was rock hard from the action. She straddled him and reached behind her. She grabbed his cock and positioned him perfectly by her pussy. She slowly sat as he slid deep inside her. Her sweat glistened in the moonlight as she slid up and down on his shaft while Tate lightly bit and nibbled on her nipples.

"You are so beautiful," he commented.

"You *feeeel* so good," she said.

Their vigorous lovemaking was like a choreographed dance as their bodies were drenched in sweat. Tate grabbed the back of her hair as she dug her fingernails into his chest. They became more vocal as their intensity increased and she took him as deep as she could stand. They moaned together as their bodies released at the same time. She dropped on top of him from exhaustion.

They laid on each other and enjoyed the breeze that blew in from the marina. Tate didn't know where this relationship might lead but damn he loved having sex with her.

"Oh my God, are you sure you're 42?" she asked as she laughed with Tate.

"Yeah, but I don't drive a 'Por-shay'," he joked.

They cuddled together and giggled until the exhaustion got the best of them. They had almost drifted off to sleep when Nicole broke the silence.

"I like you," she confessed as she fell asleep in his arms.

Tate kept staring at the ceiling. He wondered if he could ever confess his secret.

9

It was after midnight when detectives Steve Pelletti and Ramon Aguilar arrived at their destination in La Jolla. They noticed four black-and-whites, three unmarked cars, two CSI vans and three black Denali's parked in front of the mansion. *"And a partridge in a pear tree,"* was the first jingle that played in Steve's mind. He knew that the Denali's never showed up unless it was a pretty big situation. Only the upper echelon of the City and police department got chauffeured around in those bad boys.

"We got Denali's," Steve mentioned to Ramon as they got out of their Crown Vic.

"Is that some shit?" asked Ramon.

"Ever seen them at our crime scenes before?" he said as more of a statement than a question.

A few uniformed cops had just finished lining the property with yellow crime scene tape as the two detectives approached a uniformed officer. There was now a perimeter from the street all the way around the property line. It was a good boundary considering all the neighbors had gathered outside their homes or attempted to get information from the cops handling crowd control.

"What's going on?" demanded a neighbor.

"Was it a home invasion?" asked another neighbor.

Steve caught the attention of an officer trying to appease the small crowd and waved him over to them. He didn't recognize him but that meant nothing considering the size of San Diego and how many cops were on the force. He couldn't have been more than 23-years-old.

"Who's running the show?" Steve asked as he flashed his badge.

"Captain Dunn is in the house, sir," said the young cop.

"We have a body, bro?" asked Ramon.

"Uh, I'm, uh, not allowed to answer anything, Detective," the cop said hesitantly.

Steve and Ramon looked at each other puzzled as their Captain called out for them from the front porch.

"Pelletti!" he yelled as he waved them over.

The two detectives walked up to the elegant and elaborate front porch to meet him. Ramon seemed amazed at the bridge and waterfall that dressed up the front of the property.

"What's going on, Captain?" inquired Steve.

"Not good, not good," he expressed. "Follow me."

Captain Martin Dunn was in his upper-50s and had a stocky athletic build for his 6' 0" frame. His goatee was gray and definitely stood out against what appeared to be a spray tan. Steve knew after Dunn's wife passed that he had shed a few pounds and prepared for the dating scene, but he didn't think he would go with the orange skin and flashy suits. He had heard rumors that he had dated someone much younger from the District Attorney's office.

She broke up with him because he had a problem with the plumbing — as in the pipe was always limp.

Steve kind of felt sorry for him in a way. He was sure Dunn heard the snickers around the precinct. Any time anyone used the word "hard" the laughter would bellow down the halls. The rejection had to especially sting coming from a younger woman. Younger women sometimes had that effect on older men.

They followed Captain Dunn up the marble stairway to the second floor and couldn't help but gaze at the beautiful art mounted on the walls and the massive crystal chandelier that hung from the 40-foot-high foyer. They passed Crime Scene Investigators as they photographed and dusted for prints on the stairwell banisters.

"The 'vic' is a 19-year-old female college student," briefed Dunn. "Looks like she was killed in her room."

"Sexual assault?" asked Steve.

"We don't know yet, M.E. should be here soon," advised Dunn.

"So why the 10-3 and all the secrecy?" quizzed Steve.

Captain Dunn stopped at the top of the stairs and waited until his two detectives were huddled close together with him.

"She is the daughter of Jonathan Harper," he divulged. "So you can imagine the shit that's coming from downtown."

Steve remembered the name and realized the significance of the clandestine circumstances. Jonathan Harper was a billion-dollar real estate developer with ties to Washington, D.C. His foundation funded both of Mayor Villanueva's election and re-election campaigns. It was also known that Harper had aspirations of his good friend,

Villanueva, making a run at Capitol Hill and even the White House.

A few media outlets accused Harper of buying carte blanche favors from the Mayor's administration. His corporations never had any red-tape issues when it came to developing and building golf courses, hotels and condos in the region regardless of the environmental impact. He was known as the golden goose of San Diego politicians. He was also very close to Chief of Police Phillip Steward.

All of this information sent Steve's head reeling. It also brought back a tough time in his life about eight years ago.

"Let's take a look," Dunn said as he walked them into the victim's bedroom.

Pelletti and Aguilar's shoes squished on the carpet as they realized the entire floor was flooded. There was about a half an inch of standing water that had begun to irrigate the hallways outside the victim's bedroom.

"This is gonna fuck up evidence," complained Steve.

"No shit, bro," agreed Ramon.

"The bath water was running when she was found," said Dunn. "We're thinking she was getting in the bath when she was attacked."

Grace's naked body was sprawled out on the floor away from the bed and appeared completely disheveled from the trauma. She definitely didn't die peacefully. Her head was turned to the left, but her hair covered most of her face. Her skin had turned a bluish gray and the blood had settled at her back, which left blue and purple bruising. Rigor mortis had begun to set in, which caused her body to stiffen up.

Steve noticed a broken lamp on the floor next to her dresser and a blood spot with some hair on the baseboard of the wall. Shattered pieces from the porcelain base were scattered along her water-soaked floor. He had investigated hundreds of homicides in his career and knew that an abundance of water was about the worst situation when evidence was gathered and processed. This crime scene was completely compromised.

"Can we get the blood and hair on the baseboard bagged?" Steve asked a CSI Tech.

"We have to hope for semen or prints and shit, bro," commented Ramon.

"Wonder if the 'perp' planned the water or was just one lucky motherfucker," contemplated Steve.

Crime Scene Investigators photographed every inch of the bedroom, bathroom and closet to avoid having a clue overlooked but captured in a photo. They dusted for fingerprints and bagged anything that the "perp" might have touched, breathed or perspired on.

"Who found her?" asked Steve.

"The housekeeper," responded Dunn. "She's downstairs in the office. She's worked for the family since the 'vic' was a little girl."

"Notifications?" continued Steve.

"The family's been notified. They're on a plane back from Switzerland," answered Dunn.

"Is there a boyfriend?" asked Steve.

"Pretty girl," said Ramon as he glanced at a photo of the victim in happier times.

"Housekeeper said she didn't have time," said Dunn. "I think she might be a little nervous to talk with us."

"Illegal?" questioned Steve.

Dunn confirmed with a nod of his head.

"Figures, bro," whispered Ramon. "Guy is rich as fuck, too."

"We'll question her here, then," Steve said to Dunn.

A uniformed officer approached the two detectives and Captain Dunn. "Sir, two news vans just pulled up outside," he said.

"No one talks to the media! Period!" informed Dunn. "Get that message out, please."

"Has anyone dusted the bathtub knobs?" Steve called out to the Crime Scene Investigators.

"I pulled several 'fulls' and partials," responded a CSI.

"Maybe we'll get lucky, bro," commented Ramon.

"Why do I have the funny feeling we're not gonna find shit," commented Steve.

Sheila Walker sauntered into the bedroom with her coroner's bag in hand. She was in her 40's, black, and very classy looking. Steve loved working with her because she had always gone that extra mile to assist him in solving cases. She was never afraid of the horrendous hours as long as the work she put in resulted in a murder conviction. She cared about her victims and their families and had a reputation for being composed and unflappable while testifying in court.

"Nothing like being hustled out of a private Michael Buble' concert," complained Sheila. "He didn't know it yet but he was my next husband."

"You're too good for him," joked Steve.

"And I had to go up the back stairway here," she continued.

"You're like a celebrity," said Steve, "avoiding the paparazzi."

"I'm sorry for the inconvenience," apologized Dunn.

"No worries," expressed Sheila. "I've been briefed."

She looked down at her high-end Jimmy Choo platform pumps as they sloshed through the water.

"Don't know what's worse," commented Sheila, "a compromised crime scene or ruining my $500 shoes."

"Not all of us have trust funds," joked Steve. "Besides, Ramon's got you covered."

"Five hundred and shit?" yelped Ramon. "That's more than my entire wardrobe, bro."

"Yes it is," joked Sheila as she crouched by the body and opened her medical examiner's bag. She placed her magnified loop eyeglasses on her face, clicked on the LED light, snapped on her latex gloves, and went to work.

It still baffled Steve that Ramon also referred to women as "bro's". He knew Sheila was used to the term and found the moniker to be a little endearing. He also knew that she had a remarkable sense of humor. Steve always believed it was better to keep the mood light in horrible situations, and he appreciated that Ramon and Sheila agreed. The uglier the homicide — the more comedy seemed to pour out of everyone. He attempted to be in comedy mode, but also he and Sheila both noticed that Captain Dunn was too stressed out and didn't appear interested in jokes. He kept pacing in the background.

Everyone who worked in the room stopped and turned toward the windows after rays of light beamed through the glass and lit up the bedroom. Television crews turned mini-spotlights on the house to assist in the production value of their live, on-scene coverage. This caused Dunn to go ballistic.

"Get those damn lights off the house!" Dunn yelled down the hallway to the stairwell. "You," requested Dunn to an officer in the hallway, "Go down and make sure that happens."

Sheila diligently worked over Grace Harper's body and collected samples under her fingernails, between her legs, on her arms, bagged hair follicles, and observed the digital screen on her temperature gauge.

Steve and Ramon stood in the enormous closet that housed Grace's entire wardrobe and shoe collection. Ramon studied the clothes' racks that spanned each side of the closet walls. He pointed toward one of the sides.

"Has any'a you moved the clothes on the racks?" Ramon asked the two CSI's who photographed the closet.

"We didn't touch a thing," responded one of the CSI's.

"Everything is arranged and hung perfectly, bro," Ramon said to Steve. "Except this little gap and shit in the clothes."

Steve noticed there was a gap in an area of clothes near the closet's exit.

"Maybe our guy was hiding right there," concluded Ramon.

"Grab the clothes on each side of this gap and bag 'em," Steve ordered to a CSI as they exited the closet. "Captain, we think the suspect came from the closet when he attacked."

"Do we have a T.O.D.?" asked Captain Dunn.

"I'd put it around five hours ago," Sheila said. "9:00 p.m."

"Was she raped?" asked Steve.

"No apparent signs of tearing or trauma in the vaginal area or anus," she concluded. "This water didn't help but I found no traces of semen or blood. There's trauma to the back of her head. Possible skull fracture."

She pulled back the victim's hair and exposed the purple bruising formed around her neck and throat.

"But, my guess — she was strangled," Sheila continued. "I'll know more when I get her on the table."

"Is that why her eyes look bloated and shit?" asked Ramon.

Sheila pulled the rest of Grace's hair out of her face and revealed her strange-looking eyes. They appeared blood shot and swollen with a small amount of dried blood settled in the corner of her eyes. She grabbed a pair of small clamps from her bag and leaned down very close to the victim's face. She adjusted the LED light on her loop glasses and placed the clamps above the eye sockets.

"She's missing her fibrous core and the palpebral portions of the orbicularis oculi muscle," said Sheila.

Steve experienced an enormous rush of heat burst through his body, and he became extremely nauseated. He supported himself on the wall. He couldn't believe what came out of Sheila's mouth.

"In English, Doc," ordered Captain Dunn.

"She's missing her eyelids," commented Steve in a very monotone voice.

Everyone in the room looked at Steve and then looked back at the medical examiner.

"He's right," confirmed Sheila with a stunned expression on her face.

Captain Dunn appeared panicked as he searched for the right words to address his men and women on scene.

"Listen up!" yelled Dunn. "No one says a god damn thing, understood? This is coming from the top and it'll be your ass."

"The dude cut off her eyelids, bro?" asked a dumbfounded Ramon. "Wasn't that some shit a while back?"

"It's impossible," muttered Captain Dunn as he looked at Steve and Sheila. "Polski is dead."

Jack and Tate pulled up to the curb of the elementary school "pick-up" zone and opened the door to allow Sophie, 8, into the backseat of their Ford Taurus. She was a quiet little girl. Quite the opposite of Jack's other daughter, Lily, who was 10. Sophie slid into the backseat and closed the door.

"Looks like we got a prisoner," joked Tate.

"How was school, babe?" asked Jack.

"School," she answered.

"But you had a good day?" continued Jack.

"Yeah," answered Sophie.

"Did you learn anything cool today?" asked Jack.

"Not really, Daddy," she confessed.

"The good news is," Tate said to Jack. "She won't get a boyfriend if she never talks."

"Boys are disgusting," said Sophie.

"Yes, we are," agreed Tate.

"Except my Daddy," complimented Sophie.

"I'll be there to walk you down the aisle," said Jack. "Even if you wait 'til you're 50."

"Promise?" asked Sophie.

"Promise," confirmed Jack. "I'm dropping you at Grandma's."

"Oh, okay," said Sophie softly.

"You wanted to hang out with your dad, huh?" sympathized Tate as Sophie nodded her cute head up and down. "Well, your Daddy has to catch bad guys so you and your sister can be safe."

"I'm sorry, sweetheart," said Jack.

"What if you don't?" asked Sophie.

Jack and Tate were surprised that she engaged them in conversation.

"What do you mean, honey?" asked Jack.

"What if the bad guys get you, Daddy?" asked Sophie as her eyes welled up with tears.

"I won't let the bad guys get your Daddy," promised Tate as the sound of a buzzing vibration caught his attention...

It was barely 5:00 a.m. when the phone call from Rita woke up Tate and Nicole. They were cuddled up next to each other when the annoying vibration of his cell phone rattled on the nightstand next to the bed. It was extremely rare that Nicole stayed the night on the boat due to her work schedule, but they ended up falling asleep together. At least Tate believed it was her work schedule that made their slumber parties infrequent. Maybe their relationship progressed to a point where she felt more comfortable staying over instead of re-creating the college-dorm "walk of shame". Tate was too tired to contemplate his thoughts on the subject — or he just never wanted to think about it.

"Have you turned on the news, sugar?" asked Rita.

"I haven't even pee'd," whispered Tate as he slowly pulled himself out of bed.

"Why are you whisperin'?" quizzed Rita. "Oh, ya'got yourself some company n'all."

Nicole pulled the covers over her naked body and rolled over as Tate took the conversation out of the cabin and into the gulley and TV room. He made sure the door was closed so Nicole wouldn't be bothered with the noise from his conversation and the TV.

"What's going on?" Tate asked.

"A body was found in Jonathan Harper's house," she informed.

"Is it him?" he asked.

"They all say he's been in Switzerland," she stated. "They think it could be his daughter."

Tate found his remote that he could never seem to find and turned up the volume. The female news reporter, Megan Hunt, 28, could have been ordered out of a "news reporter" manufacturer's mold complete with the official "news reporter" dialect. She was reporting live outside of the Spanish-style Harper mansion. Tate noticed the crime scene tape behind a myriad of police department vehicles parked in front.

"Police department officials have had a tight lip in regards to the mysterious activity surrounding the apparent body found in the home of prolific real estate developer and friend of the Mayor — Jonathan Harper," she reported.

She mentioned that his daughter was believed to be living in the house while she went to college and that it was confirmed that Jonathan and his wife were on their way back from an overseas business trip in Switzerland. She went on and explained that there had been no official statement from the police or Harper's handlers and that there hadn't been a body removed from the property. She continued her reporting and cued up news footage of concerned neighbors.

"Neighbors want answers and feel they have a right to know if they are safe in their own homes," stated Megan.

"We just want to know what's going on," said a worried neighbor. "There's crime scene tape everywhere and I've seen the police walking in and out of the house."

"I hope it's not Grace," said another neighbor. "She's such a nice girl."

Megan continued, "The name Jonathan Harper sparks a variety of different reactions from the community based on the steady whirlwind of controversy that often surrounds his name with Mayor Villanueva and Police Chief Phillip Steward."

"With his relationship with the Mayor and the police and everything," conceded another neighbor, "we'll get information when they want us to."

"So far that statement has been true," confirmed Megan. "This is Megan Hunt reporting live in La Jolla."

Tate knew the neighbor's statement was absolutely accurate. They would only release the information that needed to be released but would hold on to anything that could be construed as controversial or damaging to the city or the department. He remembered the drill.

Phillip Steward, 51, stood with his arms folded across his chest. He could've been a stunt double for the late Clark Gable, down to the identical thin mustache.

"Detective Holloway, what the hell were you thinking?" he gasped. "Why are you talking with a reporter?"

A younger Tate paced in the middle of Chief Mario Villanueva's stately office. He had dark circles under his eyes and looked like he hadn't slept for a while.

"There is more to the story," pleaded Tate. "I have notes and theories. I think we got it wrong."

Then Detective Martin Dunn, 50, without his orange skin and white goatee, sat in a high-back leather chair next to Dr. Anita Goel, 45, the police department's in-house psychiatrist.

"You need to stop, Tate," yelled Dunn as he sat forward in the chair. "It's over! He's dead."

"You're ignoring some new facts," rambled Tate, "I may have some evidence. I think there was someone else."

Anita sat up in her chair. She was extremely beautiful but was very masculine looking with her short-cropped hair. She never married or dated men, according to some of the department gossip. Most people felt her lips were attached to Chief Villanueva's ass so much that she didn't have time to date. Tate knew she fancied women but felt that was her own business. Being a lesbian had nothing to do with why Tate disliked her so much.

"He's suffering from paranoia and having delusional thoughts," claimed Anita who spoke as if Tate wasn't in the room. "I told you to shut him down months ago before he brings down the Chief."

"I'm standing right here bitch," said Tate. "You've had it in for me since day one."

Tate never liked Anita in all the years she wandered the hallways looking to relieve cops of their badges and pensions. He felt her only concern was avoiding litigation and department lawsuits and not the well-beings of cops who truly needed her services.

"Listen to yourself, Detective," she said. "My job is to make sure the public is safe from gun-toting cops who are clinical cases like you."

"Your job's been protecting the Chief," snapped Tate.

Detective Steve Pelletti listened from the couch. He had a difficult time dealing with Tate's downward spiral and wondered if he had seriously lost his mind.

"You think all this is going to bring Jack back," asked Steve calmly.

"He's right," agreed Dunn. "We all loved him, Tate."

"But what if we didn't get the main guy?" pleaded Tate. "What if 'The Eye' is still out there?"

"And what if Santa Clause came down the chimney and had cocoa with the Easter bunny?" quipped Anita.

"There haven't been any victims in a year," exclaimed Steward. "Not one. We got him!"

"What if we were wrong?" continued Tate.

"You killed him, Tate," said Dunn. "You ended it."

"Are you guys that scared of what you might find?" laughed Tate. "An election is more important than protecting the citizens of San Diego?"

"Maybe you should take some time," offered Dunn.

"And that's not a request," commanded Steward. "Wait for me in my office."

"No need for the formal shit," Tate informed. "I'm gone."

Tate unhooked his shoulder holster and placed his gun and badge on the desk. Out of the corner of his eye he noticed that Dunn reached for his Glock when he removed his gun. Tate wondered if he seemed that unstable and insane that Dunn feared he would've shot them. He hoped it was because they knew there was some validity to his claims.

"Steve, c'mon man, you saw some of my notes," said Tate who had calmed down. "Shit, you understood my theory."

"Yes," agreed Steve, "some of it, I must admit is interesting, but c'mon, he couldn't stop killin' for this long. There's no way."

"There's never been a serial killer who murdered like this guy and then stopped cold turkey," explained Anita sarcastically. "We'd be scaring the public without merit."

"We don't need you dredging up dirt from the past," said Steward.

"This city needs to continue to heal," said a man sitting in the shadows of the dark office. Tate didn't know who he was and had never seen him before. He was in his early forties and dressed in a perfectly tailored Armani suit.

"Who the fuck are you?" snapped Tate.

"That's Jonathan Harper," offered Steward. "He's a friend of the Chief's."

Tate laughed at the comment from Captain Steward.

"It was a difficult time for the community," stated Harper. "Having the public think there could be another serial killer on the loose would be detrimental to the city and the department."

"And a Chief of Police running for Mayor," said Tate.

"Hello? Hey!" said Rita.

Rita's voice snapped Tate back to reality.

"I guess Karma's a bitch, huh?" she said. "Then ya' marry one."

"All my wives were not complete bitches," stated Tate. "I had a hand in driving them to Bitchville."

"And what about wife number four, sugar?" asked Rita. "The one laying in your bed."

"I don't want to talk about this right now," he said.

"You don't think the Harper girl was murdered n'all?" quizzed Rita.

Tate hesitated with his response and Rita picked up on it.

"Rich socialite like that?" asked Tate.

"Probably drug related," suggested Rita.

"Probably," agreed Tate.

Tate didn't want to get into the fact that last night was the eight-year anniversary of the death of his partner, Jack Runyan. That he found it a little ironic that Jonathan Harper's daughter died the same day eight years later and that her father was intricately involved in his dismissal from the police force. He was going to keep that to himself.

"No one's even confirmed that it's her," stated Tate.

Tate agreed to meet up with Rita later in the day to go over some potential clients. He wondered what Nicole would think if she knew he was going over a list of women he was going to fuck for cash. He didn't know how much longer he could live with his secret. He was ashamed that he used the term "secret". No matter how you dressed it up, it was a lie — plain and simple.

He crawled back into bed with Nicole and snuggled up behind her naked body. He never liked to cuddle with anyone before, and he wondered why it felt different with her. His mind drifted off to thoughts of Grace Harper. He wondered how someone of her stature and wealth got mixed up in drugs and jeopardized a lifestyle that average people would die for. His mind raced.

"What if she was murdered?" he thought in his head. "I'd need to know how she was killed."

VENGEANCE IS NOW

It was 8:00 a.m. when the coroner's van arrived at the Harper mansion and caused a wave of media frenzy as the news crews raced to be the first to go live on the air. The police barricaded a perimeter to keep the press out and allowed the van close enough to wheel the body out without having TV cameras shoot the event and broadcast the removal. What they couldn't account for were the news helicopters that hovered above the property. That wasn't typical protocol so the electricity in the air was evident as the news vans powered up. They knew this was something big.

Detective Pelletti and Detective Aguilar were seated in the Harper library with Captain Dunn and the housekeeper, Rosa Delgado. The library's décor was decadent and full of Ivy League panache. Floor-to-ceiling mahogany bookshelves with matching sliding ladder, high-back leather chairs, antique and first-edition books, and gorgeous Persian rugs covered portions of the Macassar ebony flooring from India.

Rosa was in her early 50's and was shaken and distraught over the death of Grace; who had been in her life since she was a little girl. Detective Aguilar handled the questioning in her native Spanish language.

"Please reassure her that we don't care about her legal status," added Captain Dunn.

"No estamos preocupados por su estatus legal," explained Ramon.

A distraught Rosa nodded her head and confirmed she understood.

"Sí," she said.

Ramon found out that Rosa asked for the night off to attend a family gathering and Grace granted her permission without any questioning. Grace always allowed her time off, especially when her parents were out of town, because Grace never wanted or needed a "servant" to be at the house all of the time. In fact, Grace encouraged her to spend time with her family instead of being at the house. Grace thought of her as a close relative and never felt comfortable considering Rosa an employee.

"So it wasn't unusual for you to take the night off?" questioned Ramon in Spanish.

"No," answered Rosa in her native tongue, "not when Mr. and Mrs. Harper were out of town. But the text was different."

"What text?" asked Ramon.

"Little Mija showed me how to text," explained Rosa with tears in her eyes. "She was so proud to teach me. She sent me a text around 9:00 p.m. asking me back to the house."

"Grace? For what reason?" questioned Ramon.

"She didn't say," Rosa said.

"Can I see your phone?" requested Ramon.

Rosa dug into her purse and handed her cell phone to Ramon. The sound of helicopters reverberated above the house.

"She said she received a text asking her to come back to the house," Ramon explained to the other detectives.

Steve listened to Ramon as he questioned Rosa, but he was completely distracted by the thoughts that ran through his head. When they discovered that Grace was murdered in the same fashion as several victims eight years earlier, he couldn't help but think of his former partner, Tate Holloway and a serial killer with the moniker, "The Eye".

Ramon looked at Rosa's cell phone and noticed the text came in from an "unknown" number. It read, *"Hey Rosa, it's Grace. Could you come back to the house around 9:30 p.m.?"* Rosa replied to the text, *"Yes, is everything okay?"* Grace never responded to her text so she ended up coming back to the house.

"So I come here and ... find her," cried Rosa.

"Tell her thank you and we'll probably need her to come down to the precinct for more questioning when she feels a little better," offered Dunn.

Rosa looked visibly shaken, as two uniformed officers escorted her out.

"Get her something to drink," Steve said to one of the officers. "She's still in shock."

"Close the door on your way out," requested Dunn.

The three men remained in the library, and Steve could see the stress and fatigue mounting on Captain Dunn's face. Steve realized the ramifications of a copycat serial killer during an election year. He knew the political suicide and media fiasco that would ensue if by chance ... no, he didn't want to think of that nightmare. He could only imagine the ulcer building in Dunn's stomach from the backlash that he could face from downtown. The daughter of the most influential man in San Diego was brutally murdered under Dunn's command. Not to mention a really good friend of the Mayor's. These were the situations that ruined careers. Someone would have to take the fall and what easier way of displaying action than to fire the Captain and replace the Chief of Police. No, this was definitely not your ordinary scenario — and Steve knew that sleep and quality time with his wife were now a thing of the past.

"This is going to be a nightmare downtown," said Dunn.

"Are we calling in the feds?" asked Steve. "Maybe a profiler?"

"Are you out of your mind, Detective?" chastised Dunn. "We need more information."

"Have you heard from the Mayor?" asked Steve.

"Let me worry about that," he snapped. "You two worry about the case."

"We can't leak any information about the method," said Steve.

"Absolutely not," Dunn interrupted.

"I'll send the phone to tech and see if we get anything from the text, bro," said Ramon.

"It'll be a throw away," claimed Dunn. "But it's worth a shot."

Captain Dunn answered his cell phone and walked to the back of the large library. Steve and Ramon continued with their case assessment.

"Someone wanted Grace dead n'shit and the housekeeper to find her, bro," stated Ramon. "Why?"

"I don't know," admitted Steve.

"It was the perfect ransom situation and shit, too," said Ramon. "And the M.E. doesn't think it was a sexual assault and shit."

"Nope, he wanted her dead and everyone to see his work," answered Steve.

Ramon saw that Steve's mind was wandering and he was having a difficult time focusing.

"This is the same shit —," added Ramon.

"—I know," interrupted Steve as he stared off into space.

"Isn't he dead and shit?" quizzed Ramon.

Captain Dunn wanted to re-engage in the conversation after he finished his phone call but noticed the silence while he approached them.

"What?" asked Dunn.

"This has to be a copycat, right Captain?" asked Ramon.

"Of course it's a fuckin' copycat," answered Dunn emphatically. "That's why we're not involving the feds. The real guy, Polski, is dead."

Steve remembered the final meeting that went down between the current Mayor, Captain Dunn, Dr. Anita Goel and Jonathan Harper. The question and statement that lingered in his mind were from Detective Tate Holloway, "What if we were wrong?" And from Jonathan Harper, "A serial killer on the loose would be detrimental to the city and the department."

His train of thought was interrupted by a knock at the library door. A uniformed officer poked his head inside.

"Sir, there was a 10-10 reported about a block and a half from here," stated the officer. "The house has video surveillance."

A 10-10 was a possible burglary in progress so Steve knew this could be a routine break-in or the killer was jumping fences during his getaway. This was a high-end neighborhood so break-ins weren't that common.

"Time?" asked Dunn.

"Around 8:15 p.m.," answered the officer.

"We may have video of our copycat killer," stated Dunn.

Tate's office, known as Holloway P.I., was located on Lovelock Street just north of San Diego's Old Town and west of the Riverwalk Golf Club. It was a nice area, and Tate knew that if he didn't continue with his extracurricular activities there was no way he could afford the space. Plus, he'd lose the boat his grandfather left him. He also found it ironic that his office was located on a street name that was an oxymoron to his job. He wasn't in the business of couples being locked in love but rather unlocking them with a messy divorce.

The space consisted of a small lobby where Rita's desk was placed and a little larger office that Tate occupied when he came into the office — that added up to about three days a week, but he still wanted a cool space.

The exposed brick walls contained old surfboards that represented different periods in Tate's life. Framed photos of famous surfing beaches from around the world adorned the walls in Tate's office. The reality was that Rita was always at Tate's desk anyway so he didn't understand why she gave the impression she sat in the lobby. Hell, she practically ran everything so why not.

"So sugar, Nicole stayed over?" quizzed Rita who sat at his desk with a headset on.

"Are you on the phone or talking to me, dude?" he asked.

"You know damn well I'm not on the phone, *dude*," she answered.

"I brought you some peanut brittle," offered Tate.

"Okay, I get the hint," she conceded.

Rita was decked out in skin-tight jeans and a cute "Mary Anne-styled" red-and-white checkered blouse that accentuated her fantastic figure. She reminded Tate of Holly Hunter — small but a spitfire.

"People are buzzing over this Harper thing," he said.

"Still haven't released a cause of death," she added.

"You'll find out when they want you to," offered Tate.

"I think I'm going to poke around a little, sugar," stated Rita.

"Just don't fly any red flags, please," begged Tate. "Any calls?"

"I have my book, sugar," she answered.

"I meant legitimate P.I. calls," said Tate.

Business hadn't been exactly booming, but sometimes he felt she allowed potential clients to walk because there was more money to be made in prostitution. He enjoyed the money and the anticipation of new encounters, but sometimes he felt better when he worked actual cases. Not only for his conscience but to keep his investigation tools sharp.

"Not today sugar," she said. "Let's talk clients. I'm sorry about the flake last night."

"It's fine," he confessed.

"Bonnie is coming to town this week," chuckled Rita.

Tate knew she was one of their top-paying customers, but every time she came to town she'd unleash a crazy request on him. Not conventional requests like a certain sexual position or taking direction in helping them achieve the best orgasm possible. Bizarre requests like dressing up in costumes and roleplaying. He had never forgotten the time she had a suite at the Manchester Grand Hyatt in San Diego.

"I'm a little nervous, Bonnie," confessed Tate.

Bonnie, 53, was a sassy brunette that reminded Tate of Bernadette Peters right down to the cute little mole above her lip. She was a corporate attorney who didn't have time for the nonsense of dating so she relied on Tate to handle the sexual itches she had to scratch. She handled high clearance security cases for defense contractors so she flew down from Seattle once every six weeks.

"It's not that bad, silly," said Bonnie. "Not like last year's Renaissance fair."

That's when Tate dressed up and appeared in public dressed as King Louis XVI to her Marie Antoinette. The fact that people enjoyed attending those conventions and truly acted out the parts completely baffled Tate. Although he admitted, "off with her head" was a kinky way of including "head" into their roleplaying. Nonetheless, he preferred losing himself and escaping this world with a bottle of amazing tequila and a little bit of weed. Not being a cop anymore allowed him to indulge in extracurricular activities that the department would frown upon. Weed being the perfect example.

"Thank God," complained Tate as he kissed down her neck and to her cleavage.

He slowly unbuttoned her blouse and revealed a stunning black-lace bra. He used his thumbs and massaged her nipples in a circular motion. She breathed deeply but grabbed his hands and stopped the arousal.

"Not so fast," she said. "Your costume's in the bag."

"Really?" he complained.

She grabbed his crotch and rubbed him seductively.

"Really," she confirmed. "With instructions."

Tate couldn't believe it when he was finally in the bathroom. He felt ridiculous. He didn't even enjoy Halloween let alone understand the fascination with costumes that Bonnie desired when they were together. Most people would tell Tate he was crazy if he turned down $2,000 for a couple of hours of sex with a hot older woman. He thought they might have felt differently if they saw him in that moment. He couldn't even look at himself in the mirror.

"Meow ... come out and play, meow," cooed Bonnie from the bedroom of the hotel suite.

Tate took a deep breath and opened the door. Not one of the more proud moments in his life. He complied with her instructions and the game began.

"Batman!" expressed Tate as he emerged from the bathroom in a movie-studio-quality Batman suit.

Bonnie was tied to the bed wearing the Catwoman suit that made 13-year-old boys tingle when they saw Halle Barry wear it on the big screen. Although, Halle's naked breasts didn't hang out of her costume and her tights weren't crotch-less.

"Come save me Batman," purred Bonnie. "And clean me with your tongue."

"Holy big tits," said Tate from the script. "I'm going to need my special tool to free you."

Tate had to chuckle at the thought of Bonnie in the Catwoman costume. She definitely wasn't conventional but at least she made their encounters interesting — just as long as he didn't have to be seen in public.

"Sugar, I'm gonna have to find you a 'plushie' n'all," laughed Rita.

"What the fuck is that?" asked Tate.

"Them weirdos who dress up like stuffed animals and screw through their damn costumes," she explained.

"Weirdos?" exclaimed Tate. "What would you call a dude dressed up as Batman?"

"A weird dude," laughed Rita.

Tate loved Rita's sense of humor, and he thought most of the shit she said was funnier in her Southern accent. He went over his "client" list and entered his schedule into his daily planner. He loved the phrase "daily planner" because it didn't reflect his way of life.

He flipped on the news in his office and placed his feet on the desk. Police Chief Phillip Steward stood at the podium and read a statement to the press.

"The body of Grace Harper was discovered last night in the Harper home," he said. "We are not releasing any details until we have further information."

"How did she die?" interrupted a reporter.

"Again, we aren't releasing any information until we know more ourselves," he continued.

Tate noticed Detective Pelletti and Captain Dunn standing next to the podium. He knew Steve well enough to know his body language and the fact he was shifting his weight from one foot to another was a classic sign of being uncomfortable. They learned the art of body language together at the academy when studying different forms of interrogation. Tate recognized when someone didn't want to draw attention to themselves, and Steve fit the bill.

"Was it a suicide?" asked another reporter.

"This is a tough time for the Harper family," added Steward, "and all they ask is that you respect their privacy as they maneuver through these painful times. Thank you."

The crowd of reporters went crazy as they yelled more questions at Steward as he exited the podium.

Tate thought Steward sidestepped the suicide question because the family would be embarrassed at the revelation that their perfect family dealt with issues just like every other family in the world. The word that stuck in his mind and increased Tate's curiosity was "maneuver". Why would someone have to "maneuver" through painful times?

"Little bit of spin on that curveball and all," stated Rita.

"Question is — what are they hiding?" quizzed Tate.

The mood was quite somber as Steve and Ramon entered the hotel room of Jonathan Harper and his wife, Lana. Their plane had landed about an hour ago, and they were hiding out at the exclusive Lodge at Torrey Pines. It was the perfect isolated locale if you wanted to avoid the press and have privacy during a tumultuous time. The last thing the family wanted was to have a camera pointed at them and be asked what it felt like to lose a daughter. A stupid question nonetheless, but one that would surely be asked.

The lodge sat on a bluff between La Jolla and Del Mar and offered amazing coastal views. Steve had always wanted to take Marcy there, but his pay-grade wouldn't even allow them to stay in the lobby on a cot. He wished he could be there on better terms. It didn't matter how rich or poor a parent was; it was always difficult to discuss the murder of a son or daughter. The parents always seemed to want specifics even though the information was typically gruesome. That part of the job never got easier.

Jonathan Harper was slouched in an over-sized leather couch that adorned the magnificent suite. He sipped on a scotch and appeared to have aged by 20 years since the last time Steve saw him. His attorney and family friend, Arthur Stein, 55, stood right behind the couch. Stein was a tall, wiry, balding man who wore circular glasses and spoke with a strong lisp. He informed everyone that Lana Harper had to be sedated and was laying down in the bedroom.

Steve could only imagine what she might be going through. He knew she would probably wake up disoriented and would wonder if it was all a bad dream. The realization that it was true would be like reliving the moment she was told of the murder.

"Why?" sobbed Jonathan. "She wouldn't hurt anyone."

Captain Dunn and Chief Steward were seated next to him in separate high-back leather chairs. Their concern for Harper was evident on their faces.

"We will devote as many resources necessary to find out who did this," said Steward.

"And we will, Jonathan," confirmed Dunn.

"Have you had any recent death threats or strange encounters lately?" asked Steve.

"Maybe a former employee or something?" continued Ramon.

"Not that I know of," whimpered Harper. "Ask my security chief for any records you might need."

"I'll get you that 'informathion,' Detective," added Stein with his lisp.

"How many people knew you were going to be away from the home and out of the country?" quizzed Steve.

Harper shook his head signifying he didn't know.

"I'll check with the travel 'thecretary' and come up with a 'listh,'" offered Stein.

Steve ignored the strong lisp but could tell that Ramon had to look down at his notes to hide his smirk. He only hoped Ramon was able to get past his 13-year-old boy mentality and understood that Stein said "secretary" and "list".

"Her eyelids?" questioned Harper. "Is it some kind of copycat sicko? Did you contact the FBI?"

The other men looked at each other and waited to see who would speak up first. Arthur Stein also anticipated an answer.

"There's no need for the feds to get involved," stated Dunn. "Our theory is a random act by a copycat of The Eye."

Steve and Ramon were shocked that the Captain would confirm a theory that hadn't really been discussed by anyone. Steve knew there were autopsy reports and collected evidence that needed to be analyzed before they confirmed a theory. Not to mention any threats or grudges that disgruntled colleagues might have carried out over sour business dealings. Steve had assumed that was a serious possibility.

"Was she ... violated?" asked Harper softly.

"We don't believe so," confirmed Steve. "But there was a lot of water contamination from the tub."

Steward's expression on his face told Steve that he didn't want the possible water-damaged forensics mentioned yet.

"There was water damage?" asked Harper. "It could affect catching the guy?"

"We won't let it get in the way of an arrest," interrupted Steward.

"We're meeting with the Medical Examiner later," offered Steve.

"We'll know a lot more after that," added Ramon.

"They're cutting my baby up," sobbed Harper.

He wasn't anything like the shrewd businessman or ball-busting negotiator he'd been made out to be. The death of a child does that to a man. He had dropped his head into his hands and was bawling a deep guttural sob. There wasn't a more uncomfortable situation for men than to be in close proximity to a sobbing man. Steve mourned for Harper's dignity and felt like an intruder in a very private moment.

"I think he 'needsth' to lay down for a while," said a protective Stein.

"We'll be in touch, Arthur," said Steward. "Detective Pelletti is my best guy."

The compliment from Chief Steward wasn't lost on Steve or Ramon for that matter. Steve couldn't grasp if he was just highly acknowledged by the Chief of Police or had been offered up as the sacrificial lamb if the case didn't unfold the way the Chief wanted. He knew that Steward was no stranger to the blame game. He'd seen it firsthand.

On the way to their car, Steve and Ramon received a call from a security company that had the surveillance footage from the possible 10-10 the previous night. This was their only significant lead so they made it a priority to pick up the video so it could be analyzed.

"Fuck, bro, that lisp," chuckled Ramon as he drove down the highway. "I couldn't keep from laughing and shit."

"You mean, '*sthit*,'" laughed Steve.

"With all that cash, bro," continued Ramon. "You couldn't get that shit fixed?"

Steve went over the case in his head as they rode over to the security company with Ramon. He was convinced their "perp" was a copycat. He truly believed that his former partner had killed The Eye eight years ago. He was also convinced that the Harpers had nothing to do with the murder. Jonathan Harper's agony was too real to be an acting job. He'd been around the block a few times and experienced some exceptionally brilliant liars, but none of them could come close to the believability of Harper's true emotions.

He also wondered how long the department could delay the murder announcement to the press. People had assumed that Grace committed suicide because of the secrecy and lack of information about the case. That they were holding off because suicide has such a negative connotation and might be an embarrassment to the family.

Harper's ties to the department and the Mayor were not a secret, and the press made sure the citizens of San Diego were aware of the connection. However, there's no way Harper would allow his daughter's reputation to be scrutinized just to keep specifics about the murder from the public. That would be the police department's problem not his. Just as long as the fallout didn't hit the Mayor's desk.

"Hopefully, we'll get something from the video," said Steve.

The detectives continued to laugh on and off about Arthur Stein's lisp until their car pulled into the parking lot of Vision Security. It was a typical metal warehouse located in the southern side of the industrial district. All the major branches in the military were represented in the San Diego region so most of the security companies that catered to the wealthy were owned by ex-military. It was the perfect transition if you were a trained soldier looking to stay in the area after your military career ended. The beautiful year-round climate was another reason to drop anchor and establish roots.

They met the owner, CJ Mueller, 32, in his office. Ramon recognized his tattoo that identified him as a former member of the 1st Marine Special Operations Battalion.

"Boo-yah," said Ramon as he pointed at CJ's tattoo. "I was 1st Battalion, 4th Marines."

"Boo-yah," responded CJ. "Always glad to help a fellow marine. Take a look."

CJ pointed the remote control at the monitor and cued up the security footage. A nicely dressed man crouched by a fence was seen entering the side-yard of a house. The man's face was hidden in the shadows, and the quality of the video was scratchy and "pixilated".

"What's wrong with the picture?" asked Steve.

"Could have been a short or a weak fuse," explained CJ. "Sometimes the signal gets scrambled if it doesn't have enough juice."

The man in the video opened the sliding glass door and walked inside the house. He quickly exited and tripped over the flowerpot. He laid on the ground for a few minutes and then got back up to his feet. He limped back to the gate and crouched. He was looking up at the next-door neighbors. His face turned and stopped in front of the camera, but the quality of the picture was so poor he was completely unidentifiable.

"Shit," complained Steve.

"Tech might be able to clean it up, bro," said Ramon.

"If they're any good," offered CJ, "they should have a program to recreate and mirror the pixels, which should produce a clear picture."

It was a start but not the smoking gun they had hoped for. Even if the man wasn't the killer, they had to identify and question him. They needed to find out if he saw anything out of the ordinary that night. He might have crossed paths with the perpetrator and not even have known it.

VENGEANCE IS NOW

I had to focus on work all day today and wonder how soon the world would know that I'm back. Is it today? Am I the scariest human being on the West Coast? Human being? That's fuckin' hilarious. The only thing human about me is my DNA — definitely not my brain or my thoughts. I'm like a game hunter who hangs out with the People for the Ethical Treatment of Animals. I have to hide my thirst for human suffering, which I've done quite well over the last eight years.

Meyers would have been so proud. But last night I opened a door that might not be able to be closed again. I have to let this play out, but my patience has to win over my demons. Sticking to the plan is more important. Tate Holloway will have his eyes opened soon enough. They all will!

When I follow my evil daydreams I have to admit, I'm really great at killing. My neighbor's dog, my cousin's cat, the rabbit in my third-grade class, the transient who was never missed, my aunt and uncle, and Doug the loser. Ah yes, Doug. Libby's molester and Mom's dreamboat of a boyfriend.

Mom was completely incoherent during that time in our lives. Doug would forge her signature on her government checks and deposit them into his own bank account. I avoided being home during that time. I'd sit on the roof of a nearby building in the 'Loin and watch the people below, observing their daily behaviors. To most people, the view would have been golden, but I wanted to see what happiness looked like. I also fantasized about killing them all. Push someone in front of a car. Drop a brick on the head of an unsuspecting normal person. Normal? What the fuck is that? If people saw into my head, they would assume I was a psychopath or mentally fucked up. They'd be correct.

I personally don't understand anyone who doesn't fantasize about murdering people. My foster brother and I would have deep conversations about killing. I met him in my fourth foster home after Mother died. The first three foster parents sensed my darkness but were too afraid to confront me so they quietly booted me out. Fuckers. Why didn't I kill them? My foster brother and I would discuss how we're only on Earth for so long. Why should we leave everything up to one "entity" to decide our fate? I didn't believe in God.

He was the only person who got me. He understood the depths of my deviancy. Some people might look at someone walking down the street and wonder where they came from or what they do for a living. I thought about different ways I could ruin their lives. I thought about how many methods I could use to kill them and inflict the most pain. That seemed more exciting for me — and normal. Show me a picture of someone who lived or worked on my block, and I'll show you detailed notes on how I would exterminate them. Some kids collected baseball cards — I collected murder notes.

Poisoning someone to make it look like a suicide or overdose thrilled me and danced around in my head like a kid curious what Santa Claus might bring them for Christmas. I knew where he kept his stash. I could tell you when his dope was getting low and when he just bought more. It was usually the day after Mother received her bi-monthly disability check. He was showing off the beer-bong his buddy had given him…

"Hey piece of shit," said Doug. "Grab three beers and load up my beer bong."

This was the chance I'd been waiting for. I went to the fridge and grabbed the cheap beer he used to drink. Not a popular product like Budweiser or Coors. This motherfucker was so cheap he bought the generic beer that had the word "Beer" printed on the white can. I knew that he just replenished his speed so I grabbed the baggie that contained the yellowy, chalky substance. He didn't realize I knew where he hid the junk. Considering he bought the cheapest beer in the city, I knew he wasn't purchasing the highest quality drugs. It was probably cut with household chemicals and contained more Comet than pure speed. I poured half of the bag into the mouth of the beer bong, dumped in some beer, and then poured the rest of the powder in. I had to wait for the foam to subside before helping "Dougie" with the process.

"How long does it take to load a bong you fuckin' asshole?" complained Doug as he chain smoked Doral Reds.

"Coming right up," I said. "Here we go."

I lifted the hose above his head, and he took every ounce of the beer into his stomach in less than 20 seconds. He unleashed a loud belch and clapped his hands with approval.

"Yeah!" yelled Doug. "Feels good! Are you in your room, Libby?"

Libby hid on the other side of the door and peeked through the crack in the doorway.

Before he could stand up, he clutched his chest and let out a long breath. His eyes bulged, he felt shortness of breath, and his skin turned pale.

"What the fuck?" gasped Doug.

He completely fell to the ground and wheezed. His body shivered like he had a fever and bubbly foam oozed out of the corner of his mouth. He reached up for me and I smiled — a smile bigger than any attempt of a smirk I tried for my school pictures. He needed me at that moment. When he died I spit on his face and stomped on his crotch with my boots. The look on Libby's face was precious — a happiness and contentment I'd never seen in her before. She received her most extravagant Christmas present — and I was St. Nicholas.

Now it was time to make my phone call.

For Tate, an early morning surf session was as much a part of his daily routine as a morning run was to joggers. He loved the one-on-one challenge of the ocean, which was essentially an individual and introspective experience that came down to him and the wave. He loved surfing Sunset Cliffs on Ocean Beach because it was difficult to get down to the sand from the steep rocks. You had to wait for low tide to safely attempt the trek down. It was also secluded enough for the locals, but it was never highly populated because of the dangerous beach access. He also loved the drive home down Sunset Cliffs Boulevard. It was as peaceful and beautiful as the surfing.

It was definitely a short board day. He had so much on his mind that he needed to blow off some steam by aggressively attacking the whitecaps. He left his long board at home for a different day when he felt like cruising and relaxing. This morning he was there to kick some ass, and he had kept his end of the bargain so far. Now he wanted one last wave to end his morning on a high note.

He couldn't stop thinking about Grace Harper. He was as anxious as the press to find out how she died. He felt confident that Rita would utilize her contacts inside the department and find out more information. The one little secret he knew about Rita was that she had sleepovers with a high-ranking official on Mayor Villanueva's re-election campaign — a *married* high-ranking official. And one of those sleepovers occurred last night. It was time she used her body for something in return rather than Tate ignoring his morals and conscience for the good of the P.I. firm's bank account.

Sandy bottom beaches made for fast and shifty swells called a *beach break*; which could produce powerful, long and shapely waves. The perfect swell rolled Tate's way, and he took off after it like a shark chased its prey. He used long strokes from his well-developed upper body to pull even with the wall. He positioned himself perfectly and caught it just before the sea foam crested at the top of the curl. He stood up and cut to the right and climbed the swell. He swiftly cut left and plunged down the wave and picked up speed. He leaned left and rode through the white mist and was completely covered by the ledge of the whitecap. He rode through the monster hollow tube and shot out through the other end before the ceiling of water collapsed on top of him. He finished his impressive run with a back flip into the water.

He pulled himself back onto his board and floated on his stomach while he caught his breath from riding that perfect wave. He thought about Nicole and where their relationship was headed. He hated that he used the word relationship. That sounded so "long term".

They had been together for about eight months now and that's usually when his internal alarm clock went off and told him to ditch whomever he was with. In fact, most women didn't even make it long enough for the alarm clock. Woman talked about how their internal clock ticked because they intensely desired to have a baby. Tate listened to his clock that signified it was time to sabotage his relationship. He wondered why the alarm hadn't gone off yet.

He was refreshed as the morning ocean breeze blew through his blond locks while he drove up Sunset Cliffs Boulevard. The way he felt at that moment was the reason why he surfed. All he needed was a nice espresso and a puff on a cigar and his tranquil morning would be complete. He had six missed phone calls from Rita, which meant her sleepover went well. There weren't too many things that annoyed Tate, but one of them was that Rita never left voice messages. She always wanted to speak directly to people and knew that Tate would realize the severity of a situation by the number of missed calls that were on his phone. Six missed calls were pretty serious.

"Talk to me, darling," said Tate.

"Have y'all seen the news?!" she exclaimed.

"I'm alone — just got out of the water," he answered. "What's wrong?"

"A mornin' quickie finally got my male friend to spill that Grace was murdered n'all," explained Rita. "But he wouldn't give me details."

"No shit," he said. "Must'a been a hell of a quickie."

"Well, sugar, I have this move — ," she confessed.

"— hey, hey, hey, Rita, please," interrupted Tate. "So why are you so upset about the news?"

"Honey, there was just an anonymous call to the press," she offered. "Someone claiming to be 'The Eye' said he murdered Grace Harper."

Tate dropped the phone. He felt numb. So many images shot through his mind.

Detective Jack Runyan, 38 and athletic, ran down an embankment and huddled next to Tate Holloway who hid behind a fence. Their guns were drawn. The air was crisp, and it was pitch-black outside. They didn't even get the benefit of the reflection from the moon because of the cloud cover. They were in a wooded area on what appeared to be a ranch up in the canyons. A white, two-story farmhouse was hidden from the road by pine trees that filled the property. Not that anyone used the old dirt road anyway. If someone didn't want to be found — this was the right place. A couple of lights were on inside the house.

"Is Polski in there?" asked Jack in a whisper.

"I know he is," confirmed Tate. "We need to move on him."

"We should call it in," whispered Jack.

"You wanna hike all the way back through the canyon just to get to the car?" asked Tate. "There's no cell service."

"Shit," Jack mumbled. "You're going to owe me a steak from Donovan's."

"Let's go," advised Tate.

Tate maneuvered over the fence and quickly moved across the embankment. Jack followed his lead. They made their way toward the house, but their footsteps snapped and crinkled dead pine needles that were scattered along the ground. It was so silent in the canyon that they feared their element of surprise would be jeopardized. They also worried that the suspect would hear their own heartbeats. A shadow urgently moved through the house to the backdoor.

Jack motioned with his head and took off to the north end of the house while Tate scurried to the south end. There was a wrap-around porch that extended the perimeter of the house. The light breeze rustled the wind chimes that hung throughout the property, which made eerie jingles. Tate cautiously approached the porch.

"Freeze!" yelled Jack from the other side of the house.

Gunfire erupted and the echo of the blasts roared through the canyon like deafening explosions.

Tate sprinted to the aid of his partner when the lights went dark in the house. Just before everything went dark, Tate thought he saw a shadow pass by one of the other windows. Everything was moving so fast he couldn't be sure.

Tate rounded the corner and saw Jack crawling along the ground.

"Jack!" yelled Tate.

"Get down!" screamed Jack.

A gunshot ricocheted off an old tractor, which forced Tate to take cover. He spotted the flash from the gun and fired two shots in that direction.

"Are you hit?!" asked Tate.

There was no response from Jack.

Tate heard movement and saw a man running with a limp toward the barn. He fired two more shots as he chased after him.

"He's going to the barn!" Tate yelled to Jack. "I think I hit him!"

Tate sprinted through the forest of trees to get to the barn, which was 50 yards from the farmhouse. He leaned against the barn doorway to get a better look inside. The floorboard creaked toward the back of the barn.

"It's over!" yelled Tate. "Give up, motherfucker!"

"Fuck ... you," gasped a voice from the barn.

Tate darted for a bale of hay in the corner of the barn and dove behind it. The wind had cleared the clouds enough for the full moon to beam down on them. The moonlight poured through the gaps in the barn walls and illuminated everything in a blue hue. The dust from the hay resembled a light snowfall as it floated around the barn. Tate saw a man slouched on the ground with one hand on his stomach while his other hand held a gun. A shadow was cast across his face so Tate couldn't see him clearly enough to recognize him.

"You're a good shot," grimaced the mysterious man.

Tate trained his Glock on the man.

"Why'd you kill all those people?" asked Tate.

The man chuckled which caused him to cough up blood.

"You'll know soon enough..." stated the man as he quickly lifted his revolver at Tate.

Tate fired his final two shots. A red mist painted the air as the bullets exploded into the man's chest.

Tate was out of his car and onto the boat before his mind was clear enough to focus on what needed to be done. He went straight down into the bedroom cabin and slid an armoire across the floor. He bent down and unlatched a hatch that opened to a secret compartment near the hull. A safe was hidden inside. Tate entered the code into the keypad that triggered an unlocking mechanism. He opened the safe and pulled out several overstuffed manila envelopes. Each envelope had "The Eye" handwritten on the front with a black Sharpie. He reached back into the safe and pulled out a Glock 9mm handgun and an ammunition clip. He snapped in the clip and slid the Glock into his waistband. He placed the files on the table and ran his hands through his hair.

He always wondered if this day would come. He thought he knew how he would handle it, but the shock left Tate discombobulated and clouded his mind. He needed to see the body. He needed to see the evidence. He needed to know the significance of Grace being murdered on the eight-year anniversary of Jack's killing. Those were three things that were going to be impossible since he no longer wore the badge. But there were three things he certainly accepted: This was going to get ugly; he knew he was going to have to break the law; and he knew he might die. Not a problem.

VENGEANCE IS NOW

Detective's Pelletti and Aguilar were summoned back to the Torrey Pines Lodge for an emergency meeting with Captain Dunn, Chief Steward, Jonathan Harper and Mayor Villanueva. Steve was certain it regarded the phone call to the press from the man who claimed to be "The Eye". This copycat murderer was going to cause a huge media uproar and raise a lot of questions that important people never wanted to answer.

"You worked that case, bro?" asked Ramon.

"Yeah," confirmed Steve.

"Didn't some detective go crazy and shit?" asked Ramon.

Steve didn't know how to answer Ramon's question. He decided it was best that Ramon know the history behind the case. After last night's call, it was all going to come out anyway.

Steve explained that he was assigned to work homicide with Tate Holloway after The Eye killed Tate's former partner, Jack Runyan. Tate couldn't let the case go and went on a rampage with his belief that the individual he killed wasn't the only serial killer involved. It was Tate's theory that it was a tandem team and that he had killed the student and not the teacher.

It was the beginning of the end for Tate as a detective and began his downward spiral in his personal life. His psyche evaluation and the fact that he spoke to a reporter regarding the death of The Eye caused a huge uproar downtown. The powers that be wanted the case closed to alleviate fear in the community and pull the focus away from the murders in an election year.

The fact that it was an election year again wasn't lost on Steve.

"Was Holloway credible and shit?" continued Ramon.

"It was an interesting theory," answered Steve. "Far-fetched, but interesting. We could never substantiate anything."

The two men entered the lobby through the door being held by the doorman who was dressed in a Scottish kilt — a long-standing tradition at Torrey Pines Lodge.

"You'd look sweet in that dress, bro," cracked Ramon.

"It's a kilt," explained Steve. "Fuckin' dumbass."

Mayor Villanueva paced back and forth in the Harper's hotel suite. He was a handsome and charismatic Hispanic man in his 50's. Captain Dunn and Chief Steward were in their usual positions on the leather chairs. A room service cart was parked in the middle of the room and contained a half-eaten burger and a few French fries smothered in catsup. Jonathan Harper sat on the couch. He looked completely exhausted from dealing with the horrible tragedy. Pelletti and Aguilar stood off near the kitchenette.

"And you're confident this is a copycat?" asked Harper softly.

"It has to be," said Dunn. "No way he's dormant for eight years."

"Does anyone have a theory about the date?" continued Harper softly. "It was eight years to the day The Eye was killed."

Steve hadn't made the connection to the anniversary of Marvin Polski's death and Grace Harper's murder. It wasn't mentioned in any of the briefings and the brass never brought it up.

"Perfect example of some sicko who 'Googled' 'The Eye'," added Steward. "It's classic copycat behavior."

"Did we know he was dormant?" asked Harper. "Are we positive?"

"There is no *'he'*," interrupted Dunn. "He was killed eight years ago, sir."

"We just ran comparisons through the system," offered Steve. "There've been no murders remotely similar over the last eight years. Nothing."

"The detective that killed him," quizzed Harper. "He had a theory there were two men?"

"It was disproven," snapped Dunn. "His credibility and reputation were ruined."

"We looked into it, and it just wasn't plausible," offered Steward.

Steve knew they looked into the claims from Tate. He just wasn't sure how closely they glared at it under the microscope. He just couldn't believe that such a prolific serial killer would just stop killing because law enforcement believed he was dead. Not when he was killing one person a week for several months. His slaughtering hit a crescendo right before he was killed. The FBI profiler assigned to the case wrote documents that explained the same impossibility.

"Who was it again?" questioned Harper.

The men in the room stared at one another before Captain Dunn took the lead and answered Harper's question.

"Detective Tate Holloway," answered Dunn. "He's a very disturbed man. Runs a two-bit P.I. firm in town."

Steve's phone beeped from a text. He glanced at the phone and looked at the screen. It read, *"Harper Autopsy complete."* He showed his phone to Ramon and excused the both of them to head off to the Medical Examiner's office. Captain Dunn wanted to make sure they called him when they found out anything.

Mayor Villanueva motioned for Chief Steward to follow him into a vacant bedroom. Captain Dunn stood up from his chair and moved closer to the door. He kept close attention to their conversation.

"We need to keep this ... controlled," advised the Mayor.

"I'm well aware of the upcoming election," confirmed Steward.

"What do you make of the date?" questioned the Mayor.

"Exactly what I said," explained Steward. "Any wackjob could look it up on the Internet."

"There's a straw poll next week," added the Mayor. "Emphasize the copycat element of the crime."

"Harper has a big say in what goes down in your campaign," confessed Steward.

"He's emotionally unfit right now," said the Mayor.

"It's his daughter, Mario," reminded Steward.

"You answer to me, *Phil*," scolded the Mayor who was not pleased to be called by his first name. "We need to be on top of this."

"Of course, Mister Mayor," offered Steward.

Chief Steward was fully aware that if something went wrong in the press or the Mayor's numbers plummeted over the murder; the ax would fall on his neck.

Grace Harper's body rested on the metal surgical table down in the morgue. A baby-blue sheet covered her face. Her skin looked porcelain white, which made the stitching from the autopsy stand out in a bright red. Steve never liked being in the morgue. He always felt the stench stuck in his nostrils and stayed with him for a few days. That's why he flunked biology in high school. He never went to class.

Dr. Sheila Walker presided over the body as she held her clipboard and wore her magnified, looped glasses.

"This smell doesn't bother you?" Steve asked Ramon.

"Shit no, bro," quipped Ramon. "Should've smelled all the burnt corpses in Iraq."

"Do you need a mask, Steve?" joked Sheila, which caused Ramon to crack up laughing.

"I'm fine," snapped Steve. "Let's get going, please."

Sheila explained that she found nothing too unusual during the autopsy. There were no apparent drugs in her system. Her stomach contents contained chicken and rice with apple juice. Her organs were healthy and their weight was normal.

"She wasn't raped," continued Sheila. "The water didn't help, but we didn't lose any DNA. There wasn't any."

"Blow to the head?" asked Steve.

"I assume she hit her head when he subdued her," Sheila added. She pointed out other points of interest on the body. "There are rug burns here and there, but nothing to make you think she fought too hard."

"She was surprised," commented Ramon.

Steve noticed the bruising around her ankles and the welt across her shins.

"What's this?" asked Steve.

Sheila told them the welts were caused by a wooden switch or a piece of wood because she pulled a sliver from the wound. She didn't have an explanation for the contusions around her ankles.

"He whipped her in the shins?" quizzed Ramon.

"Yeah, I'm at a loss on that one," admitted Sheila.

"And the official COD?" asked Steve.

"She died from asphyxiation," stated Sheila. "She was strangled."

"That's it?" questioned Ramon. "What about her eyelids and shit?"

"Patience, Detective," preached Sheila. "Hope you're not this quick with all your women."

"Women?" joked Steve. "More than one?"

"That's right, bro," cracked Ramon. "Women — plural. She knows I have game and shit."

"Take a look," stated Sheila.

Anita pulled the sheet back and uncovered Grace's face. It was a difficult sight to see such a young, beautiful woman in death. It was more disturbing to see her without her eyelids.

"Jesus," gasped Steve.

"The cut wasn't precise," explained Sheila. "It was crooked and awkward. It was definitely a razorblade."

"A box-cutter," stated Ramon.

"Sure," confirmed Sheila. "A box-cutter like The Eye used."

"So definitely a copycat and shit," said Ramon. "Right?"

"The Eye was definitely more surgical with his slice," confessed Steve.

"Wait a second," asked Sheila. "Are you suggesting it could be The Eye?"

Steve was blindsided by the question from Sheila. He'd be lying if he said the thought hadn't crept into his mind.

"Of course not," lied Steve. "And the nostrils?"

"Swabbed for smelling salt," confirmed Sheila.

Steve remembered that The Eye had used a special smelling salt that was only utilized by the military in training exercises. It still contained the same chemical compounds but differentiated from the other smelling salts that could be purchased by the average consumer.

"You should work off an old autopsy report from one of the past victims," suggested Steve.

"You didn't hear?" she asked. "I put in a file request yesterday and was told the file was missing. They can't find it."

"The Eye case files?" asked Steve. "None of it?"

"Not even the box they were in," answered Sheila. "This may shock you, but I can't always get what I want."

"Just use some of that 'va-voom' attitude to get what you want," joked Ramon.

"Honey, please," said Sheila as she eyed Ramon up and down. "I'd chew you up and spit you out."

Steve left the Medical Examiner's briefing with a few questions trapped in his mind. What if the cut wasn't precise because The Eye hadn't performed the procedure in eight years? Why Grace Harper? Should he pay a visit to Tate Holloway? He could only answer one of those questions at this point and that would require a phone call to an old friend.

Bonnie changed the time on their "date" because she had to catch an earlier flight back to Seattle. Nothing like a 4:00 p.m. booty call. He wasn't in the right frame of mind to have to try on costumes or role-play. His mind was on Grace Harper and how soon Rita's contacts could get him access to information. He understood the department was going to push the copycat angle, but he was determined to uncover the truth this time around — whatever that may be. He had less to lose than when he was a cop.

There'd be no dinner or the opera — it was going to be sex. This would truly be a "wham-bam-thank-you-ma'am" situation. Not that he was opposed to the sex, but he had to admit to himself that these encounters were becoming more and more difficult. It freaked him out that he felt a twinge in his stomach for Nicole. How would he feel if she was banging some dude to help pay off her student loans?

Bonnie pulled out her iPod and played, *"Love Will Keep us Together,"* by Captain and Tennille. She danced around the room in a 1970's-inspired sheer dress that revealed her breasts and was translucent enough to show that she wasn't wearing any panties. She tossed Tate a yachting captain's hat to put on his head.

"Come on, baby," cooed Bonnie. "We're going to pretend we're performing on the Captain and Tennille Show and you're going to take me on the bed and devour me."

"Good Lord, Bonnie," joked Tate. "That show reminds me of my parents."

Bonnie snickered as she sat on the bed. She cleverly allowed her legs to slide open enough to expose what she wanted Tate to taste.

"Let's hope you never did to them what you're going to do to me," said Bonnie in her best Mae West impersonation.

Tate began slowly licking up her calf, behind her knee, and spent some time on the inside of her thighs. Bonnie grabbed the sheets with her hands and squeezed as she reacted to the nibbling and wet kisses. He placed his tongue just outside of her pleasure zone and teased her as he blew warm air on her pussy.

"Taste me, Captain," begged Bonnie. "Make me cum."

Nicole made the rounds in the emergency room at Scripps Mercy Hospital in San Diego. She tended to a little girl who suffered from an asthma attack and was rushed to the E.R. Now that the girl was stable she wanted to follow up with her parents. The mother was thin and appeared malnourished. Nicole figured it was from drug use.

"It's really important to avoid smoking in the house," lectured Nicole. "Your daughter needs to have the healthiest environment for her condition."

"It ain't me," spouted the mother. "My dumbass boyfriend — he smokes two damn packs a day."

"You need to make the best choice for the health of your daughter," assessed Nicole. "Otherwise the state will make it for you."

She gently touched the girl's arm and gave her a reassuring smile. She hated this part of the job. Why have a kid if you're not going to give a shit about them? Odds were, the little girl would become a statistic and end up pregnant or on drugs.

She pulled the curtain closed and went on to the next bed. As she turned the corner, she was stopped by Curt Munson. He carried his black pharmaceutical bag and wore the drug rep uniform of slacks, dress shirt and tie.

"Ms. Stafford?" asked Curt.

"Yes," she answered.

"Doctor Farhadi suggested I talk to you about some drug samples," explained Curt. "Apparently he's in surgery?"

"Unless someone is having surgery on the golf course," joked Nicole, "then he's not in surgery."

Curt laughed at her witty sense of humor. He pulled out his business card and offered it to her. He looked her in the eyes.

"Five minutes?" requested Curtis.

"I'm sorry," said Nicole. "I'm on rounds right now."

"I saw you with the girl," offered Curt. "It's a shame children can't choose their parents."

"Yeah, well, you get used to it," confessed Nicole.

Curt headed for the exit door and stopped to look back at Nicole.

"Thanks for your time Ms. Stafford," he called out. "Maybe I'll see you again."

Nicole didn't hear his last statement and attended to the patient behind the next curtain.

Tate had Bonnie turned doggy style on the bed. Bonnie writhed from pleasure as Tate finished her off from behind with his mouth and synchronized his hand as he massaged her clit. She came hard and then collapsed on the bed.

"You were born to lick pussy," complimented Bonnie.

"Maybe I should put that on my tombstone," razzed Tate.

"I want you to fuck me now," begged Bonnie. "I like it when you cum inside my kitty cat."

Bonnie snickered as she maneuvered from his chest and kissed down his stomach. Tate hoped that he could get it up, but he was so distracted he had a difficult time getting his dick to respond. Images of Nicole laughing and sleeping on his chest kept dancing around in his head. He felt Bonnie pause when she got to his cock. She probably wondered why he wasn't stiff for her.

Tate couldn't believe his body reacted that way. A man's penis is like his first child. He loved it, protected it, and made sure it did well in life. He always joked that he grew up really poor and if he didn't wake up Christmas morning with a hard-on; he had nothing to play with. That was Jack's favorite joke.

Tate had been married three times and had a very active sex life. He'd never had this happen to him — ever. He was a professional — a gigolo for Chris 'sakes. He chuckled at Nicole whenever she used the stupid word, "Chris'sakes," and now he used it in his thoughts. Maybe she had more influence on him than just her vocabulary.

Bonnie licked up his shaft and took him in her mouth. She did her best to get him jumpstarted, but it didn't work.

"What's wrong?" asked Bonnie seductively. "I don't do it for you anymore?"

"It's not you at all, Bonnie," explained Tate. "I have a lot on my mind, I guess."

Bonnie leaned on his shoulder and stared into his eyes with a smirk on her face. Tate didn't want to make eye contact.

"What's her name?" asked Bonnie.

Tate got off the bed and gathered his clothes. He didn't want to talk about his feelings or get into a discussion about his love life.

"I'm sorry," he apologized. "I'll make sure Rita doesn't charge you."

Bonnie laughed hysterically as she rolled off the bed and grabbed her robe.

"Are you kidding me?" chuckled Bonnie as she flashed him her pussy. "You made me cum so hard my kitty cat would be pissed if I didn't pay you."

Tate looked at his phone and saw that he had several missed phone calls from Rita. She even sent him a text message. The fact that Rita actually texted him displayed the severity of the situation. He opened up the text and it read, "Steve Pelletti wants to meet at NuNu's at 10:00 p.m."

NuNu's was a dive bar that Tate, Jack and Steve considered their watering hole back in the day. Tate looked at his watch and realized he had four hours to kill. He knew he would spend the time wondering why the hell his former partner and lead investigator on the Harper murder wanted a sit-down.

Steve and Ramon had to dump their food in the trash in order to get to their car quickly. Crime-scene technicians had conducted a second sweep for evidence at the home on Briarwood that captured security footage of the suspected burglar. They found a box-cutter that appeared to contain blood. This was a huge break in the case. Not only did they have video of a possible suspect, but now they found a possible weapon too. Steve knew that The Eye used a conventional orange box-cutter when he committed his 25 murders. This was too coincidental to find the same night as the copycat murder occurred.

"You owe me a mega-double cheeseburger, bro," complained Ramon. "I didn't even get a bite and shit."

"Just have your cardiologist thank me," quipped Steve.

They approached the house and entered through the side gate. There were two crime-scene technicians waiting for the detectives as they arrived. They held a baggie that contained an orange box-cutter.

"Found it in the bushes behind the barbeque pit," said one of the crime techs.

"And you didn't find it on the first sweep?" asked Steve incredulously.

"It was buried pretty good," said the other crime tech. "The sun hit it just right, and I saw the reflection."

"Maybe if you did a third sweep we'd find the guy," snapped Steve.

Ramon noticed Steve's attitude and wondered why he was so bent out of shape. He took the baggie and placed the evidence in a large envelope.

"Thanks, bros," offered Ramon. "We appreciate your shit."

Chief Steward and Captain Dunn were looking over the crime-scene photos when they received the news that a possible murder weapon was found in the evidence sweep.

"The fucker dropped the murder weapon," said an astounded Chief Steward.

"This should help confirm the copycat theory," said Dunn.

"The Eye never made a mistake like this," said Steward.

"No, no he didn't," confirmed Dunn. "He was much smarter."

"Great call on the second sweep, Martin," congratulated Steward.

"I thought it'd be worth a shot," offered Dunn. "We should call Harper and let them know."

"I'll call the Mayor first," confessed Steward.

Steve answered his cell phone as they exited the gate. The video technician explained that she would have an image of the suspect by the end of the night. She used a complicated program that had to fully run its course as it mirrored and duplicated pixels that were visible as the computer recreated the portrait to a completed image of a face. Once they had the image, they would run it though the FRS (Facial Recognition Software), and hopefully find a match. The military used the same technology to identify terrorist suspects from satellite photos that weren't exactly clear. Worst-case scenario: They had an image of the suspected copycat killer.

"We should have a pic of our guy by tonight," Steve told Ramon.

"You okay, bro?" asked Ramon.

"Let's get this to the lab," suggested Steve. "Then head back over to the crime scene."

"Okay, it's just, I'm your partner, bro," offered Ramon. "If something is bothering you and shit ... "

"I'm fine," lied Steve. "Just didn't sleep much."

They arrived at the Harper Mansion after they dropped the box-cutter off at the crime lab. Steve checked his watch to gauge how long he had before he had to leave Ramon and go meet Tate. He felt compelled to talk to his old partner and pick his brain about The Eye. He knew this was a copy-cat murder, but something wasn't right in his gut. He understood the risk and repercussions if the top brass discovered his secret meeting. That's why he didn't tell Ramon he was having a drink with Tate. It was to protect him if anything negative went down, not because he didn't trust Ramon. Ramon couldn't be reprimanded downtown if he didn't have knowledge of the meeting.

Steve and Ramon surveyed Grace Harper's bedroom in an attempt to piece together a timeline of events. The Medical Examiner couldn't figure out where the bruising around her ankles and the welt across her shins had come from. They were going to try and figure it out. They established that she had turned on the bathtub water while she got undressed to take a bath.

"Bro, so our guy was hiding in the closet," said Ramon. "He's here."

Ramon hid in the space in the closet that he pointed out had a gap in the clothes.

"She comes in to change or throw her clothes in the hamper," continued Steve. "Why doesn't he grab her in the closet?"

"Maybe he didn't wait, bro," offered Ramon. "Maybe she saw him, and he had to tackle her and shit."

"So she screamed and ran to about here?" questioned Steve as he stood in the middle of the bedroom.

"She goes down and shit," continued Ramon. "He gets on top, gives her smelling salt, and then slices her eyelids off?"

"Doesn't cover the blow to the head or the broken lamp," concluded Steve.

"Or the strangling," added Ramon.

"Or the bruising on her ankles and the welts," said Steve. "Let's hope we get a hit on the security footage."

Steve and Ramon were about to get into their car when they noticed an older man standing on the neighbor's yard. He was in his 60's and had white scraggily hair and a matching beard. He had his arms folded across his chest and appeared fidgety and nervous.

"How you doing?" hollered Steve.

The man halfheartedly waved at them.

"Fine," he answered. "You here about the Harper murder?"

Steve and Ramon closed their car doors and approached the man.

"You live here?" asked Steve as he pointed to the house across the street to the Harper's.

"Yep, I sure do," said the man. "I'm Harold Reynolds. I've lived across the street from the Harpers for about 10 years."

"Did investigators talk to you that night?" asked Steve.

"My granddaughter is pregnant, and she had a false alarm," said Harold. "I was at the hospital."

"No one left a card on your door or anything?" questioned Steve.

"I didn't see one," he confessed.

"Sir, did you see or hear anything unusual that night?" asked Ramon.

"Um, no, not really," answered Harold.

"Not really?" prodded Steve. "The littlest thing could help us."

Harold shifted his weight and uncrossed his arms. "I wish I could help, gentlemen," he said. "But I didn't hear anything."

Ramon reached into his pocket and pulled out a business card. He handed it to Harold who grabbed it and eyed the card.

"If you remember anything, sir," said Ramon, "please give us a call."

"The news said it was 'The Eye'," he stated. "Do you have any leads?"

"We can't discuss the case," admitted Steve. "It's an ongoing investigation."

"Well, I hope you catch the guy," offered Harold. "She was such a nice girl."

"You knew her well, bro?" quizzed Ramon.

Steve couldn't believe that Ramon had just called an old man, "bro". He thought he'd heard it all.

"Well, just a wave here and there," said Harold.

"But you said she was nice," said Steve. "You never talked with her?"

"She seemed nice," confessed Harold.

Steve thought Harold Reynolds was a little too uptight and nervous. He even seemed a little scared. Steve and Ramon both agreed they should run him through the system to see if he had any criminal history. They also made a note to ask Jonathan Harper about Mr. Reynolds and to scold the officers who were supposed to canvass the neighborhood.

Sometimes you had to go with your gut and follow up a hunch. Steve remembered a case he caught about five years ago. Elderly people kept dying in an assisted living facility in a residential neighborhood. The sweet little lady who lived next door was more than helpful with the investigation and was very interested in the outcome. Turned out she was the one who had snuck into the facility and smothered six residents. Before her, he'd never experienced a serial killer who DVR'd episodes of *The Golden Girls*. So checking up on Harold Reynolds didn't seem like such a bad idea. You never knew when you might get lucky.

Tate pulled into the parking lot two blocks south of NuNu's Cocktails near the Gaslamp District. He never parked close when it came to an important meeting with a client or in this case — someone he hadn't seen in almost eight years. He knew the conversation would be about The Eye and the murder of Grace Harper, but he didn't know the reason for meeting at their old hangout. Was it friendly or an inquisition? Could he trust Steve? Maybe the events from The Eye had come up, and it made Steve nostalgic for Jack. Either way, he parked away for meetings in situations like this.

Rita begged him not to go because she didn't trust anyone downtown and felt that a meeting with Steve would only stir up negative memories and emotions. She felt strongly about this because she was around during Tate's demise from the force.

"Want me to go, sugar?" asked Rita.

"No," said Tate. "This was a long time coming."

"Bring your piece," ordered Rita.

"Rita," said an agitated Tate, "I'm going to listen and pick his brain as much as he picks mine."

"If it's no big deal and all, why isn't his partner going to be there?" she quizzed.

"I'll call you after," conceded Tate.

Tate sat in his car for a few minutes to clear his head as he prepared to face Steve for the first time since his dismissal. His temples hurt so badly he felt like they would implode. Forget sun damage or booze — stress was the true accomplice to aging.

Tate stumbled out of the barn after he made sure The Eye was dead. The wind had dramatically increased so there was an eerie howl that permeated the canyon. The wind chimes were dancing in the gusts of wind and sounded agitated with Mother Nature. Tate saw Jack flat on his back as he ran over to him. His shirt was soaked in blood.

"Jack!" he yelled.

Jack's eyes were glossed over, and he was barely conscious. Tate placed his hand over one of the wounds and applied pressure to help stop the blood that seeped from his partner and best friend. There are moments in life when bad things happened to friends and loved ones, and people closed their eyes and prayed for time to rewind. This was one of those times.

"Ah, man, it hurts," said Jack softly.

"Stay with me, man," pleaded Tate. "I'll get help."

Jack grabbed his hand and gave him a look that told Tate he didn't want to be left alone. Tate discovered bullet wounds in his stomach, chest and shoulder. He knew that if they had taken their time they would have been able to wear their bulletproof vests. Why didn't he wait for backup?

"Come on, man," joked Tate, "I owe you a steak from Donovan's."

"Someone else," said Jack as he struggled to remain conscious. "Something else ... ?"

Tate made sure he had his Glock at the ready with this unexpected revelation. Maybe the shadow he saw wasn't his eyes playing tricks on him.

"In the house?" quizzed Tate. "You saw someone else?"

Jack was unable to form any more words. Tate ripped his shirt open and began administering chest compressions.

"Think about Linda and the girls," willed Tate. "You always said the best day of your life would be the day you walked them down the aisle."

Each push got stronger and deeper as Tate unleashed his anguish on the situation. A bloody mist sprinkled across Tate's face and his hands and arms were covered in red as he continued his attempt to save his partner's life.

"Come on, Jack," begged Tate. "You always wanted a boy to play catch with, huh? You gotta stick around for that chance. One of the girls might have a boy. He's gonna need his grandpa."

Tate stopped long enough to check his pulse. Nothing. He continued with the chest compressions until he had another idea.

"Let's get you in the house," stated an optimistic Tate.

He grabbed Jack underneath his arms and pulled him toward the porch. The heels of Jack's shoes left two drag marks as they slid along the ground. Tate was exhausted from the adrenaline of the gunfight and the emotional devastation of Jack's shooting. He struggled with Jack's deadweight until he couldn't pull any longer. They collapsed together just shy of the steps that led up to the porch.

"I'll call it in," said Tate as he labored to breathe. "There must be a phone inside."

Tate checked his vitals one more time. Again, he couldn't seem to find a pulse.

"Jack!" screamed Tate.

Jack had such a peaceful expression on his face as he looked up to that same sky and drifted away. Tate looked up to the sky and unleashed a blood-curdling yell that echoed throughout the canyons.

"No, no, no, no," Tate begged. "God please, no!"

God didn't listen to him.

To this day, Tate wasn't sure if Jack had warned him that someone else was in the house or that he attempted to make light of his shooting with his usual line, "Ain't this something else." It was that uncertainty that fueled Tate's determination to dig deeper into the case and look at every possible scenario — the same determination and uncertainty that destroyed his credibility and killed his career. And the man he was meeting at NuNu's was directly involved in the outcome. He always felt he never stepped up and had his or Jack's back. Maybe sitting across the table from Detective Steve Pelletti wasn't as easy as he thought it would be.

He walked into the bar that he hadn't frequented since Jack's death. He thought it was interesting that even though years passed and life-changing events occurred, some things always remained the same. NuNu's was one of those places.

Established in the early 1960's, the puffy high-backed leather booths, the wood paneling, and the smell of smoke made him feel like he walked through a doorway back in time. The atmosphere was perfect as Dean Martin's song, *"Ain't That a Kick in the Head,"* played on the jukebox. Although smoking was banned in restaurants and bars throughout California, there were some watering holes where the law was never enforced and sparking up a cigarette or cigar was met with a wink and a smile. Judging by the number of smokers in the joint, there was a whole lot of winking and smiling that took place.

Tate recognized Steve as he sat in a booth in the back corner. He was occupied with his iPhone. Tate wondered how the hell he looked the same after all these years on the job. He approached the booth and sat down across from Steve.

"Angry Birds getting the best of you?" asked Tate.

He always felt that a tense situation was better met head-on with a joke.

"No, just trying to figure the fuckin' thing out," answered Steve.

"I don't get all that technology shit," said Tate. "I still miss my old pager."

"Wasn't that so much easier?" agreed Steve. "You get paged, you had to find a pay phone."

"So much easier when our wives couldn't call us all the time," laughed Tate.

"I was sorry to hear about you and Stacey," confessed Steve. "I should have called."

Tate had so much to say but didn't think it was the correct time or place to get that personal. Maybe that would happen another day. But there was a reason Steve called this sit-down, and it was much more than just a friendly reunion.

"Well, you know, shit happens," offered Tate. "How's Marcy?"

"She still likes me," offered Steve. "Still don't know why."

"You still drink bourbon?" asked Tate.

"I'll have an iced tea," responded Steve.

"You give up the sauce?" joked Tate.

"God no," said Steve. "I'm technically still on."

"So this is a business call," suggested Tate, "not social?"

Tate motioned for the waitress to come over, and he ordered a Patron and a large iced tea. He figured if he was going to have a drink, he made sure it was a good tequila to sip on. He glanced at his phone and noticed that he had four missed calls from Rita. He thought that was quite a few calls but not yet an emergency situation. She probably just called to check on him.

"No, nothing formal like that," confessed Steve. "I'm sure you've seen the news."

"You've come to tell me I was right all along," said Tate, "that The Eye is back."

"Oh, it's a copycat my friend," informed Steve. "There wasn't anyone else in the house that night. If there was someone else, he couldn't have stopped killing."

"Then why are we here?" quizzed Tate. "To tell me I was wrong again?"

Steve didn't know how to respond to Tate's question. He would be lying if he said the thought never crossed his mind, but he would never admit that he wanted to cover all of his bases just in case. He felt the more information he could share and gather from Tate, the easier it would be to confirm his theory that there was a copycat getting ready to terrorize the people of San Diego.

Steve went over the evidence in great detail. He described the murder scene and shared that the surgical procedure to slice off the eyelids was sloppy and not as precise. He shared info from the autopsy and mentioned the odd bruising around Grace's ankles and the welt across her shin. He explained his belief that the killer hid in the closet and surprised Grace with a tackle. He also told Tate that they were running samples from the nostrils to test the chemical mixture of the smelling salt.

"Did you run a black light in the closet?" asked Tate.

He reminded Steve that The Eye would leave a neon ink stamp of an eye that could only be seen with a black light.

"Yeah, nothing," admitted Steve. "That's one of the reason's we're sure it's a copycat."

"So why talk to me?" asked Tate. "Why not refer to the file?"

"Funny thing is," stated Steve. "The file's missing."

"From the evidence warehouse?" asked Tate.

"Not even an empty box," Steve concluded.

This information confused Tate. He made sure that he made copies of everything in the file before he placed the originals back in the box. It had been seven years since he broke into that evidence warehouse and copied the contents, but there wasn't a doubt in his mind — he put it back. This new information left a couple of crucial questions unanswered. Who stole the file and why?

Steve continued his evidence break down and described his uneasy feeling about the neighbor, Harold Reynolds. He planned to question him again tomorrow when Reynolds returned to town. He felt he knew more than he was saying. He even seemed somewhat frightened.

"Do you have any other leads?" quizzed Tate.

"We found gold," conceded Steve.

He explained that there was a 10-10 that night about two blocks from the Harper mansion. They felt the killer might have used the backyard as an escape route or a place to hide. He admitted that after combing that house for evidence, crime-scene techs found a box-cutter that contained blood and that the security cameras caught an image of the suspect as he entered the side gate. The image was "pixilated," but they should have a clear photo of the copycat killer after techs ran the footage through a special computer software program.

"The killer dropped the murder weapon?" asked Tate incredulously.

"Yeah, amateur hour," commented Steve.

"What street was that again?" asked Tate as he took a drink from his tequila.

"Briarwood Lane," responded Steve as he looked down at his phone after it beeped.

Tate was speechless. After he established the timeline in his head, he became flushed and began to perspire. His heart pounded through his chest. He remembered Briarwood Lane as being the street where he was supposed to have a date with the new client Rita set up. Was he the 10-10 call from the neighbors who spotted him from an upstairs window? He didn't remember seeing any security cameras but with today's technology the devices could have been tiny and difficult to notice. Was he on the footage? He took a deep breath to calm his nerves. He didn't want Steve to notice the pulse in his jugular vein if this was all a test.

"I should have the suspect's image on my phone in a couple of minutes," confirmed Steve after he read his text.

Tate downed the last of his tequila and placed the empty glass on the table. Nat King Cole's version of "*Adios Marquita Linda*" permeated throughout the old-style cocktail lounge.

"I gotta take a leak," said Tate as he slid out of the booth.

Steve watched Tate as he headed for the restroom at the back of NuNu's. He observed Tate nod his head at the bartender and then disappeared down the hallway.

Steve felt their meeting was long overdue, and it wasn't as awkward as he thought it would be. He wished he would have called Tate when Stacey left him, but at the time he wasn't the same Tate everyone knew and loved. He had changed and was so consumed with his "someone-else" theory that it got him booted off the force. A promising career snuffed out by an unhealthy obsession into Jack's death and The Eye.

"What a shame," he thought.

Steve's phone beeped again, which alerted him to an image being downloaded to his iPhone. The text from the technician read, "Running it through FRS now ..."

The image had finished the download and a clear photo was displayed on his iPhone screen. The hair on the back of his neck stood straight up and goose bumps had formed on his arms. The shock caused him to inadvertently spill his iced tea all over their table. He opened and closed his eyes to make sure they hadn't played a trick on him. He couldn't believe who he was staring at. He didn't have to run the photo through the Facial Recognition Software. It was a perfect, undeniable photo of someone he knew very well.

"Fuck me," said a stunned Steve.

He quickly slid out of the booth and drew his firearm.

It was Tate Holloway!

Steve flashed his badge to the bartender as he approached the hallway to the restrooms.

"Did he come out?" asked Steve in a whisper.

The bartender looked like a deer caught in headlights when he noticed Steve's gun.

"No," offered the frightened bartender. "I don't think so."

Steve maneuvered down the hallway with his back sliding along the wall. He pointed his gun at the men's restroom door. He was startled when a woman exited the women's restroom, and he trained his gun on her. She dropped to the ground in a panic. He stepped over her and slowly pushed open the men's door with his foot while he aimed his gun at the urinals. He heard someone using the pisser, but the person was hidden on the other side of the stall. He quickly lunged around the stall and pointed his gun at the individual who stood at the urinal.

"Don't fuckin' move," he ordered.

It was another bar patron who let go of his dick and raised his arms in the air.

"I can't stop peeing," pleaded the frightened man.

Steve turned and noticed that the bathroom window was wide open. The cool ocean breeze blew the curtains away from the window.

A "too-good-to-be-true" gift-wrapped murder weapon, getting intentionally stood up at the house on Briarwood Lane, convenient security footage that placed him at the house, his documented resistance downtown about The Eye, and his firing instigated by Jonathan Harper and the Mayor. The question that burned in Tate's mind was now evident: Who the fuck was setting him up? The 10th missed call from Rita meant one thing — a warning to get the fuck out.

Tate forced the bathroom window open and looked out into the dingy alley. He made sure there weren't any unmarked or black-and-white cop cars strategically positioned on either side of the alley entrance. He placed one foot over the window ledge and straddled the opening as he crawled out and dropped into the alleyway. He took off running south as he dialed up Rita on his cell phone. He immediately hung up when he realized his phone would eventually be monitored and tracked. He definitely didn't want to get Rita involved.

He looked back toward the bathroom window and noticed that Steve poked his head out and glanced down the alley. He'd been spotted.

"Fuck me," he said.

VENGEANCE IS NOW

Tate tried to pace himself as he sprinted down the alley to escape from Detective Steve Pelletti. He didn't know how long or short the chase would be, but he knew two things — he wasn't going to get caught, and it was painful to run in dress shoes. He also realized he had a few advantages in this chase. He knew how trained cops strategically chose their routes while pursuing a suspect on foot, and he understood how they established perimeters when they couldn't catch the suspect.

He quickly approached a chain-link fence and, in one motion, skillfully placed one foot in the link and pushed himself up and grabbed the top with his hands. He then used the strength in his arms and pulled himself up and flipped his legs over. He landed perfectly on both feet and never broke stride. He crossed over and down onto Ivy Lane and continued through the alleys that parallel 5th Avenue. Thank God for surfing or they would have found him slumped over the sidewalk blowing chunks and struggling to breathe.

Steve thought better of going through the bathroom window and settled for the backdoor as he kicked it open and began his pursuit of Tate Holloway. There was no time to digest what had just happened. He had to catch him and attempt to discern whether or not Tate killed Grace to stir up the case again or if Tate, in fact, was correct in his assessment that they got the wrong guy. Problem was Steve didn't realize whether or not the right guy was the individual he was chasing. Was Tate The Eye? Did he kill Jack that night to cover his tracks? Did Jack suspect him? How fuckin' crazy was he?

Steve hoofed it south in the alley as he spotted Tate veer down a side alley and disappear. Ramon answered his phone, but Steve could barely hear him over the mariachi music he heard in the background. Ramon sounded like he was at a club.

"It's Tate Holloway!" exclaimed an out-of-breath Steve.

"What, bro?" asked Ramon who concentrated to hear what his partner said.

"The image of the suspect," gasped Steve. "It was Tate Holloway!"

"He's the guy and shit?!" exclaimed Ramon.

"I'm in pursuit on foot," informed Steve.

"Of who?" quizzed Ramon.

"Tate!" yelled Steve. "I'm at 5th and Walnut. Call it in! Tell them I'm chasing Holloway, and he's the killer!"

"I'll call it in!" shouted Ramon. "On my way, bro!"

Steve couldn't believe the words that had come out of his mouth. Tate Holloway was the killer, and he had to take him down.

Tate looked back and saw Steve gaining a little bit of ground on him. He kicked it up to another gear and cut up the alley and onto 5th Avenue. The restaurants and bars were hopping with people, and there was a lot of foot traffic on the sidewalks. He maneuvered in and around people without sticking out like a sore thumb. At least he was dressed to look like he was going out for a drink. He should — that's what he was doing before he became a murder suspect and his evening turned into a foot chase.

"Tate!" yelled Steve.

Tate turned and saw Steve with his gun drawn as he bounced off a couple of pedestrians on his quest to catch him.

A woman screamed, "He's got a gun!"

"Run!" yelled another woman.

Panic ensued and the crowd scattered all over 5th Avenue when people noticed Steve was holding his gun. Car horns honked and brakes squealed as people filtered into the street to avoid the "gunman". Tate bent over and blended in with a small group of people who hurried into an upscale men's clothing store. Three of them were teenaged girls and the other two were a couple in their thirties. They hovered together near the back of the store. Tate perused a clothing rack and checked shirt sizes while the others panicked.

"Oh my God, like, he had a gun," stated a frightened girl to her friends.

"Totally and like he looked mad," said another frightened teenager.

A tiny, feminine Asian man in his 40's rushed out from the storeroom. He wore a salmon silk dress shirt unbuttoned to the middle of his stomach and cream-colored slacks.

"Out'a, out'a, out'a," he insisted in a funny accent. "Out'a me store!"

"There's a guy outside with a gun!" yelled the man in his 30's whose date was clinging to his arms.

"Some first date," she said.

"Oh no, good Jesus," squirmed the tiny Asian man as he ran over to the window and peeked outside.

Police sirens blared from the street. The volume of the sirens increased as they drew closer to the mayhem. Tate noticed through the store window that Steve flagged down a black-and-white. Blue and red flashing lights bounced off the back walls of the store and filled the night sky. He quickly briefed the two police officers, and they split up and took off running in two different directions. Steve spoke into his cell phone.

Tate pulled off his white shirt and slipped on a designer black t-shirt and a dark leather jacket. He tossed his old shirt behind the cashier's counter.

"You have pay fer 'dat," complained the tiny Asian man.

"Not today," said Tate. "Where's your phone?"

"Why didn't you do something?" asked the woman to her date. "You said you were a former Navy Seal."

Her date was tongue-tied and didn't know what to say.

"Busted," quipped Tate. "Don't believe everything you read on those dating sites, darling. Give me your lipstick."

"My lipstick?" she asked as she fumbled through her purse.

The tiny, feminine Asian man escaped out the front door and rushed out onto 5th Avenue. He waved his arms and jumped up and down.

Tate took the lipstick and quickly darted to the back of the store.

"Thievery, stealer, in here!" the feminine man screamed as he pointed to his store.

Tate kicked in the backdoor that led out into the alley. His escape triggered an alarm that was connected to the door.

"Shit," said Tate.

He glanced down the south end of the alley and witnessed a cop car as it slowly cruised by. The officer on the passenger side shined a spotlight up and down side streets. Tate looked at his watch and knew that from the time Steve called dispatch he only had about 20 minutes before a helicopter would be deployed. He needed to contact Rita and get somewhere safe to figure out his next move. He waited for the cop car to pass and utilized the shadows as he covertly headed south toward Spruce Street.

Steve directed the officers to split up and build a perimeter in front of Olive Park. He felt Tate might want to get shelter and wait out the search, and Olive Park would be the smartest location to accomplish that. As the officers followed his orders and left the scene, he noticed the small Asian man running out of a store waving his hands.

"Thievery, stealer, in here!" screamed the tiny Asian man.

"This way!" directed Steve to the officers who had just arrived.

An alarm sounded in the background when they ran into the store with their guns drawn.

"I like, thought you were like, the bad dude," yelled one of the teenaged girls over the sound of the store alarm.

Steve and the officers searched the clothing store room by room until they were satisfied he wasn't hiding inside. The store alarm finally stopped ringing.

"I think he ran out the back," offered the woman on the first date.

"Yeah, me too," said her gutless date.

"Navy Seal, my ass," she scoffed.

Steve used his radio to alert the outside officers that Tate could be headed in their general direction.

"Who pay fer clothes?" whined the feminine Asian man. "You pay? He pay? Me no pay."

Steve radioed out to alert his officers of the wardrobe change.

"Detective," yelled one of the officers from the bathroom. "You need to see this!"

Steve hustled to the back of the store and glanced inside the elegant bathroom. *"WAS SET UP,"* was written on the vanity mirror in red lipstick. Tate's broken cell phone floated in the toilet.

"Suspect spotted south on Upas Street," announced an officer over the radio.

"Go!" ordered Steve.

He was momentarily left alone in the bathroom. He quickly hustled out the backdoor of the clothing store and jumped into an awaiting police car.

The spotlight hit Tate's legs, and the siren alerted not only law enforcement that he was spotted but Tate as well. An officer bailed out of his police car and pursued him on foot. Tate went over to a dumpster and rolled it in place to block the small side street he took to get away. The young cop easily maneuvered around the dumpster and closed the gap between them. Tate did everything possible to shake the young, eager pursuer, but if he wanted to reach Spruce Street, his encounter would have to get physical. He saw two more cops across 5th Avenue in front of Olive Park. They also joined the hunt.

"Stop or I'll 'tase' you!" yelled the officer who was closing in on Tate.

Tate went over a wood fence only to topple to the ground as the rotted boards collapsed from his weight. He hit the ground hard and barrel-rolled to get back to his feet.

"Freeze!" screamed the young, nervous cop right before he fired his stun gun.

The barb from the Taser gun hit the ground right next to Tate missing him by a few feet. He grabbed a metal pipe and swung it low at the cop. He hit him square in the knees, which flipped the officer end-over-end into the side of a brick building. The force of the crash rendered the officer unconscious. Tate checked the young cop's pulse to make sure he was breathing and then jetted off across the street. The other two cops were close on his heels.

"Suspect crossed Thorn and headed to Spruce!" said an out-of-breath pursuer.

Steve flew down 5th Avenue in a cop car that fishtailed around Thorn Street and left smoke and the aroma of burnt tires in the night air. He had to grab the handle on the door just to keep from sliding into the driver. He saw that Tate crossed Spruce and ducked behind a building into a small opening that appeared to lead into another alley.

"All units at Olive Park proceed to 5th and Spruce," ordered Steve into his radio.

"We have an officer down in an alley off 5th," responded a voice through the radio. "Medical response has been dispatched."

"Crazy motherfucker," bitched Steve.

"Sir?" asked the cop who was driving.

"Ya think you know someone ...," added Steve to the driver.

The call for all available citywide units had begun to pay off as 10 to 12 patrol cars, sirens blaring, tore down 5th Avenue in route to Spruce Street. A SDPD helicopter that blazed overhead flanked the black-and-whites and had the large searchlight pointed down to guide them.

Steve noticed that Tate eluded the other officers and entered the alley behind the restaurants and bars that occupied the east side of the street. He motioned for his driver to head in Tate's direction.

"There! Move it!" ordered Steve. "Let's go!"

Rita was in a panic when she hadn't heard from Tate. Her evening pillow talk with an associate from the Mayor's campaign revealed the surveillance video and the murder weapon found on Briarwood Lane. She was a smart woman and had already put together the connection between Tate and the Briarwood house. She felt responsible and now understood the magnitude of the situation after hearing the All-Points Bulletin for Tate and the call of a "10-60I" through her police scanner. The APB wasn't the cause of her panic, it was the 10-60I that signified a chase or pursuit in progress.

She jumped into her car and decided to head in Tate's general vicinity in case he attempted to contact her. She realized she was his only lifeline to the outside world — and if he wanted safety, she was going to have to harbor him.

Tate slipped into the backdoor of the very colorful Jimmy Carter's Mexican Cafe on the corner of 5th and Spruce. He quickly traversed through the kitchen and up into the small dining room.

"I need a phone," insisted Tate to one of the waiters who then pointed to the front.

Tate quickly went to the hostess who worked the reservation podium. Some of the customers had already gathered next to the windows to see the commotion outside. Two huge guys, in their early 20's, wore San Diego State football T-shirts and stood next to the front door.

"This is police business," stated Tate as he flashed his P.I. badge to the two guys. "I need you to go to the backdoor and secure it so nobody comes in."

The two guys took off for the back with three other restaurant patrons who heard Tate's request.

"I need your phone," Tate ordered to the hostess.

She nervously gestured to the restaurant phone at the podium.

"Just dial 9," she said. "What's going on out there?"

"No, I need your cell phone," he ordered.

"But, it's mine," answered the sheepish hostess. "And I just posted that I'm newly single on Facebook."

"Sorry to hear that," offered Tate.

"Yeah, he was like taking me for granted—," she continued.

"—give it to me now," insisted Tate.

She reluctantly handed over her iPhone. Tate had to shake his head when he saw the red bedazzled ladybug that decorated the back of the phone.

"That door open?" asked Tate who pointed at a side door that wasn't being utilized and was obstructed with an empty dining table and two chairs.

"I think," said the teary-eyed hostess.

He slid the table and chairs out of the way and forced the door open with his shoulder. He dialed Rita's disposable pay-and-go cell phone and exited to the alley. He could hear the commotion he had created as the two football players held the backdoor closed while cops attempted to get in.

"Hey, it's me!" called Tate.

"Where are you, sugar?" asked Rita urgently. "Are we secure?"

"No, I snagged someone's cell," answered Tate over the roar of helicopters and sirens. "Someone fucked me, darling."

"I know, sugar, I know," agreed Rita.

"Meet me at that warehouse on the pier," he said.

"At the shipyard?" she asked.

"The pier at the old shipyard," Tate confirmed.

They realized how easy it would be to get "wire tapped" so they had a special language and communicated in code whenever they exchanged sensitive information via cell phone. That's why Rita was always prepared with pre-paid disposable cell phones. They certainly didn't want their dirty laundry exposed in open court if they were ever to get pinched for prostitution.

"What time n'all?" she asked. "How ya' gonna get there?"

Tate looked across the street and noticed the fire escape attached to The Inn at the Park and figured that might be his best chance.

"I haven't figured it out yet," confessed Tate. "But you'll be the second to know."

VENGEANCE IS NOW

Tate was halfway up the first-story fire escape of the Inn at the Park when he noticed two uniformed officers stop their pursuit right underneath him. They hadn't seen him yet because the streetlight in the alley was burnt out and it was extremely dark. If they only realized they were eight feet away from a career-changing capture; they wouldn't have been so eager to stop the chase. Tate would have dreamed for an opportunity that big when he was in uniform; but dreams were made to be crushed.

The San Diego Police Department displayed their impressive firepower if you considered the amount of units and the air support assigned to catch Tate. He realized he was enemy number one — and they would stop at nothing to catch the fugitive responsible for killing Jonathan Harper's daughter. Not to mention the jump in the polls the Mayor would receive when he announced Tate's capture and arrest.

"Fucker might be long gone by now," complained one of the cops.

"You see the boss?" asked the other cop as he pulled out a pack of Camel Lights.

"Nah, maybe we should hang here," he said. "Burn one while we survey the area."

"You read my mind," said the other cop as he sparked up a cigarette.

Tate didn't have a firm grip on the ladder and the muscles in his forearm began to cramp with each passing second. The rickety fire escape would be too noisy if he attempted to get a better grip so he had to gut it out while they had their smokes. The resistance strength it took to maintain his body's position caused sweat to form on his forehead. His arms began to shake, and he exerted way more energy than he wanted at this early stage in the escape. The inevitable might have to happen — and the thought made his stomach turn.

"Unit 14 back to Spruce," ordered a voice through the cop's radio.

"I'll go," said one of the cops. "Finish your smoke."

The cop snuffed out his cigarette and jogged in the direction of Spruce Street.

A few beads of sweat fell from Tate's forehead and landed on the arm of the police officer who was just below him.

"What the ...?" complained the officer when he felt the moisture hit his bare arm.

As he looked up, Tate dropped on top of him, giving him no time to react before he realized what had hit him. The force knocked the cop to the cement as Tate had his body wrapped around him and a sleeper hold placed around his neck. Tate rolled to his back while still clamped around the cop.

"Just go to sleep, dude," grunted Tate.

"Fuck ... you," gurgled the cop as his eyes rolled to the back of his head, and he fell into unconsciousness.

Tate double-checked his pulse to make sure he was just passed out. Once assured the cop wasn't going to wake up in the next few minutes, he stole his department-issued radio and turned the volume way down.

"I'm too old for this shit," stated Tate as he clamped the radio to his belt.

Tate finished climbing the fire escape to the roof of the Inn at the Park on Spruce Street. He swung his legs over the ledge and lunged onto the rooftop as he completed his ascent. He took a minute to relax and leaned against a large air conditioning unit as he caught his breath. He needed a plan. He needed to think. How did he go from such a low-profile private investigator to the most-wanted man in the city? He thought his set up could be politically motivated, but he was too dazed from the adrenaline rush to put it together at this point. Was someone hiding new evidence that would have proved his theory about another killer?

He chose the hotel because he'd experienced firsthand how difficult it was to focus on one suspect in a crowd of people. He also knew that with so many tourists and guests staying at the hotel, he would have a better chance of blending in while he figured out an escape strategy. Now that he had a police radio, he felt his chances for survival increased dramatically.

The spotlight from the helicopter blasted on the roof as it hovered above the city and assisted in the search for Tate Holloway. The entire rooftop, including the restaurant, was illuminated in bright lights that forced Tate to continue hunkering down behind the AC unit. He timed the spotlight beam as it systematically searched each end of the rooftop. He waited for the beam of light to pass by his location and then jogged along the shadows it created. He knew that if the door from the roof was locked, he would be fucked so he planned to kick it in just to be safe. An altercation on the roof of a six-story building wouldn't be his ideal situation.

He arrived at the door and led with his foot. The door almost flew off the hinges from the force of Tate's kick, and he entered the stairwell and began his descent into the hotel. He checked the stairwell door on the 6th floor to make sure he didn't need a key to open it. It reminded him of when Bonnie hunted him with a Nerf gun throughout the Hyatt, and he got locked in the stairwell and didn't have a key. Not that big of a deal in normal circumstances, but it's a little tricky when you're wearing nothing but a bull's-eye sticker across your cock. He wondered what Bonnie would think when his picture was flashed all over the nightly news. Bonnie? What about Nicole? How was he going to explain this cluster-fuck of a fiasco?

"The door on the roof of the hotel has been busted open," informed a voice from Tate's radio. "Suspect entered the Inn at the Park."

"Was probably unlocked too," quipped Tate.

All four lanes of traffic had been blocked as cop cars strategically lined Spruce Street in front of the elegant Inn at the Park. A Unit Command Center (UCC) RV arrived and parked behind the formation of cruisers. The helicopter hovered above the hotel as their spotlights crisscrossed the building and made it look like a Hollywood movie premiere. Police lights danced on the brick building and showered the streets in a red-and-blue glow. The night sky was polluted with the "whoosh" and drum of helicopter blades and the sounds of sirens.

Steve paced back and forth in front of a cop car while he received updates and reports about the situation. He had fully briefed Ramon about the circumstances of the chase but hadn't divulged the fact that he sat right across from him at NuNu's when everything went down. That would be for another time and more than likely in front of the curious eyes of Steward and Dunn. Steve dreaded the thought of that inquisition.

Ramon skidded to a stop in his burgundy 2012 Dodge Charger and hopped out of his car to join Steve.

"This shit is crazy and shit," offered Ramon.

"We've got the perimeter locked," stated Steve. "But you're talking about a six-story building. A full city block."

"What the fuck happened, bro?" drilled Ramon. "How did this—."

"—not now," snapped Steve. "We're in the UCC with brass in 10."

The two officers who had stood beneath the fire escape and took a smoke break approached Steve and Ramon. One of the officers had his hands on his hips and was being held up as he walked to the detective.

"Sir, my partner almost had the suspect," said one of the cops.

"What happened?" asked Steve.

The officer explained that he was in the alley conducting a search when he spotted Tate and tackled him. That he was just about to slap the cuffs on Tate when he pulled a gun on him and took off. It was a feeble attempt at covering one's ass.

"Why didn't you draw on him before you engaged?" quizzed Steve.

"It happened so fast," explained the cop.

"Did you radio when you saw him, bro?" continued Ramon.

"Uh, well sir," stammered the cop. "I must've dropped my radio when I tackled him?"

"Suspect is armed and has a radio," Steve barked into his radio as he shook his head in disbelief. "Scramble the channel."

"I fucked up," confessed the cop.

"We've all been there," said Steve. "You need to make sure your story is factual or the report will come back to bite you."

Steve felt a little guilty when he lectured the cop regarding honesty and truth in a report. He wondered how long he would hold his own secret.

Tate opened a linen closet near the ice machine next to the stairwell exit. He placed the ladybug cell phone on the top shelf and scoured the contents of the closet to look for anything that might assist him in his exodus. If it was Halloween he would be set. He would just use the infinite amount of white sheets and design a ghost costume. He wasn't so lucky. His perilous predicament had settled into his consciousness yet he was still able to make light of the situation. What's the point of living if you can't enjoy your moment as San Diego's most wanted?

He regained his focus and remembered "stand-off" protocol and figured he'd beat them to the punch. He grabbed a can of complimentary shaving cream from one of the shelves and placed it in his jacket. He went straight for the fire alarm and broke the glass with his elbow. He reached in and pulled out the ax and noticed a champagne bucket full of melted ice that had been set out for room service to collect. He walked over to the corner of the hallway and sprayed the tiny security camera with shaving cream that blocked the lens. He then picked up the bucket of ice in one hand and headed for the utility closet with the ax in his other hand.

He grabbed a pair of rubber gloves the maids used when they cleaned and slid them on. He located one of the power boxes in the back of the closet and took aim with the ax. He slammed the ax head through the metal casing that protected the main power and severed the wires. He felt the zing of the electricity on his hands even though he wore rubber protective gloves. The explosion was loud as sparks showered down on the closet and smoke billowed from the metal box. He poured the water from the champagne bucket onto the exposed wires that caused a sickening electrical current buzz and a small fire. The 6th floor went dark and the emergency lights kicked on from a generator. He used a sheet and snuffed out the small fire before it spread. The hallways were lit up with a green glow that resembled the view from night-vision goggles. He looked outside and realized he must have shorted the entire building as the Inn at the Park went black. Mission accomplished.

"This is an emergency," announced a voice through the hotel PA system. "Please remain calm and proceed to the nearest exit. I repeat ..."

The flow of people was evident as they gathered in the hallways and headed for the stairwell to get out. People pulled half-closed suitcases and carried laptops as they attempted to take anything valuable from their rooms.

"Single file," advised Tate. "Stay calm and filter out the lobby into the street."

A bellhop came through the stairwell door to assist in the mass exodus and assured hotel patrons and tourists that everything would be fine. Tate noticed his nametag but did a double take to make sure he read it correctly. He called the bellhop over. He had long, dirty blond hair and an infinity tattoo on his forearm.

"Ace," called Tate. "Would you mind helping me with an elderly woman in 605?"

"No problem, dude," answered Ace.

Ace used his master key and opened room 605. They entered into an empty room. The beds were made, and it was apparent that no one had occupied this space.

"Hey dude," offered Ace. "No one's in here, man."

Tate pulled his shirt up to reveal his Glock.

"Take off your clothes," ordered Tate.

"What the fuck?" asked a stunned Ace.

"You heard me," said Tate.

"Dude, I'm not smokin' your dick, man," complained Ace. "I'm not into ass rapes, bud."

"Relax," chuckled Tate.

Ace thought for a minute as he unbuttoned his shirt.

"Are you gonna pay me, man?" asked Ace hesitantly.

"Yeah, you got a batman suit?" quipped Tate. "Hurry up."

Captain Dunn and Chief Steward sat at the strategy table in the UCC while Steve and Ramon monitored a live feed of security cameras the hotel allowed them to tap into.

"We have the murder weapon," briefed Dunn. "We have the video, we have motive."

"I just wanted to bring up the fact that he wrote that he was set up," offered Steve. "That's all."

"What else is he going to write?" questioned Dunn.

"I agree, Detective," supported Steward. "It's his way of casting doubt."

"I say we take him out," ordered Dunn. "Dead or alive, this case is airtight."

"There he is bro!" pointed Ramon.

They saw Tate on the video monitor as he broke the glass on the fire alarm and retrieved the ax. He then crossed in front of the security camera and covered the lens with shaving cream.

"We lost visual," stated Dunn.

"But he's on the 6th floor," stated Steve as he and Ramon headed for the door. "We're going in."

"The snipers are in place," added Dunn. "I'm giving them the green light."

"Suspect is in dark slacks, dark shirt and dark jacket," relayed Steve into his radio.

Steve and Ramon exited the UCC and crossed the street to the entrance of the hotel lobby. They checked the safety on their Glocks and popped out their clips to confirm they contained full ammunition.

"Are you ready for this, bro?" asked a concerned Ramon.

"Yes," Steve admitted reluctantly, "the facts are facts."

"I hope so, bro," offered Ramon. "They just put a target on his back and shit."

Before Steve could respond to Ramon's statement, he heard a very loud pop and a long sizzle. One floor at a time, the entire building that housed the Inn at the Park went dark. No power.

"We're not dealing with an amateur, Ramon," stated Steve.

Tate stood in room 605 wearing Ace's bellboy uniform as he finished tying his hands to the bed with the chord from the iron. He allowed him to put on some of Tate's clothes so he wouldn't be found in his boxers.

"Is Ace your real name?" asked Tate.

"Nah, it's Bartholomew, dude," he confessed. "I just go by Ace."

"Wise move," agreed Tate. "I'm gonna need your car keys."

"It's a blue Honda parked on 6th, dude," offered Ace. "Hey, man, it's got a sunroof."

"Thanks for your generosity," said Tate as he was about to place a gag around Ace's mouth.

"Wait, dude, is there any way you could leave a cool scar or bruise on me for my dudes to see?" asked Ace. "You know, man, nothing drastic."

Before Ace could finish saying the word, "drastic," Tate hit him in the jaw with a crisp right hook that rendered him completely unconscious.

"That should leave a mark," said Tate.

He propped Ace's head up and leaned him against the bed so his airway would stay open. He calmly exited room 605 and turned left down the hallway. He checked behind him to make sure there were no cops in the vicinity. Everything was clear.

He glanced at his watch and realized he still had to get to Rita. She probably arrived at their meeting location and was chewing her fake nails to the bone worried about him. Or she could be positioned outside with a rifle ready to lay down ground fire for his escape. He just never knew with his redheaded jewel. But first things first, he had to get to room 405 if he was to get to 6th Avenue and find a blue Honda.

He slipped into the stairwell and began his descent to the 4th floor.

Steve and Ramon jogged through the elegant lobby and entered the stairwell that led to the upper floors. They attacked the stairs two at a time with their guns drawn. They arrived at the second floor, but the stream of evacuees headed down the stairs hindered their speed. A woman panicked when she saw their guns, which caused a wave of terror as the people knocked over other hotel guests as they attempted to flee the building.

"Stay calm!" screamed Steve.

"We're cops and shit!" added Ramon.

Steve and Ramon checked as many faces as possible but were overwhelmed with the thought of Tate sneaking by them in this crazed melee.

"He has to come this way," said Steve. "There's no other way down except the fire escapes, and they're all covered."

"No other way, bro," agreed Ramon.

"He's gonna try to blend in," stated Steve.

They continued up to the 3rd floor but much slower with all the chaos in the stairwell. A call over the radio informed them that Tate took a young hostess' cell phone and that a tech was running the number to pinpoint his location and intercept possible audio feeds from his phone conversations. If they couldn't find him they wanted to know who he was calling and where he was going.

Tate used the stair railing to hop from one set of stairs to the next as he avoided a couple of evacuees. He heard a woman scream from below which echoed up the stairwell. Panic ensued and he could hear people falling and tripping over one another.

"Stay calm!" screamed a man from below.

"We're cops and shit!" added another man's voice.

Tate made it down to the 4th floor and entered the stairwell door into the hallway. He now realized they were only one floor below him. He quickly hustled down the hallway in search of room 405.

Tate wondered what his Grandpa Holloway would have thought if he was alive to see him in this predicament. He always supported his theory of there being two killers. He also agreed that no one downtown wanted anyone digging deeper into the case and that it was more than likely politically motivated. He always encouraged Tate to stand up for himself and keep searching for the truth. Tate had abandoned the case after his death but now suddenly realized he had to finish what he started eight years ago. Not only for Grandpa Holloway but also for the families and loved ones of the victims.

He used Ace's master key to open room 405 and entered undetected. The people had pretty much cleared out of the upper floors so as long as the electricity stayed off he was going to be okay. He understood how hotel security surveillance systems worked, and they wouldn't have enough juice in a power outage to feed video to the Unit Command Center that was sure to be parked outside.

Steve and Ramon reached the 6th floor and entered the hallway cautiously but in proper police formation. Their guns were drawn, and they carefully traversed the hallway as they maneuvered throughout the hallways. They had a difficult time seeing through the eerie glow from the green emergency lights. They checked closets and trained their guns on the corridor that led to the elevator. Nothing.

"Do we have a visual?" asked Steve into his radio.

"We're still trying to reconnect enough juice," answered Dunn through Tate's radio. "Should be in the next 15."

"SWAT has been notified," added Steward. "He won't get out without someone seeing him."

"Bro, we're gonna have to go door to door," informed Ramon.

"Fifteen fuckin' minutes," Steve complained to Ramon. "He could be at the border by then."

"We've assembled teams to search the rooms on each floor," Steward's voice boomed through the radio.

"Perimeter is sealed, and we have eyes in the sky," followed up Dunn.

"Give me the master key and shit," said Ramon. "How many rooms?"

"Eighty-two," answered Steve.

Ramon used the key and swiped it through the lock mechanism attached to the door handle. The green light flashed, and they charged through the doorway with their guns drawn. Nothing. Ramon moved to the bathroom and searched the shower while Steve pointed his gun underneath the bed.

"Clear," yelled Ramon.

"Clear," added Steve. "Shit! Fuck that hurt!"

"What?" asked Ramon.

"Hit my fuckin' shin on the bed frame," complained Steve.

"It's dark as shit, bro," said Ramon.

Tate went straight to the closet located in room 405. The glow from the emergency lights didn't spill into the room enough for him to see clearly, but he remembered the layout from the 6th floor guestroom. He took the hotel-issued laundry bag from a hanger and sliced the top corners open with the pocketknife from Ace's keychain. He placed the plastic laundry bag over his head and pulled it over his bellhop uniform as if he was putting on a shirt. He placed each of his arms through the two openings that had been cut and completed his plastic bag poncho.

Tate pulled the ironing board down and spotted a cherry-wood cupboard door located against the back wall of the closet. The cupboard door was about two feet wide and three feet long. He pulled it open and revealed a thin wooden panel with a circular metal handle. He placed his finger around the circular handle and slid the panel open.

Tate took a step back and smiled.

"Fuck me," he said.

A large number of cops infiltrated the stairwell with their guns drawn and raced up the stairs. A team of five peeled off on each floor and entered the hallways in search of Tate. The entire Inn at the Park had 25 cops split up and comb through each room on every floor. They didn't have the master keys so Steve realized the city would be hit with a hefty bill. They'd have to replace the hinges that were about to be dismantled from the doors when they got kicked in. Bam! Bam! Bam! One door after another was busted down as cops poured into various guest rooms.

Steve and Ramon remained on the 6th floor as they supervised the massive sweep.

"He could hide for days in this building, bro," commented Ramon.

"Not his style," said Steve. "He won't stay still for long."

"Good luck and shit, bro," joked Ramon. "It's like Pelican Bay around here."

"People have escaped from Pelican Bay," informed Steve.

Tate reached into the pitch-dark opening and ran his hand along the back of the old dumbwaiter shaft. He located the rope that was connected to the pulley system and gave it a tug to test the strength. The tension in the rope caused the guide rails to squeak and the small wooden cart to wobble.

When questioned about a possible escape route, Ace had explained to Tate that some of the hotel staff covertly used the old dumbwaiter to transport weed between the kitchen and room 405. Those locations were the only access to the dumbwaiter. He went on to explain that room 405 used to be part of a 4th-floor parlor and bar that existed in the 1950s. They just never sealed the dumbwaiter when they replaced the parlor and built guestrooms. Tate knew the city's history pretty well and figured that the hotel staff hadn't utilized the dumbwaiter in decades — not exactly a comforting thought.

Tate wrapped towels around his hands to protect himself from rope burn and crammed inside the wooden platform. He sat with his legs crossed, which enabled him to descend the shaft without his knees getting lodged. The plastic laundry poncho protected his bellhop uniform from dirt and grime that had settled over the years. If he was going to blend in he didn't want to look like he had just surfaced from a coal mine.

Hand-over-hand Tate slowly released the slack and lowered himself into the dark abyss. The pulley joint squeaked with every yank of the rope, and he quickly realized he had to keep his core balanced or the platform would flip. Thank

God for surfing. Not being able to see his hand in front of his face had its advantages — he wasn't able to recognize how high up he was or for that matter; how far he'd fall. He told himself to focus on the task at hand and not the actuality that his life depended on a dumbwaiter cart that hadn't been serviced in decades. He weighed 203, and he knew damn well the only other passenger on this rickety piece of wood was maybe an ounce of pot and a glass bong. Tate wasn't much for heights, but you would never know it the way he had finessed fire escapes and rooftops tonight.

He realized he descended past the next level when his shoulder grazed the former opening to the 3rd floor that had been sealed and closed off. He figured counting sealed dumbwaiter exits would be the easiest way to judge the distance he had left to travel.

He intensified his pace and felt comfortable with his smooth descent to the kitchen when the sound of wood splitting echoed throughout the shaft. The sound resembled the creaking of a wooden-boat hull that was tied to a dock in rough weather. Just as his mind processed the potential danger, the wooden platform snapped and dropped out from underneath him. The rope coiled around his wrist and his body swung into the shaft with a painful thud. The platform smashed into the ground below. He was able to grab the rope with his right hand and dangled until he had the wherewithal and grabbed a piece of the rope with his left hand. He used his upper body strength and rappelled the final 25 feet toward the bottom of the shaft. His arms ultimately gave out and he dropped the last eight feet. His legs hit and his body crumpled from the force.

Steve and Ramon were caught off guard by the radio calls that came in back-to-back to one another. The search crew discovered a young white male in room 605 who was stripped down and tied to the bed frame. A dark jacket covered his lap. He was groggy and couldn't respond coherently to any of the questions from the officers. Steve thought he would take a shot when he arrived in 605.

"What happened?" asked Steve.

"I ... didn't ... suck ... dick, dudes," answered Ace with grogginess still heavy in his voice.

Steve didn't know if he was a casualty of Tate's attempted escape or was abandoned amongst the chaos by a frightened, sadistic homosexual lover. Either way he was useless to them in this condition.

"The jacket, bro," stated Ramon as he pointed to Ace's lap. "Is that Tate's?"

"He changed clothes again," stated Steve into his radio.

They were quickly summoned to guestroom 405 to evaluate a discovery that needed their immediate attention.

"Get an EMT up here and keep asking questions," ordered Steve as they exited room 605 for the 4th floor.

They jetted down two flights of stairs, and Steve noticed that Ramon was breathing heavier than he was.

"Burritos catching up to you, huh?" teased Steve.

Ramon glared at him, but Steve couldn't figure out if he was pissed at the comment or if he agreed. He would never admit it either way. They arrived to find three officers in room 405 that were eager to disclose their discovery.

"What do we got?" asked Steve as he and Ramon hustled into the guestroom.

"We found the ironing board tossed on the ground," said the officer who helped search the room. "Then we felt cool air and noticed this ..."

Ramon saw the small cupboard door opened in the closet. He felt a crisp breeze that escaped the opening and chilled the air. He grabbed the officer's flashlight and lit up the dumbwaiter shaft.

"Holy shit, bro," commented Ramon. "We got a tunnel rat."

"Find out where this goes?" stated Steve to one of the officers.

"I'll update command, bro," Ramon told Steve.

"Tate!" yelled Steve down the shaft. "Turn yourself in and let's talk!"

Tate rolled out of the dumbwaiter shaft and rested on the floor while he mentally assessed his body. He'd been demolished by 20-foot waves a few times in his life but was surprised by the force that shot through his body when he landed in the shaft. He stood up to stretch his back and tore off the plastic poncho and tossed it into the nearest trashcan. He leaned behind a prep table in the kitchen and waited as two officers jogged past the kitchen entrance. He noticed a sous chef on the very far side of the enormous kitchen. The sous chef pulled food products out of the enormous stainless steel refrigerator and placed them into an ice chest. In the mayhem of everything that had gone down in the hotel, Tate chuckled at the fact that no matter the circumstances; there were always asshole bosses.

"Hey, I need your help," begged Tate urgently.

"I was told to save the perishables," explained the sous chef.

"I'll do that," offered Tate. "The manager sent me."

"In pursuit! Suspect being chased through the lobby!" exclaimed an officer's voice through Steve's radio.

"All units move!" ordered Dunn through Steve's radio.

"All units to the front of the hotel!" yelled the officer's voice through Steve's radio.

Steve and Ramon attacked the stairwell while the other officers followed closely behind. They jumped three stairs at a time for the race to the lobby.

"We have a green light on suspect," ordered Dunn. "Repeat, green light on suspect!"

Steve couldn't digest the fact that Tate took the time to write that he *"was set up"*. Who stops to write a message while under a citywide hunt? He knew he'd never find out the answer to that mystery if Tate was gunned down in the street. He also noticed the glare he got from Ramon after Dunn's announcement as several different voices from officers blared over the radio.

"Where is he?" asked one voice.

"I don't see him!" yelled another.

"There he is!" added another.

"Tate!" echoed a male voice down the dumbwaiter shaft. "Turn yourself in and let's talk!"

"Shit," Tate said to himself.

He glanced out the backdoor that led to the alley connected to 6th Avenue. He noticed the stakeout units that established the perimeter behind the hotel and realized this was the most opportune time to continue his deception.

"All units to the front of the hotel!" yelled Tate into the radio.

He knew they must have found the cop he "sleep-held" in the alley because they scrambled their radio signals. Tate might not be good with numbers, especially in his checkbook, but he had what many considered a photographic memory. He remembered the formulas they used to scramble the channels and worked backward until he found the frequency they were using. There was so much chaos he figured he'd create a diversion to manage his escape by calling out false claims and visuals.

Steve and Ramon sprinted out through the lobby to join in on the capture of Tate Holloway. A man dressed in a hotel uniform quickly ran out of the hotel as he hurriedly wheeled a room-service cart out the front door. The tablecloth covered the surface of the cart and hung down low enough to hide any cargo that might be underneath. A dozen cops surrounded the guy with their guns trained on the possible accomplice.

"Freeze!" ordered one officer.

"Don't fuckin' move!" ordered another.

Steve aimed his gun where the tablecloth covered the bottom of the cart.

"Come out, Tate!" ordered Steve.

Nothing. He lifted the tablecloth and revealed two cases of bottled water. The hotel employee stood with his hands in the air. He was the sous chef from the kitchen.

"It's free," whimpered the frightened sous chef. "The guy told me to bring it to you guys, ASAP."

"Suspect hiding under room-service cart!" informed Tate into his police radio.

Tate saw the units as they responded to his request to hurry to the front of the hotel and vacated their perimeter posts. He simply walked out the backdoor and calmly made his way through the crowd that had gathered to watch the fiasco unfold. To an observer, Tate appeared like any other bellhop headed to his car after a long day's work.

An older bystander in the crowd noticed Tate as he crossed the alley behind the hotel and walked right by him.

"Is it crazy in there?" asked the bystander in his 60's.

"Sir, you have no idea," answered Tate.

"He must've broken the radio scramble," complained Steve.

"He was using the damn radio, bro," said Ramon. "Fuckin' played us and shit."

Captain Dunn and Chief Steward approached the chaotic scene.

"How did we miss him?" asked Dunn. "I don't understand it."

"Where did we go wrong?" questioned Steward. "I'm the one who has to call the Mayor, Detective."

Steve kicked the garbage can next to the hotel entrance out of frustration. He informed them about the breach of the radio signals and how Tate pulled the units off the rear of the building. Over Steve's shoulder, in the far background, a blue Honda turned left down Spruce Street and disappeared into the night.

An officer ran up to the group as they stood and wallowed in their loss of Tate Holloway.

"We'll go to the press," offered Dunn.

"He was right under our noses all these years?" questioned Steward. "How were we so wrong about him?"

"I always knew he was fucked in the head," confessed Captain Dunn.

"Sir," the officer interrupted. "The techs pulled audio from an intercepted call the suspect made on the stolen cell phone."

"And ... ?" continued Steve.

"We know where he's headed," stated the officer.

Edgar Allen Poe said it best, *"I became insane, with long intervals of horrible sanity."* I couldn't agree more. That's the existence that's pumping through my veins. The years of being dormant left me aching to inflict sorrow and pain. If I would have killed over the last eight years, the pure exhilaration I'm feeling wouldn't tempt me to slaughter again.

The chaos I've created proves my allegiance to Meyers. He would be so proud. Fuck Tate Holloway! The extraordinary intoxication of watching the life leave Grace Harper makes me want to take a bite out of Satan's apple, slit Adam's throat, and fuck Eve from behind. I don't fear God because he ignored me when I was a kid. He turned his holy back when I chose to be a disciple of the Angel of Death. My hotel suite is already booked in hell, and God's not going to waste his time saving someone like me. Wonder if my penthouse suite in hell will have a dumbwaiter?

I must admit I might have underestimated my prey's will to survive. He's hard to catch. I just have to change the bait. My plan is still going accordingly, and in the end, I will taste the sweet wine that is vengeance. I remember my first taste of wine. I was 10 years old. Mother left out her cheap box wine on the counter one afternoon — and I used it in a celebratory toast.

Our neighbors in the apartment complex found a puppy, and I watched Libby sit by the window next to the balcony and gaze at it for hours. She wanted a little puppy of her own, but Mother wouldn't allow it. Shit, we never had enough food to eat so there was no way we could feed a puppy. It was a white cocker spaniel named Brenda. Who the fuck names their dog Brenda? Stupid fuckin' neighbors. I should have killed them, but they had a nice TV.

That fuckin' dog would whine and bark every morning. It was cold out, and the idiot neighbors would leave Brenda leashed to the balcony guardrail. I knew it was safe because they were passed out from coming down on whatever drug they were using the previous night. I crawled over the neighbor's guardrail and kicked the mutt off the 3rd-story balcony. The leash was still tied to the railing, but the choker was doing its job. Brenda could only manage a groan and some wheezing as she dangled from the balcony. I was watching her little legs scratching and clawing on the side of the building, trying to gain enough traction to loosen the choker around her neck. I slowly hoisted her up by the leash and helped her get to the balcony before she went unconscious. I loosened the choker and watched as her eyes came back to life.

I remember she licked and kissed me and was so thankful I was there to help her. She was a really cute puppy. I tickled her pink belly, and she started to yelp and bark with excitement. Her tail was wagging like crazy, and she rolled over to play some more. What the fuck was

I doing? I wrapped my hands around her tiny throat and squeezed. Her eyes bulged with fear.

William Shakespeare was so profound when he said the eyes were the windows to the soul. Eyes *are* the windows to the soul, but also the eyes are the barometers of pain. According to Brenda's eyes, the barometer level reached capacity — extreme agony. When the life left the puppy, I tightened the choker and hung her back over the balcony to make it look like an accident.

I went inside and felt the need to celebrate so I pressed the valve on the box wine and filled my *Fugitive* TV show cup. I used to wish David Janssen was my Dad — it turned out my birth dad was a real fugitive. He didn't play one on TV — and he definitely wasn't innocent. So I slammed my wine to commemorate a few milestones in my young life. Brenda was my first murder of a domestic animal. Don't get me wrong, killing and skinning rats and mice were weekly occurrences. In fact, later in life, Meyers and I would have contests to see who could kill the most living things. Our foster homes were full of rats and mice so it was easy.

The rodents' eyes were more difficult to read and appreciate. Their eyes were more like dark, empty pomegranate seeds. At least they felt that way when I squished them between my fingers. And I didn't count killing the cockroaches in the apartment either. I was addicted to the popping sound the roaches made when I used my thumb and pressed them into the floor. It was almost as addicting as popping the bubble wrap companies used to protect shipping packages. No, that was the first kill of something people loved and would miss. It was also my first victim with a human being's name — Brenda.

But the most important milestone at the time was I ended some of my sister's sadness. It was the first time I was able to do that for her. I was able to eliminate the grief Libby felt when she watched Brenda through the sliding glass door. No more puppy — no more sadness in Libby's eyes. And no more waking me up at the crack of dawn.

I just have to sit tight and allow my plan to unfold. It got knocked a little off track, but the damage has been done. Not the ultimate damage that will soon befall him but enough to fuck up his life. But one thing is quickly becoming apparent to me. I'm feeling that burn in my chest — and that tingle in my loins. The only euphoria that releases enough serotonin to make my cock hard. I won't fuck up the plan, but once the genie was let out of the bottle — he's not going back in after eight years. Not today. Not ever. If I had some box wine I'd make a toast to Meyers. Let him know my work is almost complete.

I will have to alter my method and modify my process, but I will not be able to contain my hunger for death. I will not deny the inevitable — someone else has to die. I just don't know who. Sometimes the hunt is just as fun as the kill ... sometimes.

Steve and Ramon led the convoy of cop cars as their Dodge Charger skidded to a stop at the gate in front of the old shipyard. The police helicopter hovered above the scene as the spotlights lit up the grounds around the shipyard warehouse. They jumped out of their car and checked the lock that hung on the gated entrance.

Thanks to Ace, they knew at this point that Tate took the keys of an older blue Honda and more than likely escaped through the rear of the hotel dressed as a bellhop. The car was parked on 6th Avenue so he would have to travel west to get to the shipyard.

"Nobody saw anything?" Steve asked into his radio.

"Negative," answered the helicopter pilot. "No sign of the Honda."

"Shit," complained Steve.

"He could've dumped the car, bro," stated Ramon.

"But he was still coming here," said Steve.

"This is the place and shit?" asked Ramon as he cut through the padlock with a deadbolt cutter.

"We heard the phone call," stated Steve. "He said the old shipyard plain as day."

"Do we have anything on his accomplice?" asked Chief Steward who approached them at the gate.

"No," stated Steve. "We couldn't get a hit on the disposable. He works with a Rita Jones."

"Why is that name familiar?" asked Steward.

"She used to work in dispatch," answered Steve.

"Find her," ordered Steward. "And Holloway?"

"He either changed his mind," offered Steve, "or he played us again, sir."

"The entire property is clear," informed the helicopter pilot. "Please advise."

Steve looked to the Chief for guidance. He was smart enough to respect authority and not make a decision while he stood next to the Chief of Police.

"He could be anywhere by now, Detective," complained Chief Steward. "Send him home."

"Return home," ordered Steve into his radio. "Thanks for your help."

The helicopter peeled away from the shipyard and took off toward home base. The surrounding area instantly went dark without the helicopter spotlights. They had to rely on their vehicles and the glow from the red and blue cop lights.

"He's not here," offered Ramon. "He's in the wind, bro."

"He used to live on a boat in one of the marinas," informed Steve. "Let's send a unit to his office, too."

"I'm on it," said Ramon as he stepped away from them.

"Where's Captain Dunn, sir?" asked Steve.

"I sent him to Jonathan Harper's to help brief the Mayor," he answered. "I'm headed there now."

"We'll keep you posted, sir," informed Steve.

"*You* keep us posted Detective Pelletti," ordered Steward as an obvious jab at Ramon.

"Yes, sir," offered Steve who was somewhat confused by the slam at his partner. He thought Ramon handled himself pretty well in this fiasco.

"Oh and Detective," scolded Steward. "I'm getting tired of being played."

Tate stretched his legs on Rita's couch while he assessed the damage the escape caused to his body. He was thankful to have a friend and partner who lived such a clandestine and secretive life. Not many people are able to own a "safehouse" in the canyons that is completely untraceable and owned by a fictitious person. She also had a vehicle stashed in the garage that was registered to the same fake name. He always thought Rita reminded him of Andy Dufresne in the movie, *The Shawshank Redemption*, where he created a fake identity to help hide the funds that were scammed by the prison warden. Way smarter than your average criminal and just smart enough to never get caught.

He didn't know much about her prior history before they had met at the precinct. She was completely honest about everything after that point, and he obviously trusted her with his life. Maybe it was better if he didn't know her entire story. Maybe some things were better left a secret.

He realized there was no one better equipped to help him get out of this dilemma than Rita. Her contacts ran deep, and they weren't just police department and city officials either. This was a military town, and she knew influential people who knew how to keep secrets.

She entered the living room and carried a tray that contained two hot cocoa mugs. She chuckled when she saw Tate in his bellhop uniform.

"I feel like I should hand you my luggage n'all," chuckled Rita.

"As long as you leave a tip," said Tate.

"Kahlua with a little coffee, sugar," said Rita. "My Momma used to give me this me when I was a child."

"That explains a lot," said Tate. "Think they're searching the shipyard?"

"And you laughed at the code n'all," chuckled Rita.

Rita had come up with a simple code to use if they were ever in a situation where they were desperate to convey sensitive information and had to use a mobile device. Everything they said that regarded a location was completely opposite of what was actually spoken. If they said desert, they meant the ocean. If they said the city, they meant the canyons. It was basic but if people secretly listened to their conversation they would have to take the information at face value.

Rita flipped on the TV and watched the media frenzy unfold. Reporter Megan Hunt broadcasted live outside the Inn at the Park on Spruce Street.

"The manhunt for former SDPD detective Tate Holloway continues as the evacuation at the Inn at the Park caused mass hysteria and chaos. The way the scene is clearing out, you'd have to assume he got away. There has been no official statement from the police or Mayor's office other than to name the suspect and release this photo minutes ago," reported Megan.

An image of Tate's face from the surveillance video filled the television screen as Megan continued her breaking-news segment.

"He's seen here on security footage while he fled from the Harper home after he committed the murder. Not only is he wanted in the Grace Harper slaying but a person with direct knowledge of the case told us that Tate Holloway could be a possible serial killer with several undiscovered victims. Sources went on to tell us that seven years ago his obsession over 'The Eye' led to his forced resignation from the department, and he was considered mentally disturbed," stated Megan Hunt. "Did Tate Holloway claim to be 'The Eye'?"

"No reward offered, sugar?" joked Rita as she muted the TV. "I need to get my titties lifted n'all so I figured I'd use the reward money."

An image of Rita Jones was displayed on the TV screen. Tate pointed at the TV and chuckled as Rita turned up the volume.

"His accomplice could be his business partner, Rita Jones, who also used to work for the police department ...," continued Megan Hunt.

"No reward for you, either?" laughed Tate. "I could've used it to pay off the boat."

"At least they used a good photo of me n'all," expressed Rita. "I don't look like Ted Bundy caught in headlights."

Tate realized how his life would change from the media attention.

"This hurts everything, Rita," confessed Tate. "I have to get to Nicole."

"No, sugar," ordered Rita. "They'll be all over her if they aren't already."

"Can we hide her up here?" asked Tate.

"Have you lost your damn mind?" yelled Rita. "To her right now you're a mentally disturbed murderer who lived a double life n'all. How long 'fore they find out you screw for money? This hurts everyone — including yours truly."

Tate was so focused on the escape that he forgot the impact this would have on his personal life. He knew Rita was right. There was no way he could trust Nicole. He understood exactly how the game was played. They'd use her to get to him. He needed to redirect his feelings for her and concentrate on finding out who set him up and why. He needed to accept the reality that their relationship was over and nothing would be the same; but he wanted her safe. She would be a liability if she stayed in town. She could also be in danger. That still didn't ease the pain of the inevitable. Even if he proved his innocence she would never take him back if it was revealed that he slept with other woman for money. Women marry murderers on death row. They don't marry gigolos. Period.

"Who would want to set you up?" asked Rita.

"I've been racking my brain since this went down," admitted Tate. "I have no idea."

They evaluated the evidence that had mounted against Tate: a call to the media claiming to be "The Eye" confessed to Grace's murder; a new gigolo client set up a date at the house on Briarwood; a security video of Tate at the Briarwood house; and a blood-stained murder weapon also conveniently found at Briarwood. They needed to find out who called Rita to set up the date.

"Let's take a look at the old case file with fresh eyes n'all," said Rita. "See if something doesn't fit."

"That's gonna be a problem," confessed Tate.

Steve and Ramon hovered over Tate's Jeep that was located in a parking lot two blocks west of NuNu's. They glanced through the windows and noticed an item of interest in the backseat — a dark blanket covered what appeared to be a box of some kind. They waited as an officer tried to operate a Slim-Jim tool to open the Jeep door. He wasn't having much luck getting it unlocked.

"We don't have all day, officer," said Steve.

"I can't seem to get it, Detective," confessed the officer.

Ramon walked over to the passenger side of the vehicle and smashed through the window with his elbow. He cleared some of the shattered glass, reached inside, and unlocked the door.

"Got it, bro," said Ramon said to the officer.

They reached in and tossed the blanket to the side, which revealed a medium-sized cardboard box. Steve pulled the box out and set it on the hood of the Jeep. He opened the top and saw a stack of files labeled, *"The Eye."*

"What the fuck?" asked a bewildered Ramon.

"The missing case file," confirmed Steve. "He had it the whole fuckin' time."

"He was set up, bro?" questioned Ramon. "Yeah, my ass."

Steve heard Ramon's comment but didn't know how to respond. The cloud of doubt that formed in his head when he read Tate's message in the bathroom had suddenly dissipated. The insurmountable evidence against Tate led to only one conclusion in Steve's mind. Tate Holloway went crazy and killed Grace Harper for revenge. He thought that Tate might have wanted to get back at Jonathan Harper who encouraged his dismissal from the force. He wasn't convinced that Tate was "the other guy" he always referred to or that he was in fact The Eye —that would have to shake out in the investigation.

He'd have to take a look into Marvin Polski again. He was the man who Tate killed and was confirmed to be The Eye. Maybe Tate knew him? Did Tate have something to do with Jack's murder? It always bothered him that Tate and Jack were by themselves at the cabin the night Jack was killed. Why didn't they call for backup? So many things that made sense to Steve this morning made absolutely zero sense tonight.

"We got a gun," informed one of the officers who searched Tate's Jeep. "A Glock .40."

"That's Tate's preference," stated Steve.

"I thought he pulled a piece on a cop and shit?" quizzed Ramon. "With his gun in the glove-box, bro?"

"You have more than one gun?" Steve answered with a question.

"This shit is off the charts crazy," stated Ramon.

Steve couldn't agree more.

"I'm going to need a gun," said Tate after putting on a black T-shirt to go with his jeans. He felt more human after he ditched the bellhop uniform.

"You should get some rest, sugar," advised Rita.

"I need to be somewhere," he said.

"You're safe here," convinced Rita. "We can start piecing the puzzle together in the mornin'."

"I'm gonna need your car keys and a gun," ordered Tate. "You have an extra gun?"

Rita knew how stubborn Tate could be and recognized the determination on his face. She let out a sigh and walked over to a bookcase on the far side of the cabin's living room. She entered a code into a keypad that was mounted on the wall and the bookcase slid open to the side. Tate stood there dumbfounded. He couldn't believe his eyes. A secret room behind the bookcase housed an entire arsenal of weapons.

Numerous SIG550 assault rifles, M-4 carbines, SWAT HK machine guns, 50 caliber sniper rifles, Glock .40 semi-automatic handguns and M1014 shotguns hung methodically on the walls. Strategically placed track lights illuminated the weapons like a gallery would showcase an artist's paintings.

"I got one or two," answered Rita.

VENGEANCE IS NOW

Harold Reynolds pulled his car into the driveway in the dead of night. He flipped his headlights off and checked the street for any police activity. He only noticed the same squad car that had been parked in front of the Harper mansion every night since the murder. He realized the cop was there to preserve the crime scene and keep out any unwanted trespassers.

Harold clicked the garage-door opener and slowly rolled his Cadillac XT sedan into the driveway and the safety of his three-car garage. He clicked the opener again and watched the door glide closed behind him before he exited his vehicle. He seemed fidgety as he unlocked the door that led into the house. He flipped the light switch on in the kitchen and called for his cat.

"Precious?" he called out. "Here, Precious ..."

He entered the PIN number of the alarm code into the keypad next to the door to the garage. Nothing happened. He entered it again but the touch screen indicated that the alarm was off. He shrugged his shoulders and hit the light switch as he passed through the living room. The lights didn't turn on. He continued toward the hallway and tried those lights as well. Nothing. A door closed by the kitchen and startled him.

"Precious ...," called Reynolds nervously. "Where are you sweetie?"

He hit another light switch. Nothing. His heart rate soared when the kitchen light suddenly turned off. He was standing in the middle of the living room in complete darkness. He panicked when he heard a shuffling noise by the kitchen.

"Who's there?" whimpered Reynolds.

He slammed his leg into an end table while he quickly tried to click on a lamp that he scrambled to locate. The crystals that decorated the lampshade jingled when he couldn't find the button and his elbow knocked into the shade. He found it! He pressed the button. Nothing. The lamp didn't come on. Harold nervously pulled his cell phone out of his pocket and pointed it at the floor. The phone's blue light created a ghostly glow in the room and every piece of furniture bounced shadows off the walls.

"Have a seat Mr. Reynolds," said a creepy voice.

"What do you want?" exclaimed a frightened Reynolds. "Don't hurt me! I don't have anything to take!"

"Sit down," ordered the voice.

The mysterious man was seated in a chair by the fireplace. He positioned a flashlight underneath his chin and pointed it up to the ceiling. He clicked it on and revealed himself to be Tate Holloway. He was almost unrecognizable with the creepy light bouncing off his face.

"Who are you?" begged the petrified Reynolds.

"I'm like a cop," stated Tate.

"Well, do you have a warrant or something?" continued Reynolds. "What are you doing in my house?"

"I'm not that kind'a cop, Mr. Reynolds," informed Tate.

"What kind of cop are you?" he asked.

Tate pulled a silver-plated, semi-automatic Glock .40 out of his waistband and placed it on his lap.

"One that doesn't have rules," informed Tate.

"I don't understand," whimpered Reynolds. "What can I do?"

"Give it to me," ordered Tate.

"I don't know what you mean," answered Reynolds. "I already told the detectives everything."

"No, no you didn't Mr. Reynolds," rebutted Tate.

Tate hopped the back fence into the backyard of Harold Reynolds' house after he parked several blocks away to avoid being detected by the officers assigned to babysit the Harper mansion. His mug was plastered all over TV stations and Internet news sites so he had to be extremely cautious whenever he had to be in public. If he was going to find out who set him up; he'd have to be in public a lot.

Rita made some calls and was able to download the blueprint and schematics of the house and inquired about the home's security system. He was much better prepared for this outing instead of the one earlier with Steve. He still couldn't believe he made it out of the hotel alive.

From the street, Tate had noticed that a window in the attic faced the window directly across from Grace's bathroom window. He remembered Steve had said that something wasn't right with Reynolds and that he wasn't being forthcoming. Considering Tate was enemy number one now, he knew they weren't too interested in what the retired college professor had to say. This was the perfect time for Tate to find out what he may or may not be hiding.

He walked past the enormous custom pool and covertly located the alarm box mounted on the opposite side of the guesthouse. The pool was gorgeous. It had an upper and lower level and the water spilled down through a rock waterfall that had a swim-up bar underneath. Tate now understood why college tuition was so expensive. How the hell could a college professor afford to own this extravagant property?

He took out what appeared to be a small iPad tablet. He pulled a wire from the tablet and connected a USB cable to the keypad of the alarm box. He entered the code Rita had uncovered by hacking the security company's computer system and de-activated the alarm to the house.

He picked the lock to the French doors that led into the dining room and closed the doors behind him. He headed directly to the staircase. It was dark but with his flashlight and the memory of the blueprint; he knew exactly which way to go. The home was elegant with wood floors and extravagant furniture. He noticed the exquisite woodwork and attention to detail in the architecture. Again, how the hell could a retired college professor afford to own all this?

He quickly traversed the stairs to the second floor and searched for a door that led to the attic. Something grabbed Tate's leg! He dropped the flashlight and noticed the glowing yellow eyes that stared up at him. It was a white cat that purred and clawed again at Tate's leg. The shock almost sent him into cardiac arrest.

"Holy shit," exhaled Tate.

He picked up the cat and tossed it safely into a bedroom and shut the door. He glanced down the other end of the hallway and spotted the attic door. He thought it was odd that the professor, who lived alone, would need a padlock on a door to the attic. What was he hiding? He reached back and made sure the safety was disabled on his Glock and proceeded to work the padlock with his small metal pick.

He opened the door and pointed his flashlight up the wooden staircase that led to the attic. The wooden stairs creaked with every step as he slowly made his way up the skinny staircase. He survived the dumbwaiter, but the creepy atmosphere in the house was driving him crazy. He fully expected Nicole Kidman's character from *The Others* to walk around the corner at any moment.

He reached the attic and pointed the flashlight near the window that faced Grace's bathroom. He smiled. A high-tech HD video camera was bolted to a tripod and pointed in the direction of Grace's bathroom window. The camera had an extended night-vision zoom attached to the end of the lens. Tate looked through the eyehole. The image was in a green hue from the night vision and a little fuzzy because the zoom lens kept recalculating the focus. Nonetheless, he could clearly see into Grace's bathroom.

"Someone's been naughty," muttered Tate to himself.

He noticed a lockbox located next to the base of the computer that the camera was connected to. There was a small key lock over the latch so Tate busted it open with a hammer he found on the floor. The lockbox contained several

DVDs that were labeled in red Sharpie pen. They consisted of women's names and dates. He filtered through the DVDs and noticed dozens and dozens that contained Grace's name. He looked at the dates and realized that the DVD from the night of the murder was missing from the collection.

"You sick fuck," muttered Tate.

Tate noticed the car headlights that beamed through the attic window and glanced outside. He saw a Cadillac XT sedan as the headlights turned off, and it slowed down in front of Harold Reynolds' driveway. He grabbed the lockbox and headed back downstairs.

Tate continued his interrogation as he sat in the chair with the flashlight casting an eerie light across his face. Harold sat in the chair opposite Tate's.

"I know you're a sick fuck," stated Tate. "I've got most of your DVDs."

"I can explain," whined Reynolds. "I can't go to prison."

"Prison?" chuckled Tate. "You'd love prison. You could spy on people showering every day. 'Course they'd have something a little different between their legs."

"What do you want?" asked Reynolds.

"I want last night's DVD, now," ordered Tate.

"You couldn't see who it was," argued Reynolds. "It was too dark."

"But you let it happen," argued Tate.

"No, I ... I watched the footage after the fact," explained Reynolds.

"You filmed her every day?" snapped Tate.

Harold Reynolds dropped his head into his hands and began to sob.

"You saw nothing unusual?" questioned Tate. "A vehicle not normally in the neighborhood? Anything?"

"Well, I did see an old maroon sedan," answered Reynolds.

"I'm listening," commented Tate.

"I noticed it twice in the last couple days," helped Reynolds. "I'd never seen it before."

"Just driving by?" asked Tate.

"Yes," he continued. "And it was parked across the street."

"See, that wasn't so hard," Tate said calmly. "Now get me the DVD."

Reynolds grabbed his leather attaché case and reached inside. He pulled the DVD out of the side pocket and placed it on the end table.

"What happens now?" whimpered Reynolds.

"Make me a copy," he said.

"Then what?" quizzed Reynolds.

Tate held up a thin yellow piece of rope and smiled.

VENGEANCE IS NOW

It was 3:00 a.m. and Jonathan Harper paced impatiently in front of the fireplace at the lodge. Dark circles had formed under his eyes and his cocktail glass hadn't been empty. He had been apprised of everything that had gone down, and he wasn't very enthused with the way the San Diego Police Department have handled the investigation. The Mayor stood off to the side with his arms folded across his chest. Captain Dunn and Chief Steward took the brunt of Harper's aggression while his attorney, Arthur Stein, stood nearby.

"So he just strolled out of the hotel with 50 cops surrounding the building?" he asked incredulously.

"We believe he used his knowledge of law enforcement protocol to aid in his escape," answered Steward. "Unfortunately, he was able to obtain a police radio."

"Jesus Christ," said the exasperated Mayor.

"He may be a nutcase, but he had 12 years on the job," agreed Captain Dunn.

"And you're positive he killed my baby?" asked Harper as his voice cracked with emotion.

"The evidence is undeniable," stated Chief Steward.

"It's iron clad, Jonathan," reassured the Mayor.

"Where have I heard that before?" questioned Harper. "Haven't we already been down this road?"

Arthur couldn't allow his client to get too heated or say something he would later regret. He knew he was powerful, but he also didn't want his client to alienate the city's Chief of Police and Mayor Villanueva. Politics were all about relationships and favors.

"Pleasth, gentlemen," offered Arthur with his severe lisp. "Can't we —."

"This is different," interrupted Steward.

"Is it?" continued Harper. "Holloway has been in the equation from day one."

"I assure you that we —," promised Steward.

"Assure me?" interrupted Harper with an exasperated laugh.

Jonathan Harper took the final swig of his scotch and placed the empty glass on the bar. He plunged his hands into the ice bucket and splashed the melted ice water onto his face. Chief Steward and Captain Dunn watched as Harper dabbed his face with a towel and took a deep breath. It was all he could do to keep from having a breakdown. He was a genius political strategist, but the death of his daughter never played into his ability to conduct nefarious negotiations or business deals. He was understandably out of his element of control.

"Arthur, we need the room," requested Jonathan Harper.

"But —," protested Arthur.

"Please," insisted Harper.

Arthur reluctantly stepped out of the room to appease Harper's request and give the men their privacy. He looked back at Jonathan Harper and glared. He slowly shook his head from side to side before he closed the door behind him.

"You too, Mayor," said Harper.

"You don't think this involves me?" questioned the Mayor. "I was the Chief of Police."

"Yes you were," snapped Harper, "and I'm the one who made you mayor, Mr. future Congressman."

"So I stay," stated the Mayor.

"Suit yourself," said Harper. "How does Marvin Polski play into all this?"

Marvin Polski was the man Tate shot and killed at the remote cabin eight years ago. He was labeled and confirmed to be The Eye after CSI discovered all the evidence in his secluded cabin in the canyons. It was a considered an airtight case at the time.

"He was Holloway's accomplice," said Dunn. "Holloway must've killed him after Jack was already shot. He could look like the hero while still hiding his true identity."

"So you think Holloway is The Eye?" asked the Mayor.

"With Polski dead," offered Steward, "all he had to do was stay dormant."

"Then why'd he go on and on about someone else?" asked Harper. "It makes no sense. He was free and clear. Why bring this on himself after all this time?"

"He was delusional," confirmed Captain Dunn. "You remember Dr. Goel's diagnosis and recommendation."

"I remember something else too," snapped Harper to Steward and the Mayor. "You think he knows? Is that why he killed Grace?"

Chief Steward and Mayor Villanueva searched for a way to answer Harper's questions. They knew people's jobs and reputations depended on the outcome of this fiasco but were also surprised at how flippant Jonathan Harper was with his questions. They figured the murder of his child trumped concealed secrets and melted away the hard surface of guarded discretion.

Captain Dunn had no idea what they were talking about. He was a detective when The Eye went on his rampage. He wasn't privy to some of the information they had access to at the time because he wasn't in the loop.

"Does he know what?" quizzed Captain Dunn.

"It doesn't concern you, Captain," silenced the Mayor.

"We don't believe he knows," offered Steward, "but we're keeping a detail on site for your security."

"He just evaded the entire police force," stated Harper. "If he wants to get to me, he will."

"He won't get to you," said the Mayor. "You can share my detail."

"We do have a green light on his head," offered Captain Dunn. "I assure you this will all be over soon."

"Maybe for you, Captain," reminded Harper. "But I still have to bury my daughter."

Steve and Ramon responded to a 9-1-1 call that came from Harold Reynolds' house phone. The call registered but there was no one on the other end of the phone. Protocol is to send the nearest black-and-white but considering what had happened at the Harper mansion the call went immediately to Detectives Pelletti and Aguilar. They both agreed that Professor Harold Reynolds seemed a little off and was hesitant to speak with them. They were going to give him a little time and then interview him again but plans changed. After they discovered Tate was the murderer, questioning him simply wasn't a priority anymore.

The officer who was assigned to watch the Harper's residence met them.

"Lights are off," briefed the officer. "I checked the perimeter and windows. No activity."

"How 'bout the door, bro?" asked Ramon as the three of them walked up the front porch. "You ring the doorbell?"

"Well, no, I thought I'd wait on you guys," he responded.

"Smart choice," said Steve as he pulled out his Glock and burst opened the front door with one swift kick.

"Hello?" yelled Ramon as he flicked on the light to the chandelier that hung in the foyer. "Anyone in here and shit?"

The men traversed the foyer and noticed Harold Reynolds tied to a chair with a gag in his mouth. They hurried over to him and removed the gag.

"What happened, bro?" questioned Ramon.

Tate noticed a piece of paper on the end table with a DVD sitting on top. He took a closer look and saw *"Pelletti"* written across the paper. He picked up the DVD and read the note.

"I need my medication," complained Reynolds. "I can't breathe."

"Relax Mr. Reynolds," assured Ramon as he finished untying him. "Whatcha' got, bro?" he asked Steve.

The letter quickly explained the situation with Harold Reynolds, his fetish for peeping, the HD camera in the attic, the other DVDs, and most importantly — the DVD that contained an image of the killer in Grace's bathroom. The last part of the letter also caught Steve's attention:

"Check out a dark maroon sedan that Reynolds noticed. Have the image on the DVD enhanced through your techs. The killer is on camera." But it was the last line that guaranteed another confrontation with Tate, *"I'll be in touch ..."*

"What is it, bro?" Ramon asked again.

"Looks like we have a peeping Tom," announced Steve as he handed Ramon the paper. "And we're Chris Hanson from *Dateline* NBC."

"Is that a fact?" chuckled Ramon who read the note.

"He said he wouldn't say anything if I told you about the maroon sedan," whined Reynolds.

"Holloway?" mouthed Ramon not wanting Reynolds to hear him.

Steve nodded his head to confirm that it was indeed Holloway.

"Get a team in here and bag everything," Steve requested to the officer.

The officer headed outside to call it in. Ramon unclipped the handcuffs from his belt and dangled them in front of Reynolds' face. Steve grimaced and pulled up his pant leg to see the source of his pain. He noticed a long skinny bruise across his shin, which initiated the most bizarre epiphany.

The bruise on his shin appeared identical to the mysterious bruise on Grace Harper's shin.

"Get up," ordered Ramon who noticed a large sticky-note stuck to Reynolds' back. "What's this?"

Ramon pulled the sticky-note off his back and started cracking up.

"Check this out and shit, bro," cracked up Ramon.

He held it up for Steve to read, *"Kick me — I'm a pervert."*

Steve couldn't help but laugh at Tate's sense of humor. He remembered him as someone who could make you laugh. This entire situation kept getting more and more strange. Why would Tate help them? Why kill after all these years? Why tell them to enhance the image if he's on the tape? Those were some of the questions that bounced around in his skull. Questions he didn't feel comfortable sharing with Ramon. The cloud of doubt had re-emerged in his head, and he tried to squash the one question he didn't want to deal with at this point: What if Tate was set up? "No, impossible," he thought but didn't say aloud.

"Does any of this shit make sense to you, bro?" asked Ramon as the other officers entered the house to bag the evidence.

"No," agreed Steve. "But I want to show you something. Grab the black light from the trunk."

VENGEANCE IS NOW

Tate and Rita sat at a large computer table with three separate monitors and the latest state-of-the-art computer technology. She had the police department's secure website pulled up on one of the monitors and a police scanner running in the background. Rita could accomplish many things, but one of her best assets was the ability to hack high-security firewalls and retrieve classified personal information.

They watched the HD footage of the murder on the large flat-screen monitor in the center of the console. They clearly saw Grace Harper going back and forth from the bathroom to her closet. On her last trip to the bathroom her body suddenly disappeared. They played it back in slow motion and could see the shadow of someone as he crawled on top of her.

"Holy shit," said Rita.

"Can we get in closer?" asked Tate.

"It's grainy but let's see …," she offered.

The image of the shadow on top of Grace crawled along the ground and then disappeared out of frame. The green night vision made it difficult to make out anything but shadow figures.

"You have a silhouette as the killer, sugar," said Rita.

"That's the best we can do?" asked Tate.

"The quality is what it is, n'all," stated Rita.

"This keeps getting better and better," complained Tate. "I get a piece of evidence that could exonerate me, and you can't see shit."

"I'll send it to a guy I know," offered Rita. "See if he can minimize the night vision n'all."

Steve and Ramon entered Grace Harper's bedroom with the aide of the officer assigned to protect the integrity of the crime scene. Steve had sent the DVD off to the lab for their technicians to enhance, but he wanted to follow up a hunch and confirm a fact that Tate had revealed to him during their short meeting at NuNu's.

Steve explained to Ramon about the bruise he had on his leg and how it looked identical to the mysterious bruise on Grace's shins. He told Ramon that he bumped it on the wooden bed railing in the guestroom at the Inn at the Park. He had pulled up the autopsy report on the laptop in their car and confirmed the measurements of the bruise in relation to the placing on Grace's shins.

"So she had the bruising here," stated Steve as he pointed to his own shin.

"And she had the bruising on the back of her ankles and shit," confirmed Ramon.

Steve stood close to the bed and re-enacted what could have happened in his head.

"She had a slight skull fracture from her head hitting the ground flush," continued Steve. "So her legs had to be swept out from under her."

"So the bruises on the back of her ankle ...," added Ramon.

"Could have been caused by grabbing and pulling," informed Steve.

He demonstrated his legs being pulled and his shins hitting the base of the wooden bed frame.

"He's under the bed, bro," stated Ramon.

"Exactly," confirmed Steve. "Hand me the black light."

Steve crawled under the bed and Ramon handed him the light. He turned it on and scanned underneath the bed. There it was as plain as day.

"Fuck me," whispered Steve.

A neon stamp of an eyeball missing the eyelids illuminated from the inside of the bed frame. Just like Tate reminded him when they were at NuNu's — The Eye always left a neon stamp of an eyeball at a crime scene. This triggered a reminder that sent shivers down Steve's spine — that information was only brought to the department's attention when Dr. Goel, the department psychiatrist, came to that conclusion four years after the case was closed.

Apparently, she did an independent profile of The Eye for a book she was going to write — and that information was never made public. It was also three years after Tate's forced resignation. Tate had no access to that inside information because he was no longer on the force. Steve only knew about Dr. Goel's conclusion because he overheard Chief Steward inform the Mayor via speakerphone. He had a meeting with the Chief about another case and entered the enormous office without Steward's knowledge. He didn't want to interrupt their phone conversation so he backed out of the doorway and re-entered after the phone call ended. He didn't think anything of it at the time because the case had been closed for a few years.

Steve showed Ramon the neon stamp and shared with him the conversation at NuNu's he had with Tate regarding the stamp. He also explained the timeline and the fact the information wasn't made public.

"Does the Chief know you heard them and shit?" asked Ramon.

"No, it was a few years ago," answered Steve.

"We're going to need this bed taken apart and the wood frame brought to the lab," Steve requested to the attending officer.

"You got it," he answered.

"So, bro, now you think Holloway's the original Eye?" asked a confused Ramon.

"I don't know, man," confessed Steve. "I have no clue."

"How else would he know that shit, bro?" quizzed Ramon. "He wasn't even on the force anymore and shit."

Steve felt the intense demand to know the answer to that question. How *did* he know? He would ask when and if Tate contacted him again.

Rita ran every model type and year of maroon sedans registered in the San Diego area. It was a remote long shot but maybe a familiar name would pop up in the search through the DMV database. They had over 2,000 names to peruse and that's assuming the individual didn't have his or her car painted maroon after they bought it from someone else. Exactly what Tate thought — a remote long shot.

She also logged into the Department of Transportation's system and checked any surrounding street cameras to see if they picked up a maroon sedan leaving the area. She had the street camera footage rolling through one of the monitors, but so far they hadn't spotted the vehicle.

"And you're taking care of the Nicole situation?" asked Tate who couldn't get her off his mind.

"Consider it done, sugar," assured Rita. "Everything will be okay."

"Shit, I'm going crazy sittin' here," complained Tate. "It's time to reach out. Without a clear image of the killer's face, I have nothing else to go on."

"Think, sugar," assured Rita. "What was the profile you put together?"

"Bad childhood, poor, cruel to animals," remembered Tate. "Raised by a single mother and possibly sisters."

"Why?" asked Rita.

"Most of his earlier victims were female and wealthy," stated Tate. "He strayed from his pattern when he went on his killing spree at the end. He got sloppy."

"And you didn't think Marvin Polski fit the profile?"

Rita was inquisitive because Tate never really shared the entire story and background of The Eye with her. She only heard precinct gossip. They didn't become close until after he left the force and decided to become a private investigator. She had heard rumors of his mental collapse, but she always felt it was warranted because of the death of his partner, Jack. She knew he had carried the burden of Jack's death with him since it happened. She couldn't blame him if he felt strongly about finding what he felt to be the truth.

"No one knows for sure," said Tate. "He was a transient with no family. There was no record of his existence before the age of 18, and no one, to this day, could conclusively confirm his identity. They let it go because he was dead."

"And that was good enough n'all?" she asked sarcastically.

"The evidence was overwhelming," added Tate. "He was at the cabin with the box-cutters. He had the mementos he swiped from the victims and the crime scenes. He shot Jack and I shot him. Case closed."

"And you threw away your career searching for another killer," reminded Rita.

"It never felt right," he said. "The closer I got to the truth in my mind, the harder they pushed me away."

"Well, sugar, who pushed the hardest?" questioned Rita.

Tate absorbed Rita's question and then snapped into action, "I'm going to need a disposable. I have a call to make."

Rita handed him a disposable cell phone.

"It's time to push back," warned Tate.

The gorgeous sunrise turned the morning clouds pink and puffy white as the rays reflected and shimmered off the calm marina water. Those were one of the picturesque moments that made Steve appreciate the city he lived in. It also made him wonder how people could do such horrific things in such a beautiful setting. He figured bad people did bad things in any location regardless of their surroundings. Bad people enjoyed ruining people's lives and leaving families to mourn loved ones. He couldn't and wouldn't accept that fact no matter how long he continued on the job.

A team of crime-scene investigators and uniformed police officers scoured Tate's boat for any forms of evidence that might be used to confirm the Harper murder or shed some light on whether or not he could be The Eye. He watched the other majestic sailboats as they danced across the smooth water and headed out to sea. What a dire contrast to what was taking place on Tate's boat.

"Looks like blood on these pants," announced a CSI from the boat. He held up a pair of black slacks. "The pant leg is ripped."

"Let's get those to the lab," said Steve as he finished off his second large coffee. "Run the blood against the victim's."

"You think it'll match, bro?" questioned Ramon.

"In this case?" said an exasperated Steve. "Who fuckin' knows? The more evidence we get the less it makes sense."

"Looks like we got a girlfriend," said a uniformed officer as he held up a recent photo of Tate and Nicole. They were on the beach holding their surfboards.

"We need a name, please," Steve called out to the officer. "Maybe he reached out to her."

Ramon glanced at his notepad and then stared off into space. Steve had seen that look before, and he knew his partner was attempting to make sense of theories in his head about Tate and the murder.

"Why would he meet you and shit?" quizzed Ramon. "Think about it, if he's the fuckin' killer — why show up at NuNu's, bro? It just doesn't shake with me and shit."

Steve was surprised it took Ramon this long to start asking him tougher questions about Tate. He knew Ramon was too smart of a guy to ignore the fact that some of the evidence was extremely contradictive.

"Maybe he wanted to pick my brain. Find out what I knew," offered Steve. "But he didn't scare until I mentioned getting the surveillance image from Briarwood. He left his Jeep. He left the files. He could have killed me on the spot — but he ran."

As the partners pondered their theories with one another, a call came in on Steve's cell phone. It was from an "unknown caller".

Nicole stepped out of the shower and checked her cell phone. She was surprised to see so many missed phone calls from friends and family members. Although, nothing from Tate yet. She had a text from her Dad who lived in Arizona, *"Did you see the news? I'm coming to get you."* Another text from her best friend, *"OMG, are you okay? Call me girl!"*

Nicole assumed that there was an earthquake or some kind of disaster that happened overnight that she was unaware of. She just worked a double-shift the night before and her sleep pattern was all screwed up. She started to panic a little bit as she grabbed the remote and flicked on the TV. She was just about to call her Dad when an image on her television sent a shockwave through her body. Her mouth dropped open and tears welled in her eyes. She froze. She couldn't believe what she was staring at. The image was Tate Holloway and the text underneath his photo read: *"Fugitive: Considered Extremely Dangerous."*

The news reporter, Megan Hunt, continued with her account of the events that unfolded the previous night. Tate Holloway was confirmed as the killer of Grace Harper and led police on a citywide chase and standoff that resulted in his escape. That an anonymous source close to the investigation revealed that Holloway was deemed mentally incapable of performing his duties and was forced to leave his job as a detective seven years earlier. That the murder of Grace Harper was a vengeance killing and done to get back at the department and the Mayor who was the Chief of Police at the time.

"Allegedly," continued Megan Hunt, "this had something to do with the controversial close ties between the

Mayor and Jonathan Harper. If you see Tate Holloway, please call the authorities. He is considered armed and extremely dangerous ... "

Nicole dropped the remote from shear panic. Before she could get her bearings together and focus, a gloved hand covered her mouth, and she was pulled to the floor.

Steve knew to activate the tracer software on his cell phone whenever he suspected the caller might be Tate Holloway. The software wasn't department issued and he was conducting the trace on his own — no department knowledge. He would have to keep him on the phone long enough for a reverse trace. Even if Tate used a disposable cell phone they'd still be able to pinpoint and locate a small area based on the nearest cell tower.

"This is Pelletti," answered Steve.

"You like my work on Reynolds?" joked Tate.

"The 'kick-me' sticky note was classic," offered Steve.

"People like him never think they'd get arrested," added Tate. "They never do."

"What about people like you?" asked Steve.

"I told you," stated Tate. "I was set up."

"Set up?" questioned Steve. "Then explain to me how you happened to be at the Briarwood house, on camera, where the murder weapon was found?"

"It's complicated," answered Tate.

"Un-complicate it," ordered Steve.

"The weapon was planted," explained Tate. "I was meeting ... someone at that house."

"Who?" asked Steve.

"A date," offered Tate.

"I need a name to co-oberate," stated Steve.

"I don't have one," confessed Tate. "If I did, I would tell you."

"So your alibi is a woman who asked you to meet her there who doesn't exist?" stated Steve with a chuckle. "That's airtight, man."

"Told you it was complicated," offered Tate who knew it sounded ridiculous. He couldn't tell him he was meeting a new client to fuck for cash.

"You have a nice boat," complimented Steve. "Was this your Grandpa's?"

There was a moment of silence on the other end of the phone that baffled Steve. Did he hit a nerve with Tate?

"You do what you need to do, Steve," said Tate. "But please show a little respect for his boat."

"I have a cop with a broken knee cap and one you immobilized after taking his radio," explained Steve. "Forgive me if my sympathy for your boat isn't at the top of my list."

"I didn't have a choice with the cop in the alley, and I feel bad about that," confessed Tate. "The beat cop was a moron taking a smoke break during a manhunt. It was like taking candy away from a baby."

"We found the missing files in your car," stated Steve.

"Look closer, Detective," advised Tate. "You found *copies* of the files. I left the originals in the evidence warehouse."

Steve was quiet as he digested the information about the files.

"Why'd you run?" asked Steve. "You know as well as anyone that innocent people don't run."

"I told you," emphasized Tate, "I was set up. Someone is looking to frame me."

"Why?" he quizzed.

"I'm not sure, but I'm getting close," revealed Tate.

"How'd you know about the neon stamp?" asked Steve. "That was never made public."

"I have my sources in the department," informed Tate. "The questions are — who discovered it and why was someone working a closed case? I hear that's detrimental to a career."

Steve wasn't sure if he should reveal that he heard about the stamp while stepping unannounced into Steward's office and that the voice on the other end of the conference call was Mayor Villanueva. He was also surprised at how much sense Tate made with his assessment of the situation.

"I don't know," said Steve. "Why don't you tell me."

"Those cell phone tracers sure do take a long time to work," stated Tate. "You forget I was a cop all those years?"

"Come in and we can talk about it," offered Steve.

Click. Tate was gone. No trace.

Captain Dunn and Chief Steward strolled up the hallway toward Jonathan Harper's suite at the Torrey Pines Lodge. It had been five days since Grace's murder, and they had just arrived with their morning coffee and wanted to touch base with Harper and the Mayor. Captain Dunn held Steward back. He had been agitated all night and there were a few things he wanted to get off his chest.

"I get the feeling I'm not being kept in the loop, Phil," complained Dunn. "I feel like there's something I don't know."

"Listen, Martin," said Steward, "if this all goes bad the finger of blame is going to be pointed at me. I'm the Chief of Police, damn it. My head will be served on a platter."

"And what's going to happen to me?" he asked incredulously. "I don't have your title but at the end of the fuckin' day, my career is over too. You were in my shoes eight years ago."

"This is very sensitive," confessed Steward.

"I heard Harper ask, 'If he knew?'" said Dunn. "Was he talking about Holloway?"

"Yes," answered Steward quietly.

"Tell me what he might know," demanded Dunn trying to keep his voice down. "I might be able to help."

"The Mayor and Jonathan just — ," said Steward hesitantly.

" — it's my ass, too," interrupted Dunn.

"A couple of years after the thing with Polski at the cabin," informed Steward, "a construction crew was remodeling and found a diary hidden in one of the walls. They turned it over to the police. It was written by The Eye."

"What was in it?" quizzed Dunn.

"Crazy rants and mumbo-jumbo crap," revealed Steward. "We made the decision to keep it quiet. There was no need to get people asking questions again."

"Where is it now?" asked Dunn. "Why aren't we utilizing it to help us?"

"There hadn't been any murders in three or four years," explained Steward. "There was no need to log it into evidence. We got the sonov'a bitch."

"Did you destroy it?" quizzed Dunn.

"Harper gave it to Dr. Goel after she retired," said Steward. "She was going to write a book. Would have made the Mayor look like a hero."

"Did she ever write her book?" asked Dunn.

"Never did," answered Steward. "She was told to get rid of the diary."

"We need to do whatever it takes to stop that information from getting out," agreed Dunn.

Curt Munson backed his pickup truck to the end of the loading dock at the medical and pharmaceutical warehouse. A dockworker used a pallet jack to deliver a box to the truck's tailgate.

"That's all I'm supposed to do, man," said the dockworker. "My union don't let me lift nothing."

"That's quite all right," offered Munson. "I've got it."

He bent down and lifted the enormous box onto his tailgate and slid it inside the bed of the truck.

"Shit, dude," commented the dockworker. "You work out?"

"Yes, yes I do," answered Munson.

Munson covered the box with a heavy quilt. He pulled the blanket over the side of the box, which revealed the name of the contents in bold blue letters: "Embalming Fluid".

Chief Steward, the Mayor, and Captain Dunn finished their coffees as they watched Jonathan Harper finish buttoning up his shirt. They could see that these few days had been difficult on Harper. Who could blame him?

"We want to go back to the house," stated Harper. "My wife wants to be at home when we make the funeral arrangements."

"I'm not sure that's the best idea, Jonathan," said Mayor Villanueva. "The press will be all over you. Not to mention Holloway's still out there."

"It's more of a safety issue at this point," offered Steward.

"He's capable of anything," added Dunn.

"Where is he? Where are we at with everything?" quizzed Harper.

Chief Seward filled him in on everything, from Reynolds to the bloody pants to the discovery of Nicole, Tate's girlfriend. He also believed he had an accomplice named Rita who used to work on the job but now ran Holloway's P.I. firm. They were still trying to locate her. He also informed him that Steve and Ramon were on their way to Nicole's house to check on her safety and for an interview. He assured Harper that the evidence was there to convict — they just needed to find him.

"Why would he hand us Reynolds?" asked an agitated Harper. "Who goes on the run but makes sure he collars a pervert?"

"He was obviously trying to destroy the DVD of him ... in your daughter's bedroom," explained Dunn cautiously.

He didn't want to use the phrase, "murdering your daughter," out of respect for the Harper family.

"So he leaves a note with the DVD so we'd destroy it for him?" asked Harper sarcastically.

"He knew the quality wasn't sufficient enough to ID him," intervened Chief Steward. "Helping us makes him look ... innocent."

"I need to get out of here for a while," confessed Harper. "I feel like a prisoner in this damn room."

"Give us 24 hours," suggested the Mayor.

"If Holloway's not in the morgue by then," added Steward, "we'll make sure you return home."

"Trust them to do their jobs, Jonathan," asked Steward.

Jonathan flopped down onto the couch and released a deep exhale. He ran his hands through his hair and rubbed his temples in an effort to ease some of the stress and confusion.

"So take down Holloway and everything goes away nice and clean, eh?" asked Harper with a hint of sarcasm. "That's the plan?"

"We feel that's the best solution," advised the Mayor. "We need to handle it and move forward. Bury anything that could come back to haunt us from the past."

"If he's guilty," snapped Harper, "why would anything from the past haunt us? Unless you think someone else could be responsible?"

"Of course not, Jonathan," stated the Mayor.

Harper understood that Villanueva was favored to win a seat in Congress next year. After all, Harper was the mastermind behind the scenes pulling the necessary strings in the last decade to make that happen. The Mayor was handsome, he was smart, and in California where the demographics swayed in his favor — he was Latino. Jackpot. If they stayed the course and stuck to his plan, Mayor Villanueva could make a run for the White House. But the murder of his daughter distorted the pursuit of his ultimate dream — direct access to a President of the United States of America.

Harper knew all along that he and the mayor buried the diary, and they did so when they realized Goel found something unusual. His quest to protect and elevate the mayor was clouded by the fact that his own daughter was murdered now. He wanted justice for her more than a desire to protect the mayor, which was why he had his attorney meet with Rita to make a deal. He started to feel that Tate might not be the killer, and he wanted the truth more than he wanted the mayor to be elected to Congress.

Once the men exited his hotel suite, he reached for his cell phone and made a call. He held the phone up to his ear until someone answered.

"Go ahead and do it," ordered Harper into the phone.

VENGEANCE IS NOW

Steve and Ramon arrived at the Seaside Village condos and parked in front of the gate that led to the luxurious courtyard. They wanted to make sure Tate's girlfriend was safe and also interview her for any information that might help disclose his whereabouts. They knew that Nicole was a registered nurse at Scripps Mercy Medical Center, and according to her supervisor wasn't scheduled to work that day.

They ended up playing it safe and had two black-and-whites parked on the next block. They didn't want to take any chances in case she had been harboring him at the condo — she was his girlfriend after all. Steve had been on the job long enough to be shocked more than a few times at the type of people who would hide suspects. He'd encountered sweet elderly ladies over the years who would stare right into his eyes and tell him they hadn't seen the suspect he was looking for. Meanwhile, their fugitive grandson would be on the other side of the door with a loaded shotgun. Blood is always thicker than water and significant others fit under that description.

Steve and Ramon's car ride from the marina was uncomfortably silent. Steve couldn't believe he had broken his oath and a cardinal sin in regards to a police investigation

— never withhold crucial information from your superior officers. He realized Tate's phone call fit under the "crucial-information" category, but something in his gut told him to ride it out a little bit longer. He needed to wrap his head around a few more facts before he revealed their conversations. Cops were always taught to listen to their guts. He was listening.

He also realized Ramon wasn't pleased with how the investigation had been handled so far — that he felt completely out of the loop because he wasn't involved with the previous case. He didn't share the intense history with The Eye that Steve, Captain Dunn, Chief Steward and Mayor Villanueva shared. Ramon wasn't the type of guy to hold back his opinion. He had a short fuse for bullshit — and his fuse was almost burned down to the dynamite.

"So we're gonna pretend the call never happened and shit?" asked Ramon incredulously. "We're running all over fuckin' town looking for a guy with a target on his back. He's wanted dead — or dead. No *alive* in that equation, bro."

"I know," conceded Steve.

"And you fuckin' talk on the phone like you're planning a barbeque and shit," continued Ramon.

"Listen, Ramon," explained Steve, "if shit goes down I'll make sure you're not touched. It'll be on me."

"Bro, we're partners," expressed Ramon. "I'll follow your lead every day and shit. I'll go over the cliff with you, bro. But I need to know what the fuck's goin' on in your head."

"I'm starting to believe there's more to the story," admitted Steve. "I know Tate. He's trying to put things together."

"That's what I've been thinking, bro," exclaimed Ramon. "With Reynolds and shit, leaving us the DVD."

"We're still chasing," stated Steve. "That's what the brass needs to know. I'm just not going to put a bullet in him if we find him."

"It's like that *Fugitive* movie, bro," expressed Ramon, "where Indiana Jones goes on the run and figures out that crime with the one-legged man and shit."

"Harrison Ford," corrected Steve. "And it was a one-armed man."

"Exactly, bro," agreed Ramon.

As they made their way through the courtyard, they saw Nicole's condo address and headed to her front door. Ramon glanced through the side window and noticed a chair tossed upside down. He looked closer and saw an end table flipped on its side. He pulled his Glock from his holster.

"We have a problem," informed Ramon.

"On three …," said Steve.

They busted through the front door and methodically trained their Glocks in every room and down each hallway. There were signs of a struggle evident throughout the condo.

"Nicole?" hollered Steve.

"Clear," stated Ramon as he came in from the back bedroom. "Her curling iron and shit are all over the sink. She had a full cup of coffee on the bathroom counter."

"Signs of a struggle here," said Steve as he pointed to a broken lamp next to the coffee table.

"Holy shit," said Ramon. "What the fuck is going on, bro?"

Steve reached for his cell phone and made a call to Chief Steward. He had to inform him what was apparent to both the detectives.

"Sir, Nicole Stafford has been abducted," stated Steve.

Rita couldn't wait to get a hold of Tate who'd been holed up in her safe house where he scanned traffic camera footage for the last two hours. She understood he needed to recharge his battery, but also she knew he still wanted to be productive. He could sleep when he was dead. She received a game-changing phone call and needed to share the information with Tate.

It had been a long night for Tate and his mind reeled from the uncertainty of the crazy events that unfolded in the last 48 hours. He racked his brain trying to figure out who wanted him set up and why. His disposable phone rang, and it snapped him out of his investigative trance.

"Honey, I just received a call," informed Rita.

Dr. Goel grabbed her luggage from the carousel and headed for the airport exit. One of the great perks of living in a city with an airport meant reduced travel time and easier accessibility when she had to fly to speak at one of her psychiatry conferences. It was also easier to get to and from the airport when she utilized a car service. That way she didn't have to deal with her own vehicle or worry about long-term parking fees.

She was fully aware of Grace Harper's murder and the manhunt for Tate Holloway. The added police presence at the airport reminded her that he was still on the run. This revelation stirred mixed emotions inside her and brought to mind conversations she had with the Mayor that she desperately wanted to forget. She changed her return flight plans after she received a call from Chief Steward and Captain Dunn. She wanted to be readily available in case they called upon her to assist in the investigation. It was a simple return trip from Sacramento — a 50-minute flight away.

She located her driver who held up a small sign that read, "Goel." He was a tall man with a beard dressed in a black suit. He promptly assisted her with her luggage and led her to a black Lincoln Town Car.

"How was your flight, ma'am?" asked the driver politely.

"Got bumped off one flight and put on another one," answered Dr. Goel. "After that stress, it was fine."

"Well, feel free to smoke 'em if you got'em," offered the driver as he placed her luggage in the trunk. "Doesn't bother me a bit."

"No, thank you," she answered. "Gave it up a few years ago."

"Then you're much stronger than me," joked the driver.

She slid into the backseat, and he closed the door for her.

Steve had just informed Captain Dunn and Chief Steward about Nicole's abduction when the phone call came in from the medical examiner, Sheila Walker. He placed the call on speaker so Ramon could contribute to the conversation.

"The smelling salt on the Harper girl came back a match," informed Sheila. "Same stuff used in all the other murders over the years."

"How would a copycat know about the special military chemical blend?" pondered Steve. "It was never made public."

"Unless he was still alive and shit or passed it on to someone else," added Ramon.

"Anything else?" asked Steve.

"Thanks to a new program from Homeland Security," she said, "we're able to enter the chemical compounds of the smelling salt into the system and it provides a list of manufacturers."

"Okay," said Steve not knowing where she was headed with this information.

"Turns out it was made by a company in San Francisco," stated Sheila. "It was only made for the military up until 1968. They've been closed for almost 35 years."

"You sayin' this guy got a hold of a stash of this shit before 1968, bro?" questioned Ramon.

"He could've bought some at an army surplus store," answered Sheila.

"No," interrupted Steve. "This guy had a stash from back in the day."

"What are you sayin', bro?" asked Ramon.

"Tate Holloway is the original Eye," stated Steve, "or he's completely innocent."

"Tate couldn't be the copycat killer?" questioned Sheila.

"There is no copycat killer, bro," stated Ramon as he caught on to Steve's theory.

"I'm lost," confessed Sheila.

"Marvin Polski wasn't The Eye," offered Steve. "The Eye is back."

"We just don't know if it's Tate," said Ramon.

"We don't know if it's Tate," agreed Steve.

It was late afternoon when Megan Hunt conducted her live report from the steps outside the police precinct. She had been the face and voice of the manhunt and investigation from the beginning, and her national credibility rose from the story being picked up by CNN, MSNBC, Fox News and all the other cable outlets.

"The manhunt continues for Tate Holloway with a series of new twists and turns to the story," reported Megan. "His girlfriend, Nicole Stafford, a nurse from Scripps Mercy, is now missing. Was she a victim or an accomplice? To add to the strange story, we've had two accusations from women — who wish to remain anonymous — who accuse Holloway of being a high-priced gigolo. A murderer and male prostitute? Mayor Villanueva made this statement at a fund raising luncheon for his upcoming Senate election ..."

Mayor Villanueva stood at a podium in a banquet hall at the Hyatt on the Marina.

"We have full confidence that Tate Holloway will be brought to justice for the murder of Grace Harper," announced The Mayor. "Our team has been diligently investigating and following all possible leads to bring an end to this unfortunate scenario."

"Since the murder of the daughter of the Mayor's largest political contributor, his lead in the polls has increased to nine percent over the Republican incumbent," stated Megan.

Dr. Goel watched the buildings and scenery glide by as her Town Car sped down the Harbor Freeway. Being back in San Diego triggered some overwhelming emotions regarding The Eye on the trip home. She decided to listen to her gut and changed her itinerary on the spot.

"I've decided to change it up a bit," she said to the driver. "I need to go downtown."

"Sure, no problem, ma'am," said the driver.

They drove in silence for the next few minutes as the doctor pondered the situation. A lot had happened in the last eight years. Chief Villanueva was elected to Mayor, Captain Steward moved up to the Chief of Police, and Detective Dunn became a Captain. The only individual on the short end of the stick, other than Jack, was Tate Holloway. The Town Car continued down the highway as Dr. Goel watched her exit blow by the window.

"Excuse me," she said to the driver. "We should've taken that last exit."

"I need to know about the diary," emphasized the driver.

Dr. Goel's breath escaped her. Her pulse escalated and her arms tingled from shock. Sweat beads accumulated above her upper lip.

"Excuse me?" asked a breathless Goel.

"The diary," said the driver. "I need to know what you discovered."

It wasn't until she looked at his face through the reflection in the rear-view mirror that her conscious alerted her that the driver sported a fake beard. She didn't pay much attention when he helped her to the car, but now she recognized his eyes.

"Tate Holloway …," whispered a stunned Dr. Goel. "Where are you taking me?"

Dr. Goel tried to open the door but her handle was disabled. She reached into her purse for her cell phone.

"Don't bother," stated Tate. "The locks are rigged, and there's a signal scrambler implanted in the windows."

"Dunn and Steward are expecting me," said a frightened Goel who realized the tint on the windows was too dark for her to motion other drivers for help.

"What did you find out?" interrogated Tate. "Who is setting me up?"

"I … I don't know what you mean," pleaded Dr. Goel. "I didn't find anything …"

"You're in a lose-lose situation, Doctor," stated Tate. "Everyone thinks I'm crazy and a murderer. If you don't tell me what I need to know I will have no other choice but to make you."

Dr. Goel began to sob in the backseat. Tate pushed the speedometer over 90 mph and quickly took an exit off the freeway.

"Why didn't you write the book?" demanded Tate. "Tell me!"

"It just never came together," she explained.

"The serial killer of the decade?" continued Tate. "You had a front-row seat on the action. The book would have made you famous."

"No," said Goel.

"Probably sell the movie rights, get a big payday," he continued. "Consult on a TV cop show."

"That's not true!" she exclaimed.

"I'll tell you why you didn't write it," lectured Tate. "Because you found something in that diary. Something that convinced you that Marvin Polski wasn't The Eye."

"Stop, please," she pleaded.

"I always said the profile was off, *way* off," concluded Tate. "But nobody listened to me. Not even you, Doctor."

"There were things I didn't know at the time," scrambled Goel.

"You value your reputation too much to write a book about catchin' a killer you knew was still out there," chastised Tate. "I know that about you. You're thorough. You take your job seriously. You had me labeled as a mental case!"

"I did what needed to be done under the circumstances," pleaded Dr. Goel.

"The circumstances have changed dramatically, Doc," stated Tate. "You can make things right. Tell me what I need to know!"

"It's not that simple," she whimpered.

"Where's the diary?" demanded Tate. "They're going to hang me for this!"

"It's in my safe," confessed Dr. Goel.

"Honey, I got a phone call," informed Rita.

"From who?" asked Tate hesitantly as the street camera footage continued to roll in the background.

"I can't say, sugar," pleaded Rita. "You'll have to trust me."

"I'm listening," responded Tate who was used to these kinds of requests from Rita.

"There was a diary," stated Rita. "It was found at the cabin a year later n'all. It was written by The Eye."

Tate sat in stunned silence — things started to come together in his head.

"Where is it?" he asked.

"Steward and the Mayor knew about it n'all," continued Rita. "The Mayor gave it to Dr. Anita Goel, sugar."

"She was going to write a book," added Tate.

Tate filled her in on his conversation with Steve regarding the neon stamp and her writing a book about the case.

"Yes," she agreed. "But it never happened."

"Then she retired," stated Tate as he realized the timeline. "Took a position in the mayor's office. She found something, Rita."

"You read my mind," agreed Rita.

"Where is she now?" quizzed Tate.

"Sacramento, sugar," informed Rita. "Got a hit on her credit card, and she shortened her trip. She's flying back in an hour, but I'm going to bump her to a later flight n'all."

"How ironic," he said sarcastically. "I think I should be a gentleman and make sure she's picked up from the airport."

"I'll have the Town Car your way in about 30 minutes, sugar," stated Rita.

Tate used a universal remote control and opened the garage door to Dr. Goel's house. He pulled the Town Car into the garage and closed the door behind them. He pulled his Glock from his waistband and unlocked Dr. Goel's door.

"After you," said Tate politely as he took her cell phone.

The distraught Dr. Goel led him inside her house and into the den. Nude paintings of women adorned three of the four walls — nothing pornographic or offensive. These were high-quality works of art. Her licenses and certificates were displayed on the other wall along with several photos of her and the Mayor at various events.

"Tell me your profile," ordered Tate. "I need to hear it."

"You're not going to want to hear it," said the doctor as she looked down at the floor in shame.

"Try me," urged Tate.

"You were spot on," confessed Goel. "According to his writings, he had a horrible home life. All women in his household. Single mother. Dad died when he was young. He mentions a sister named Libby."

"Marvin Polski was too sloppy," agreed Tate. "He didn't match up."

"You were right," she agreed. "I think he was his apprentice or partner. For how long? I'm not sure."

"How about a birthplace?" asked Tate.

Dr. Goel slid open a panel next to a bookcase, which revealed a wall safe. She spun the combination and opened the safe's door. She pulled out a book that was covered in a plastic sheath. She handed it over to Tate.

"He kept referring to the 'Loin,'" stated Goel hesitantly. "I pinpointed the references to the Tenderloin district in San Francisco."

"Was that as far as you went?" asked Tate.

"I stopped when I realized the truth was still out there," confessed Goel as her voice broke from emotion.

"Who knew?" pressed Tate.

Dr. Goel broke down in tears. Her body shook as she sobbed uncontrollably in front of Tate. A small part of him felt sorry for her. It must have been tough keeping her findings to herself after she discovered Polski wasn't the guy. His pity was short lived when he realized how dramatically his life changed due to Goel's secrets.

"I can't …," whimpered Goel.

"How high does it go?" demanded Tate.

Her silence seemed to manifest from fear of some kind. He sensed that she wanted to tell him, but there were even bigger consequences branded in her mind. She was in a fetal position now as she whimpered on the floor. A far cry from the steel persona she proudly exhibited during her illustrious career.

"I'm sorry," whispered Dr. Goel.

Her allegiance to the cover up indicated to Tate that the corruption went to the top of the food chain. Mayor Villanueva? Chief Steward? Or God forbid, did Jonathan Harper know about the diary and what the writings should have alluded to? That Marvin Polski was not The Eye. Tate had to prove that he wasn't the serial killer either, and he found the most important piece of the puzzle — the diary. But he was going to do more than just prove his innocence. He was going to find The Eye — and he was going to kill him. *Vengeance is now.*

A uniformed officer stood next to the luggage carousel at San Diego International Airport. He kept glancing at the arrivals monitor that hung from the ceiling and reached for his radio attached to his shoulder.

"She's not here," said the officer. "She must've missed her flight."

Chief Steward and Captain Dunn sat in the Mayor's office when the call came in. Mayor Villanueva paced in front of his floor-to-ceiling windows that overlooked the Pacific Ocean.

"What?" exclaimed Steward. "What do you mean she missed her flight?"

"I've been here an hour, sir," said the officer. "No sign of her."

"Stay an hour more," ordered Steward as he ended the phone call. "We'll check the passenger list to see if she jumped on another plane."

"What the hell is going on?" questioned the Mayor. "Holloway's girlfriend and now Goel?"

"I'll reach out to my contact at the FAA," said Dunn as he headed for the door.

"We need to find her," stated the Mayor as Dunn exited his office. "This is getting out of hand."

"I assure you — ," started Steward.

"—You haven't assured a God damn thing," interrupted the Mayor. "He's still out there running around causing havoc, and I have an election in seven days."

"Detective Pelletti and his partner are on their way in for a briefing," informed Steward.

Tate drove the Town Car down side streets and back roads as he headed back to Rita's safe house in the canyons. She wasn't that shocked to hear the revelations from Tate's encounter with Dr. Anita Goel, but, they were both shocked at the revelation about Tate being a man-whore. Which client squealed? Was it really another client or another ruse from whoever set him up? Did Nicole hear the news? He understood the horrific ramifications when she finally heard the rumors about his extra-cirricular activities. He was too deep into the investigation to think about that conversation. He would have to save face another day. Today, things were beginning to unfold and Tate was excited to use Rita's contacts and computer skills in their effort to find clues in the diary. He also reminded himself that when this entire fiasco was over, he wanted to find out Rita's background before she worked in dispatch. Now he had to stir the pot. He had his disposable cell phone to his ear as Steve Pelletti answered the phone.

"I just found a huge piece of the puzzle," stated Tate.

Everything is spinning in my mind. I'm so dizzy. The fuckin' cops are idiots. I handed them that son of a bitch on a platter, but these morons can't even contain him when they have a building surrounded. I admit, I underestimated his ability to escape and drag this out any longer. I make very few mistakes, and this was one of them. Who the fuck was helping him? The ringing in my ears won't stop. He took my best friend — and I took his. Now it's time to finish my game. Tate Holloway is a dead motherfucker. My spine aches from fatigue. I haven't slept in days. I miss my sweet Libby. I loved you. Mother was sick. She was really sick. I'm sick.

Dr. Goel made sure her doors were locked and her alarm was set. She wanted to tell Tate the truth, but her involvement ran too deep. A lot of the blame would be dropped on her. The people implicated were too powerful to blow the whistle. She worked her entire life to get into the position she was currently in.

She was retired from the force with a great pension. She had a thriving private practice that allowed her to work her own schedule. She also had speaking engagements at conferences around the world. She was a renowned psychiatrist whose opinion was highly respected and sought after. How would the world react if they knew what she had done — secrets that she kept? And now more lives had been lost.

She had to lay down on the couch to collect her thoughts. She laid her head back and took a deep breath. She knew Steward and Mayor Villanueva would be calling soon to find out where she was. They were nervous and now they had reason to be. Tate Holloway had the diary. She didn't want to be bothered with anything until she figured out what she was going to do. She turned her phone to silent. Would she tell the truth?

She knew the Mayor couldn't overcome the scandal that would ensue if the press found out he buried the diary — that she came to him to share her theory and updated profile based on the new information she uncovered. That she wanted to reopen the investigation, but he told her to forget writing the book and never speak of the diary.

She also realized she was guilty for taking an advisory position with the Mayor's office, and accepting the early retirement perks he bestowed on her when she agreed to conceal her findings. Would she allow things with Tate to unfold? Would she listen to her conscience? How could she allow Tate to go down for this when she already ruined his career?

Steve sat next to Ramon as they cruised back to the Mayor's office to present an update on the case. His cell phone rang, and he noticed another call from an "unknown number". He answered his cell phone and placed it on speaker so Ramon could hear their conversation.

"This is Pelletti," answered Steve.

"I just found a huge piece of the puzzle," stated Tate.

"Is Nicole a piece of that puzzle?" questioned Steve. "Or did you know she was missing?"

"I know she wasn't safe out in the wind," explained Tate. "She could've been a target by whoever framed me."

"So she's safe, bro?" asked Ramon.

They took his guarded silence as confirmation that she was safe. Tate understood that his relationship with Nicole wasn't salvageable, but he couldn't stand the thought of her being in possible danger. Rita used her contacts and established a way to get her out of town and to the safety of Nicole's dad's house. They extrapolated her from her house and convinced her dad that their abduction and delivery of his daughter was in connection with the investigation. It was to keep her safe from Tate.

"I know about the diary," stated Tate.

"What diary?" asked Steve with a confused expression on his face.

"A diary was found at the cabin a couple years or so later," informed Tate. "It was written by The Eye."

"Where'd you get this?" asked Steve.

"Just listen," ordered Tate. "It was given to Dr. Goel to write a book, but she declined because the new profile she put together completely exonerated Polski as The Eye. She buried the results and was told to destroy the diary."

"By who?" questioned a stunned Steve.

"She wouldn't tell me, but she was scared, man," confessed Tate.

"Wait, what?" he asked. "When did you see her?"

"I just left her house with the diary," admitted Tate.

Steve didn't know how to respond — this was jarring and unexpected news. If Polski wasn't The Eye and Tate was framed — who the hell was the true Eye? Was Tate truly at Briarwood Lane because he was hooking? Could Jack's killing have been averted? Did Grace Harper have to die?

"This is off topic, bro," offered Ramon, "but how does a guy go about being a gigolo and shit?"

"Ramon," scolded Steve. "Really?"

"Sorry bro," apologized Ramon. "But that would be some shit."

"Did you get anything else from her notes? asked Steve.

"She thinks he grew up in San Francisco," stated Tate. "The Tenderloin district."

This information rocked both Steve and Ramon. They informed Tate about the smelling salt being manufactured in San Francisco. The advancements in crime technology enabled them to enter the chemical compounds into a computer program, and it revealed the background of the company, Oxford Manufacturing, and that Oxford shut down in the late 1960s.

"So our 'perp's' from the 'City by the Bay' and shit," noted Ramon.

"So now what?" asked Steve.

"I want you to inform the brass that I have the diary," ordered Tate. "I want you to see the expressions on their faces."

Steve understood the consequences if he informed Steward and Dunn about his phone calls with Tate — and that he purposely didn't inform his superiors. That his omission of facts would be considered hampering the investigation of one of the biggest manhunts in San Diego history. But if Tate was telling the truth — some situations were bigger than any one individual and that included Steve Pelletti.

Dr. Goel felt a warm breeze on her face when she realized she had dozed off. She still hadn't adjusted her eyes because the lights were off, and it was dark in her office. The time changes always made it get darker much earlier which she always hated — especially living in San Diego. She made a move to get off the couch but was unable to get up. Her chest felt tight. Her breathing was challenged. She squinted and noticed the reflection of two eyes staring down at her and the smell of garlic on his breath. There was someone in her house! Her heart stopped as she attempted to move, but the man who hovered above her had his hand around her throat.

"Where's the diary?" demanded the man. "I need it!"

She tried to remove his hand from her throat, but he wedged his knee against her chest to immobilize her. She couldn't make out his face as she struggled to break free.

"The harder you try to move the tighter my grip, you fuckin' bitch," he warned.

"I don't have it," she whimpered.

"Don't make me tear your fuckin' house apart," he threatened. "This house is too nice for a butch doctor. Did you wanna feel my cock? Bet you haven't felt one of those in a long time."

"Your voice ...," realized Goel.

He lifted her up off the couch by her throat and threw her onto the hardwood floors. Her arm crashed through the glass end table and the chards of glass embedded in her forearm. The blood drained from her wound and smeared on the throw rug. He kicked her in the ribs hard. A deep thud echoed, and a sound of cracked bone filled her office. Then he grabbed her by the hair and smashed her face down on the broken glass. He rubbed her face in it like you would rub the nose of a dog in its own piss. He pulled her head back and revealed the gashes in her face. Blood splattered all over the walls and the desk. Her lower lip was severed and hung by a thin piece of skin. She had a gap in her bottom gums from her teeth being knocked out from the force of the impact.

"Where's the fuckin' diary?" he screamed.

"I don't have it," she said as blood bubbled from her mouth.

He dropped his elbow on the bridge of her nose and shattered her cartilage. She couldn't see from the blood in her eyes.

"I gave it ... to Tate," she mumbled incoherently.

"No!" the man screamed. "No you didn't!"

She grinned as blood dripped from her nose and mouth. Her left eye was disengaged from the socket and stuck to the side of her cheek. Her nose was splayed open across her face — a truly gruesome sight.

"He has it," she breathed.

He screamed from the bottom of his lungs. He was crazed. He was insane with despair and frustration. He pulled out the box-cutter from his jacket pocket and began slicing her face uncontrollably. With each swipe of the blade, a spray of blood painted the furniture and walls like a painter who created a work of art in his studio. He was out of control.

Crimson blood covered his body as he looked down at Dr. Goel to see what he had done. Her facial skin was sliced into pieces and hung from her face. He saw her bones and muscles. Her skull was exposed. One last slash of her throat ended any possibility of a miraculous recovery and frankly, no one would want to survive such a horrific attack.

"Why?" screamed the man.

He pushed himself off her mutilated carcass and stumbled to the bathroom. He flicked on the light and panicked. He was covered in Dr. Goel's blood. He would have to shower and get out before they came and discovered what he had done. Not a masterpiece by any stretch of the imagination, but a killing that had to be done. She knew too much.

He turned on the faucet in the sink and cupped his hands with water. He splashed his face to rinse away the blood and looked at himself in the mirror. The reflection revealed a crazed *Captain Dunn* — The Eye.

VENGEANCE IS NOW

Steve and Ramon entered the Mayor's office with weighted anticipation of sharing their information about the diary and the phone calls with Tate. They immediately recognized that Chief Steward and the Mayor were extremely stressed and uptight. They had barely entered the stately office before they were bombarded with questions.

"Anything new on Nicole Stafford?" questioned Steward.

"Any Holloway sightings?" followed the Mayor.

"Can you believe they're saying he's some sex addict, male escort?" commented Steward.

"Where are we at with everything?" continued the Mayor.

"Where are we at with everything?" continued Steward.

They brought the men up to speed on the conventional investigation, which wasn't anything new. Nicole was missing although Steve and Ramon knew that Tate had her safe somewhere. They couldn't divulge that fact. They also admitted they had no other leads on the location of Tate

Holloway. Their bosses were disgruntled at the lack of progress with the case.

"Where's Jonathan Harper?" asked Steve.

"He's emotionally incapable of remaining involved in the investigation," informed the Mayor.

"Understandably so," agreed Steward.

Steve knew this was the best possible time to end their stalemate with the investigation and reveal what they had recently ascertained.

"I've spoken to Tate Holloway twice," offered Steve as Ramon looked down at the floor.

Chief Steward and Mayor Villanueva paused as they digested what Detective Pelletti had just told them.

"I'm sorry, what did you say?" asked Steward.

"I've had two phone conversations with your suspect," announced Steve. "Tate reached out to me twice."

"Just right now?" asked an exasperated Mayor.

"No, one this morning and one about 45 minutes ago," confessed Steve.

"And you're just bringing this to our attention now?" barked Chief Steward.

"There were things he said," informed Steve. "Things that didn't make sense or add up. I mean, c'mon, he gift wrapped Reynolds who ended up being a lifetime 'perv'. He has an excuse for being at the Briarwood house. He was meeting —"

" — Why didn't we trace the damn call?" interrupted Steward.

"I tried, but he's smarter than that," offered Steve. "He's been around the block a few times."

"Detective Aguilar," snapped Steward, "were you aware of this?"

"Ramon had no knowledge of my communications with Holloway," informed Steve. "In fact, he's the one who made me come forward."

"Is that true, Detective?" asked The Mayor.

"With all due respect, sir," said Ramon, "I think we should be focusing on catching the killer of Grace Harper and sh—stuff."

"I thought we were focused on Tate Holloway," stated Steward.

"What else did he say?" quizzed the Mayor.

Steve and Ramon looked at each other and Ramon nodded his head. Time to check out their facial expressions.

"He said he got a diary from Dr. Goel," informed Steve. "Said it was found at the cabin and was written by The Eye."

The Mayor abruptly stopped pacing. Chief Steward looked like a deer caught in headlights. Their reactions solidified Steve's belief that Tate was innocent, and there was a possible cover-up involved.

"When was this?" demanded the Mayor.

"Right before the last call," said Steve. "Forty-five minutes ago."

"And what was his ridiculous theory?" questioned Steward.

"It wasn't his theory," informed Steve. "I mean, initially it was, but Goel told him the diary confirmed in her mind that Polski was an accomplice and that The Eye was still out there."

"That's preposterous," snapped Steward. "Lies from a sick man."

"That's not all," stated Steve.

"That's all we need to hear," ordered the Mayor.

"There's more and shit," stated Ramon.

The men stared at Steve in anticipation of more information they didn't really want to deal with. This situation was becoming a public relations nightmare.

"Goel said she came to the department with this information and was told to bury it and destroy the diary," explained Steve.

"Ridiculous!" exclaimed the Mayor as his cell phone rang. "Holloway's been playing us from the very beginning! Chief?"

"You knowingly broke your oath and withheld pertinent information in an ongoing police investigation," stated Chief Steward.

"No way, bro," complained Ramon. "Don't do this. That's not — ."

"Let it go Ramon," interrupted Steve. "This isn't your fight."

"As of now, you are suspended effective immediately pending review from the board," continued Steward. "Your union rep will be notified."

Steve handed over his gun and shield to the Chief of Police. It was at that very moment that Steve completely sympathized with Tate Holloway and all he had to endure eight years ago. He now understood what went through Tate's mind when his theories and profile didn't fit what the department wanted to hear. He wished he would have spoken up and defended Tate when his forced resignation went down; but there were ways to make amends. There were ways to make things right. Steve Pelletti was ready to make those sacrifices.

Mayor Villanueva answered his cell phone and turned his back to the actions taking place between the Chief and Detective Pelletti. His heart hadn't stopped racing since he heard the phrase, *"Tate got a diary from Dr. Goel."*

"Do I need to remove you as well Detective Aguilar?" asked Steward more as a statement than a question. "Or are you ready to lead this investigation?"

Ramon looked over at Steve and recognized that stare from his partner. He'd probably get his ass kicked if he declined.

"Yes sir," answered Ramon.

"What?" yelled the Mayor into his phone. "When?"

"Mayor?" asked Steward curious about the content of his phone call.

The Mayor covered the phone and addressed everyone in his office. He almost seemed relieved at the newfound revelation.

"So much for Tate being innocent," stated the Mayor. "You just ruined your career for a desperate man, Detective."

"What is it?" asked Steward urgently. "Did we get him?"

"Captain Dunn's on the phone," informed the Mayor. "Dr. Goel has been found brutally murdered."

VENGEANCE IS NOW

Tate and Rita poured over the diary from cover to cover while they sat in front of her elaborate computer station.

"Who do you think talked?" asked Tate.

"None of my girls, sugar." stated Rita. "I've been over it in my head n'all and the leak had to come from whoever set up the date."

"Think she was an accomplice or a victim?" asked Tate.

"Thinking back," offered Rita, "as scared as she seemed on the phone and all, she might have had a gun pointed at her head."

"Her body won't be found," stated Tate. "She could be my alibi."

"Unless she's involved and we don't know it yet, sugar," claimed Rita.

"I'm just glad your name didn't come up," said Tate.

"I'm just glad I don't have to explain everything to your lady friend, sugar," admitted Rita.

Tate knew that the hole he dug for himself over the Nicole situation just got a hundred feet deeper. He couldn't think about that right now. He had to continue on his quest for the killer and put Nicole in the back of his head — where she would probably punch him if she ever decided to see him again.

They continued with the diary, and what they read horrified them equally. They had been in law enforcement for many years, and they had witnessed and encountered the most heinous people who walked the planet. The Eye belonged on a planet of his own.

They also agreed that they had never dealt with such a disturbed sociopath. There were stories of animal mutilations, kicking a puppy off a balcony and strangling it, the fascination with inflicting pain, and the intense desire to be noticed. The writer definitely expressed his disdain for people with money and anyone who grew up with a "normal family". There was mention of watching his sister being raped. That his mother was a drug addict and alcoholic who suffered from several mental disorders. They read a passage about how he painted a large eye on the inside of his closet with neon grease paint. It was the only way he felt he was being noticed and given attention.

Tate and Rita chronologically accounted for his spiral into absurdity and his descent into being a crazed serial killer — the perfect construction of a madman.

"There's reference to Oxford Manufacturing here," pointed out Rita.

"*I sat on Oxford across from my dump,*" read Tate. "*Enjoying a view of where I belong. Day dreaming of dropping bricks on the people below.*"

Rita pulled up a satellite photo of the Tenderloin district as it stood in the early 1960s. She ran it through a three-dimensional processing program that allowed her to manipulate the image and have a 360-degree view.

"So let's say he was on the roof of the Oxford," offered Tate.

Rita worked the mouse and moved the view to the roof of Oxford Manufacturing. The point of view of the computer monitor was as if you were perched on the roof of the building. The program she ran the image through enhanced the view into high-resolution and high-definition-quality graphics.

"How do you have access to this type of program?" asked Tate.

"Let's keep focused, sugar," commented Rita who obviously avoided the inquiry like a master politician.

"*Across from my dump*," continued Tate. "Okay, his apartment, right?"

"I'm with you n'all," agreed Rita as she entered the coordinates and the view changed to three apartment buildings across the street from Oxford.

"Okay, we have three possible buildings n'all," added Rita. "*Enjoying a view of where I belong?*"

"Wait, move the view down to the last building on the corner," requested Tate.

"What'a ya seeing?" questioned Rita as she maneuvered the image perfectly to Tate's request.

"*Where I belong*," quoted Tate. "Holy shit, look in the background."

In the background as clear as day, Alcatraz could be spotted from the roof of Oxford Manufacturing.

"You can see Alcatraz," he confirmed.

Answers to the riddle were coming together, and Tate could feel his vengeance on the horizon. He felt he was getting close to The Eye, and his quest to seek justice was within reach. The resolution to eight years of turmoil wouldn't bring Jack back, but Tate would be able to look his daughter in the eyes and tell her he never gave up. He was sorry he didn't protect her dad like he promised, but the killer wouldn't be able to take away anybody else's dad.

"He lived in the building on the corner," stated Tate. "So run the names of all the residents who lived there going back to the late 1950s."

"I'll cross check welfare and financial aid recipients," added Rita. "Cross check DMV and employment records n'all."

"Welfare should also have records of the children of recipients," stated Tate. "We need to find anyone named Libby."

"I'm on it, sugar," assured Rita.

"He had to practice his craft when he was younger," mentioned Tate. "Look for any unsolved murders in the area where the victim was missing eyelids."

Tate stared at the apartment building on the computer monitor. He pictured a disturbed young man sitting on the roof with the same exact view. Instead of enjoying the beautiful views of San Francisco; this future serial killer was fixated on Alcatraz and fantasized about killing the people down below.

Rita's police scanner beeped which indicated a widespread alert from dispatch. She pointed a remote control at the scanner and increased the volume.

The dispatcher requested all available units to Dr. Anita Goel's address. They reported a 187 and a 10-55. Someone was murdered inside Dr. Goel's house, and they needed the coroner.

"He was lookin' for the diary," suggested Rita.

"He killed Goel," agreed Tate. "Fuck me."

"Holy shit buttons," sighed Rita.

"Can you get me to San Francisco?" asked Tate. "I need to get in that apartment building. We need a name fast."

The perimeter around Dr. Goel's house mirrored the crime scene at the Harper Mansion. Crime-scene tape, black-and-whites and the coroner's van invaded the front of the property.

Ramon and Chief Steward covered their mouths when they caught a glimpse of the damage done to Dr. Goel's mutilated body. It was apparent to both men that a crazed homicidal maniac performed this handy work. No one in their right minds could even fathom such a horrific crime scene. Blood splattered the nude paintings that adorned her walls. Blood, hair and brain matter were spread across the wood floors. Dr. Goel was completely unrecognizable.

Sheila Walker, the medical examiner, hovered over her body with her loop glasses on her face and her evidence kit opened.

"I don't even know where to begin," admitted Sheila as she desperately attempted to keep her professionalism.

"This is the worst scene I've ever been associated with and shit," confided Ramon.

"Tate is much more disturbed than I imagined," stated Steward.

"How does a guy go from precision and attention to detail to this shit?" questioned Ramon. "This was a sloppy murder by a desperate guy who knows his game is almost up, bro."

"I'm not your bro, Detective," chastised Steward. "You don't have much experience dealing with serial-killer psychosis. So keep your uneducated opinions to yourself. And don't speak to the press."

Chief Steward walked away as he dialed his cell phone. Ramon assumed he was going to inform the Mayor about this unorthodox murder scene.

"Where's Steve?" asked Sheila quietly.

"Suspended and shit," informed Ramon. "He was asking the wrong questions to the wrong people."

"What?" asked an exasperated Sheila.

"There's some shit I can't talk about, bro," explained Ramon covertly. "There's much more going on here."

Megan Hunt stood outside the Goel residence as the police activity was in full swing behind her. She went live for her report as a small crowd of neighbors gathered on the sidewalk and became voyeurs to the activity.

"The Tate Holloway saga has taken another grizzly turn as he continues to evade law enforcement and is the main suspect in the gruesome murder of former police department psychiatrist and consultant to the Mayor, Dr. Anita Goel. Holloway has eluded authorities after the murder of Grace Harper and the alleged kidnapping of girlfriend, Nicole Stafford. Chief of Police Phillip Steward released a statement minutes ago," reported Megan Hunt as she read the statement: *"Tate Holloway is considered extremely dangerous, and the police department is exhausting all avenues to bring him to justice for these horrific murders. This investigation is too crucial to the safety of the citizens of San Diego, and there is no room for error. With that in mind, we regrettably had to remove and suspend the lead detective for conduct unbecoming of a police officer. Tate Holloway is a sick individual who will stop at nothing to avenge his termination from the force seven years ago. That theory is evident from the murder of the psychiatrist who diagnosed his mental illness, Dr. Anita Goel.'"*

Tate knew he didn't have much time before he was getting picked up, but he couldn't get Nicole out of his head. He felt horrible that she had been mixed up in the whole cluster-fuck of a fiasco. Now that his gigolo gig had been outed in the press, he didn't realize how much he cared what she thought about him. The old saying, "You don't know what you got, 'til it's gone," couldn't have been closer to the truth for Tate. He was going to ignore Rita. He already had Nicole's number dialed before he considered the negatives that could result from his call. He didn't care.

"Hello," answered Nicole.

He knew the only shot of her answering his call would be because of the "unknown caller" moniker that would be splashed across her iPhone screen.

"Nicole, it's me," stated Tate hesitantly. "Please don't hang up."

"I don't even know what to say," responded Nicole. It was obvious to Tate that she had been crying. Her voice was shaky.

"Just listen," pleaded Tate. "Hear me out."

"They say you killed that girl," stated Nicole. "They have a picture of you fleeing the scene. That was the night you made love to me on the boat and I stayed over."

She was becoming angrier with every revelation that spilled from her thoughts.

"And you're a fucking male escort? Really?" she exclaimed.

"For not knowing what to say ...," joked Tate as he tried to ease the mood.

"This is funny to you?" yelled Nicole. "I have to tell them I'm on the phone with you. I hope they catch you. You are a sicko!"

"Just listen," urged Tate. "Tell them we're talking, I don't care. I want you to know that the truth will come out."

"They said it could be no one else but you," she continued. "You don't have an alibi. You were there. What is wrong with you? I'm so stupid!"

"I promise you," replied Tate.

"Promise?" she asked incredulously. "Are you fuckin' kidding me? You told me you retired from the force. You were fired for being crazy! Were you ever going to tell me about the other women? Was I just a fucking game to you?"

"Please, just keep an open mind," pleaded Tate. "I'm innocent, and I'm going to prove it."

"You're sick," stated Nicole over her tears. "Don't ever contact me again."

Click. She was gone. Tate felt a new low, but he knew he didn't deserve her. He had lied to her since day one — and now he expected her to get over the fact that he was a wanted murderer and he slept with other women for money. All he could do was hope.

35

Tate hated flying in small planes but considering his face was plastered all over airports, bus terminals and train stations; he didn't have much of a choice. Rita's contact dropped Tate off after they landed at the San Rafael Airport. It was a privately operated airfield that catered to the wealthy business elite who wanted to avoid the logjams and crowds at the traditional airports in San Francisco and Oakland.

Another one of Rita's contacts made sure he had a ride to the Tenderloin district, and the drive took about 30 minutes of travel time. Rita established a cover for Tate with the apartment building owner for him to get inside without breaking and entering. He was in enough trouble in San Diego; he didn't need to get arrested in San Francisco.

"I've crossed-referenced names from the welfare database and the school district records, sugar," informed Rita via cell phone. "I have yet to find a girl named Libby n'all, but I narrowed the single moms with daughters during our timeframe to three possible apartments."

"Could be a nickname," offered Tate through his disposable cell.

He sported a mustache and wore a blue work shirt with a red stitched name patch that read, "Henry." He was posing as an inspector with the United States Department of Housing and Urban Development and needed to conduct health tests in a few apartments in the building.

"How you coming with unsolved murders?" continued Tate.

"There's been a few in our timeframe, sugar," informed Rita. "I'm waiting on autopsy reports n'all."

"Let me guess," added Tate. "Another one of your contacts?"

Tate approached the first apartment as the owner ordered the tenants into the hallway so "Henry" could run chemical safety tests.

"I don't have pay for this?" questioned the owner in his thick Russian accent.

"The State covers the expense," informed Tate.

"This first I heard," the owner explained. "I'm cautious, no?"

"I would advise you to stay in the hallway," explained Tate. "You don't want to be exposed."

The Russian owner complied as Tate entered one of the targeted apartments and headed for the first bedroom. He placed an earpiece in his ear to communicate with Rita and carried a bag with him as he opened one of the closets. It would have been almost 50 years since The Eye would have occupied an apartment in the building, but Tate knew that grease paint was difficult to cover. According to Rita's investigation, there was a renovation to the building in the 1980's. The exposed brick was covered by sheetrock, and the walls were finished.

He pulled out a small crowbar and lifted the sheetrock away from the closet wall, which revealed the original brickwork. He quickly realized that the construction crew didn't bother to paint over the brick, but there was nothing unusual in that apartment. After he checked all three closets he exited out into the hallway.

"It all looks good in there," Tate informed the Russian owner.

"They go back now?" the owner asked.

"I would wait for two hours," suggested Tate. "Unless you want to be exposed."

Tate went upstairs to the second apartment on their list. The same routine played out as the Russian owner made sure that particular apartment was empty. Tate pulled the sheetrock from the closets in the second apartment — and the walls were exactly the same as the first set of closets. Nothing.

Curt Munson maneuvered the dolly perfectly as he positioned a large box into his basement laboratory. He had been waiting on the new equipment for over a month. It was so large he had to remove the railing from the basement stairwell just to get the box down the stairs. His basement resembled a high-tech research laboratory that had just been newly assembled. All of the beakers and instruments looked brand new and computers still lined the back wall in their factory-sealed boxes. He took an orange box-cutter and sliced through the packaging tape. He opened the box and took out a smaller box that was labeled, *"Electric Plaster Cutter Saw,"* and another box labeled, *"Amputation Saw."*

He pulled back a sheet and revealed a brand new gurney and chrome instrument table. He opened the boxes and meticulously placed the amputation saw in an open space between a brand new scalpel and a surgical clamp. He took the plaster cutter saw out of the packaging and plugged it into the wall socket. He held it close to his ear and pressed the power button. The high-pitched whining of the small circular saw blade made him smile ...

Tate entered the third apartment and went through the same routine. His frustration began to increase when Rita interrupted him with a phone call.

"We must be off on the building," complained Tate.

"Hold your britches, sugar," joked an enthusiastic Rita. "There was a double murder in 1973: James and Melanie Ostrowski."

"I'm listening," anticipated Tate.

"Both strangled in their homes, sugar," stated Rita.

"No sexual assault?" asked Tate.

"None whatsoever," confirmed Rita. "The M.E.'s report listed Melanie as missing her damn eyelids."

"Okay, so what's the connection?" prodded Tate.

"Their obituary listed a sister, niece and a nephew as next of kin," exuberated Rita. "The niece's name was Libby. The victim's sister's name was listed as Sarah Lindeman. I ran the name against the tenants going back to 1950 n'all and apartment 312 was listed under a John Lindeman. He died in 1960, but his widow and kids lived there until Sarah's death in 1971."

"I'm on my way to 312," stated Tate.

Chief Steward and Mayor Villanueva sat in a parked car down the street from the circus at Dr. Goel's house. The Mayor took drags off a Marlboro Red to ease the tension in his shoulders and the stress built up in his stomach.

"I have to meet with Harper, and I haven't a clue what to tell him," confessed a nervous Mayor.

"What's in the diary?" asked Steward hesitantly.

"What's your gut on Pelletti?" questioned the Mayor in his attempt to change the subject.

"He won't talk to the press," stated Steward. "He'd lose his pension."

"And Detective Aguilar?" continued the Mayor.

"He'll toe the line," assured Steward. "He's ex-military."

There was a very uncomfortable silence as the Chief tried to pick his words carefully.

"How bad is it?" inquired Steward.

"We need to find Holloway or we're all going down," confided the Mayor.

Tate warned the owner of the building that he needed to get into apartment 312 to check a possible mold situation. It amazed him that people were so gullible if you had an official title and worked for the government. He immediately felt the negative energy that engulfed the entire apartment when he went inside. He noticed the table set with plates and felt a little bad that he interrupted someone's meal. There would be other meals, but he had to make sure there'd be no more murders.

He had no luck in the first closet he checked, but he felt deep in his gut that this might have been the place. This apartment was where The Eye grew up. The next-door neighbor's balcony was probably where he killed the puppy. This place was the lair that spawned his wickedness. Was he born that way or did the environment determine his sadistic fate?

"Sugar?" asked Rita while she stayed in contact through Tate's earpiece. "You might want to hop, skip and a jump a little faster n'all. The owner just called the answering bank I set up for the scam."

"Are you fuckin' serious?" asked Tate.

"He's checking you out, sugar," warned Rita.

He used the small crowbar to wedge out the sheetrock in the second bedroom closet. He knew right away this closet was different. The brick behind the sheetrock was painted almost like a primer. He reached into his bag and pulled out a can of paint thinner and connected a small plastic hose to a spray bottle mixed with other chemicals. He slid the clothes on hangers to one end of the closet so the brick wall would be exposed. He sprayed the chemical cocktail all over the brick wall and waited for the liquid to dissolve the paint.

"Uh, just pinged a 9-1-1 call from the building owner's cell phone," stated Rita urgently. "He's calling the cops, sugar."

"Fuck me," sighed Tate.

"You don't want to find out if that old building has a dumbwaiter n'all," joked Rita as she attempted to keep the stress level down.

"Just about done," said Tate.

The dissolved paint ran down the dilapidated brick wall and dripped onto the floor. There it was — the reason for the primer was revealed. Half of an eyeball painted in a neon grease paint stared back at Tate — a reveal that was a metaphor to the case history. The past was being exposed and soon so would the killer.

"Holy shit," said Tate to himself as he pulled out his camera and took a few pictures. "This is it, Rita baby. This is where he lived."

"Okay, school records have a Jeffery Lindeman at that address until his mother died in '71," informed Rita.

Tate quickly packed up his tools and headed for the fire escape out the window.

"Until how old?" asked Tate as he cruised down the fire-escape ladder.

"Why are you out of breath, sugar?" wondered Rita.

"Don't ask," stated Tate as he dropped onto the sidewalk and walked to the car that waited for him to complete his deception.

"In 1971 he was 16 years old, sugar," informed Rita.

"That makes him what?" quizzed Tate. "Fifty-eight now?"

"Why can't ya manage your checkbook better with those math skills n'all?" teased Rita.

"So his mom and dad are both dead before he's 16," pondered Tate. "He had to live somewhere. Was there anything about foster care in the diary?"

"That could've been mentioned in the damaged pages, sugar," informed Rita.

"Run it," requested Tate.

"Running him through foster care records now," stated Rita as she mastered her elaborate computer system. "On another note, Steve was suspended today. Saw it on the news n'all."

"He asked the wrong questions," admitted Tate.

Tate felt horrible about the news on Steve's suspension. There are times when something bad happens to a friend and people can't think of what to say so they use the ambiguous phrase, "I know what you're going through." Most of the time they do not. This was one of those times that Tate could commiserate. He knew exactly how Steve felt.

"Here we go, sugar," stated Rita. "Lindeman was removed from eight foster homes in an 18-month period n'all. Arrested for petty theft, vandalism, and here's the kicker — animal cruelty."

"Is there a mug shot?" requested Tate.

Rita perused arrest records as she attempted to get any kind of photo of Jeffrey Lindeman.

"Waiting for the search," exclaimed Rita.

"Why don't you run Marvin Polski or any foster siblings that got popped for animal cruelty, too," suggested Tate.

"You're pretty damn smart for a man-whore," complimented Rita.

The computer screen popped out a name that matched Tate's request.

"No Polski but ...," hesitated Rita. "I have a Greg Meyers. They were foster brothers in five of the homes. Animal cruelty charges."

"Pull them up, my Southern dream," joked Tate.

"Got Lindeman!" exclaimed Rita. "And a mug of Meyers!"

Her excitement turned to shock. She recognized the mug shot of Jeffrey Lindeman. Very few things in life left her speechless — and this was one of them. Tate picked up on it.

"What's wrong?" questioned Tate.

"You need to come back, sugar," advised a stunned Rita. "Should be coming through to your phone n'all."

Her computer monitor displayed a photo of Jeffrey Lindeman's mug shot from 1972. He was much younger but there was absolutely no doubt about it. *The Eye was a youthful-looking Captain Martin Dunn.* Greg Meyers' mug shot came up as well. His 1972 photo was also recognizable — *a youthful Marvin Polski.*

His phone beeped alerting him to a text attachment. He looked at the photos and didn't know what to say or how to respond. He was angry at how simple it was to put the pieces of the puzzle together and realized innocent people didn't have to die. In fact, he was fuckin' pissed.

"I'm going to need the Mayor's personal cell number," requested Tate in a very monotone voice.

VENGEANCE IS NOW

Mayor Villanueva sat alone at his desk with a bottle of blue-label Johnny Walker opened in front of him. He poured himself another glass and pondered his dire situation. Did Tate know the truth? How long before everything went public? Did Tate discover the true killer? These were questions that ate at his stomach lining. He needed a plan B or everything he had worked for his entire life would be destroyed.

His personal cell phone rang, and he prayed it wasn't his wife. He didn't think he could conceal the mass depression that had settled in. The number was an "unknown caller".

"Yes?" answered the Mayor.

"Can you feel the noose tightening around your neck?" asked Tate.

"Who is this?" demanded the Mayor.

"Are you feeling a little guilty about Dr. Goel?" continued Tate.

"Tate Holloway," commented the Mayor. "Feeling clever are you?"

"I know everything," informed Tate. "Right down to the killer's identity and everyone's involvement, including yours, Mister Mayor."

"What do you want?" pleaded the Mayor. "How can I make this go away?"

Libby where are you? Why couldn't you be with me? Maybe I should have ended my life long ago. Killed the demon that pulls the strings on my impulses and muted my conscience. Meyers was the only person who understood me. We were going to rid the planet of every human we deemed dispensable. He was my best friend and that motherfucker killed him. He was the only brother I knew. He was my partner in watching life escape the eyes. He was the one who suggested our name changes to get a fresh start in death. He was the one who pushed me into becoming a cop to help cover our tracks of destruction. I release souls to purgatory. Send the ungrateful to the bright yellow light. They say people see dead relatives when they pass; fond memories of loved ones. I hope I get to see all the fucks I've killed over the years. Nothing would be greater than to hear their voices explain the sorrow and remorse of leaving this world without saying goodbye to their loved ones. I'd laugh in their faces. It was time to laugh in Tate's face.

The weather and time of night were identical to the evening eight years ago at the same hideaway cabin owned by The Eye. The wind howled throughout the canyons and the cool night breeze made the wind chimes dance an eerie jingle. The pine needles were dead and dried and covered the ground around the abandoned cabin. It was a beautiful property. The cabin was perfectly secluded enough for anyone interested in buying a place for weekend getaways; but the history of the cabin was a nightmare for any realtor who abided by disclosure laws. Not such an easy sale when the previous owner was thought to be a notorious serial killer.

A maroon sedan approached the property with the headlights off and parked in the dirt driveway. Captain Dunn exited the vehicle. He wore a black sweat suit and black knit cap. His eyes were bloodshot and crazed. He pulled out an ammo clip and snapped it into his Glock .40. He slipped the remaining ammo clips into his jacket pocket. He glanced around the property, and it brought back great memories. He missed Greg Meyers aka Marvin Polski as much as Tate missed Jack Runyan. Now was the time to reunite Tate with Jack.

"Tate Holloway?" yelled Dunn. "I'm gonna fuckin' kill you tonight!"

He pulled out an orange box-cutter, slid the blade into the protective sheath, and giggled to himself.

"You're gonna pay for what you did to Polski!" manically screamed Dunn.

The battle cry echoed throughout the canyon and seemed to bring the temperature down a few degrees.

Tate sat at the old wooden kitchen table in the freezing cabin and waited. He could see his breath. His Glock .40 was placed on the table right next to the diary. He knew his plan would work, and he couldn't wait for the showdown. He had worked alongside Dunn for a few years and never once detected any kind of unusual psychosis. He thought he was a little odd but was always fair with Tate. The rumors of his erectile dysfunction made sense now when Tate considered none of the female victims were sexually assaulted; but to hide the fact he was clinically insane so easily proved one thing to Tate. He couldn't begin to understand the depths of his wicked soul.

Rita wasn't very happy with the ultimate plan, but she realized Tate wouldn't be denied. She knew there was nothing to say to change his mind. He wanted to end it on his terms. His way. For Jack.

Tate heard the rumbling of a car's engine and the crunching of pine needles underneath tires. He smiled. He disengaged the safety on his Glock .40 and made sure his clip was full. Jeffrey Lindeman — The Eye — had finally arrived.

Not much had changed in eight years. The cabin was cold and eerie. The electricity was disconnected to the cabin because the property was vacant. Tate lit candles throughout the cabin to compensate for the darkness. The shadows that danced around the walls from the flicker of the candle flames created the perfect atmosphere for what was about to go down.

"Tate Holloway?" screamed Dunn from outside. "I'm gonna fuckin' kill you tonight! You're gonna pay for what you did to Polski!"

Tate got up from the table and moved to the window by the front door. He peeked out the window and spotted Dunn taking cover behind a tree.

"No, I killed Greg Meyers!" yelled Tate. "Isn't that right, Jeffrey Lindeman?"

"You're a better cop than I gave you credit for!" countered Dunn. "And the only name that matters is what's on your tombstone! Was Jack Runyan's name spelled correctly?"

"This ends tonight!" responded Tate.

Tate aimed his Glock at Dunn and unloaded three rounds in his direction. The gunshots sounded like thunder throughout the canyon. The tree bark exploded above Dunn's head as he ducked for cover. Dunn leaned out and returned fire as two rounds shattered the glass and slivered the remaining plywood that covered the window.

"Why?" yelled Tate. "Why'd you do it?"

"That may be the question in your head," replied Dunn. "You think I'm not normal. But the question in mine is why wouldn't you kill? It seems so natural to me."

Dunn crossed to another tree and fired two more rounds in Tate's direction before he crouched to take cover.

Tate heard the crunched pine needles and knew Dunn was on the move. He scurried from the window to the back of the cabin and covertly exited out the rear door. He yelled in the direction of Dunn and hoped he would respond to reveal his general location.

"How'd you stay dormant for so long?" questioned Tate. "How'd you stop killing?"

"It was so hard!" yelled Dunn. "I was plotting my vengeance against you. You killed the only person who appreciated me! I wanted to make you suffer like I did!"

Dunn fired off a few more rounds in Tate's general direction. More out of fury than actual aim.

"Getting me to Briarwood," announced Tate. "How did you know?"

"I'd been watching you for a while," answered Dunn. "Fucking for money ... you're life wasn't supposed to be so good."

"And the girl who made the phone call?" asked Tate.

"Her eyelids are in my car," he answered with a maniacal laugh. "You won't find the rest of her."

Tate popped off three more rounds in Dunn's general direction.

"And Grace?" hollered Tate who double-checked the ammo clips in his jacket. He only had three more clips. "You waited for the anniversary!"

"She woke me up!" screamed Dunn. "It was an easy way to tie you to the case! Talk about a sweet piece of ass!"

"But you couldn't do anything about it!" yelled Tate as he quickly jetted off the back wrap-around porch and hid behind an old, rusted Ford pickup. "You can't get it up!"

"Fuck you!" screamed Dunn as he unleashed more ammo at Tate.

"But you slaughtered Dr. Goel!" hollered Tate.

"That bitch had my diary!" responded Dunn. "Meyers said he destroyed it. Too many secrets to reveal."

Dunn's voice sounded as if he was close to the dirt walkway that led to the barn. Tate saw a shadow race in that direction. He chased the shadow but led with his Glock. He unloaded more rounds to lay cover so he could reach the tree near the barn entrance. The moon was full, and a blue-hue illuminated the entire property. It was déjà vu for Tate. He could almost hear his cries for Jack bounce around in his head.

Dunn entered the barn and flipped over an old bale of hay and created his own concealment. His breathing was heavy. His adrenaline aided in his strength.

"You couldn't keep your mouth shut!" hollered Dunn. "Had to keep poking around. Even now!"

Dunn emptied his clip in the direction of Tate's voice. He popped out his ammo clip and quickly inserted a fresh one.

"It must have been hard knowing Meyers got all the credit for your work!" goaded Tate.

"No," yelled Dunn, "he was like the brother I never had!"

"But he wasn't as good as you," responded Tate. "He was sloppy. Made you look bad."

"Sometimes he wouldn't listen," responded Dunn. "He had no patience!"

"But he got the credit for being The Eye," reminded Tate. "You knew he wasn't as special as you. He took all the glory for your vision!"

"And look what happened to him!" replied Dunn.

"But you were a lowly detective," added Tate. "Villanueva and Steward benefitted from everything."

"I became Captain," defended Dunn.

"C'mon, Jeffrey," said Tate sarcastically. "No one gives a shit about a Captain. They knew about the diary, and they didn't even keep you in the loop. That had to make you feel insignificant again. Just what your mother and Libby would do to you!"

"Leave Libby out of this!" screamed Dunn. "She was a good girl!"

Tate fired a couple of shots toward the barn, and the bullets pinged and ricocheted off some old farm equipment. He covertly maneuvered next to an old piece of iron that leaned against the side of the barn. He could see through the broken boards that Dunn was behind a bale of hay.

"She followed in your mother's footsteps," baited Tate.

"No!" protested Dunn as he turned in Tate's direction and fired more shots that missed above his shoulder.

"She was a druggie whore just like her mother!" screamed Tate.

"I watched her die before it came to that," confessed Dunn. "I loved her!"

Tate trained his Glock on a shadow that appeared to be Dunn's shoulder. He fired a shot that clipped Dunn and spun him around behind the hay. Dunn grimaced with pain.

Dunn quickly got back to his knees and took cover. The chaos sent small particles of hay and dust floating in the barn. The moonlight made the hay appear like dancing snowflakes. He checked the wound near his bicep. He could feel the warmth of his blood as it trickled inside his sweat jacket.

"Is this where you tell me to give up so we can talk about it?" mocked Dunn.

"No," responded Tate calmly. "This is where I kill you."

Tate ripped off several rounds as he crashed through the aged boards and rolled behind an old tractor. Dunn returned fire but missed. His clip was empty. He urgently reached into his pocket for another one, but his cold hands couldn't keep a grip, and he dropped the ammo. He quickly slid in a spare clip.

Out of nowhere, Tate flew over the hay and tackled Dunn and his gun dislodged from his hand. They rolled to the ground, and Tate swung a right and connected with Dunn's forehead as he ducked. Dunn countered with a left but missed to the right of Tate's face.

"I heard Jack whimpered like a little baby," sneered a crazed Dunn.

Tate had some of Dunn's blood smeared on his chest as they circled one another like prey. Tate was focused and determined.

"Meyers tried to give you up at death's door," snapped Tate. "He was going to rat you out, but he choked on his own blood."

Tate took a swing at Dunn but missed to the left of his head.

"Jack's little daughters cried like little bitches at his funeral," teased Dunn. "And his wife wouldn't even look at you."

Tate attempted a slide kick, but Dunn was able to leap over his leg when it kicked by.

"You want to kill me so badly," giggled Dunn. "Doesn't it feel good? What a rush!"

Tate lunged at Dunn again and caught him with a right to the side of his neck. Not exactly where he aimed, but it landed. Dunn was surprisingly quick and nimble for a man his size and age.

"When you're dead," warned Tate, "I'm gonna make sure the press thinks you were Meyers' sloppy copycat. They're gonna think you were the hack."

"NO!" screamed Dunn.

The thunder of helicopter blades engulfed the canyon with a deafening rumble. Headlights from cars approaching the property lit up the barn like spotlights. Tate was able to see the gunshot wound on Dunn's arm and landed a swift kick right above the injury. Dunn grimaced but came back with a solid punch to Tate's ribs. He wrapped his arms around Tate to throw him down, but Tate headbutted him in the bridge of the nose to get free. Dunn's nose suffered a gash, and the cartilage separated from his face. Tate followed up the head-butt with an elbow to the side of the head, which left Dunn dazed and wobbly.

"You mother fucker!" screamed Tate.

Tate landed a shot to his left cheek, another blow to his mouth, and a hard right that popped Dunn's eardrum. Tate dropped an elbow on the crown of Dunn's forehead that tore open a gash down to his eyebrows. He still wouldn't go down.

Dunn dove at Tate's legs to take him down but was met with a knee to the shoulder. He rolled off, but Tate fell on top of him.

"You ruined me!" yelled Tate as he landed a perfectly placed shot to Dunn's jaw. Then he landed a blow to his right cheek. Then another to his nose. Blood flew everywhere.

Dunn broke free and was up and ready to defend himself. His strength was remarkable. He pulled the box-cutter from his pocket and exposed the blade. Tate was ready for anything. He grabbed an old 2x4 and waved it around the air as he waited for Dunn to make a move.

Ramon drove up in his vehicle with Chief Steward seated next to him. It was a long, uncomfortable drive in silence as he could sense Steward's apprehensiveness to the upcoming situation. They arrived and exited the car as three black-and-whites and a SWAT unit slid to a stop in front of the cabin.

"Gunshots reported by a dude at a cabin down the road and shit," informed Ramon as they exited their vehicle.

"They're in the barn!" announced one of the officers on site.

With their guns drawn, Ramon and Steward hustled to the barn entrance and recognized Tate and Dunn entangled in a fight. Dunn's face was a mess, and it was clear Tate had the upper hand. Dunn circled with a box-cutter in his hand and Tate held up an old 2x4. Steward trained his gun on Tate. The other officers and the SWAT team flanked the barn and trained their weapons. There were now 14 guns pointed at Tate and Dunn.

"That's it Tate!" yelled Steward over the thunder of the helicopter blades. "We got it from here!"

"This is my game to finish," warned a determined Tate. "You guys can referee."

Dunn's face was covered in blood, and he struggled to keep his balance. Ramon continued to cover Dunn with his weapon. He waited on Steward's command.

"The Chief of fuckin' Police ladies and gentleman," laughed Dunn. "Keeping the citizens of San Diego safer from the likes of me. How? By burying his head in the fuckin' sand.

Maybe someone else will write that book about me since Dr. Goel doesn't have a face."

Steward noticed the box-cutter in Dunn's hand. He had made several poor decisions over the past eight years that significantly altered many people's lives — including Tate Holloway's. He finally had a chance to make things as right as he could.

"Stand down," ordered Steward to the other officers and SWAT members.

"Sir?" asked one of the officers who continued his aim.

"Disengage!" ordered Steward as the officers put down their guns.

Ramon disengaged but kept his eyes on Chief Steward. He didn't want him to have an opportunity to do anything he might regret. After Ramon was briefed that Captain Dunn was The Eye, he had been watching his back. In this mess, he didn't know who could be trusted. He knew there was so much more to the story.

"Let's go fucker!" yelled Dunn as blood sprayed from his mouth with every word.

Tate swung the 2x4 and smashed Dunn's forearm with a thud. He swung back around and landed the board into his shoulder, which knocked him down. He went for the final blow to the head, but Dunn swiped the blade across Tate's arm. Dunn swiped again but missed which left him open for Tate's foot to crush the side of his head. He went down, and Tate pounced on him like a panther. He squeezed his neck and kept slamming Dunn's head into the ground.

"You left two daughters without a dad," screamed Tate who was also covered in blood. He continued to pound Dunn. "Jack was a good man!"

Steward and Ramon quickly ascended on Tate before he killed Dunn in cold blood. Tate had a wild look in his eyes.

"That's enough, bro!" yelled Ramon as he grabbed him by the shoulders and pulled him off.

Dunn was lying on the ground with a maniacal smirk on his face. He noticed his gun was next to a spare tractor tire on the ground.

The helicopter slowly hovered above the barn's roof and then landed in the open field next to the barn. The noise added to the chaotic scene that unfolded inside the barn.

"As much as you deserve to," admitted Steward over the chopper blades, "I can't let you kill him in front of everybody."

"He's done, bro," assured Ramon. "It's over. You got him and shit."

"Yeah," agreed an exhausted Tate. "It's finally over."

"Cuff that piece of shit, bros," ordered Ramon to the officers.

The cops moved in to subdue Captain Dunn, but he strategically rolled over and grabbed the gun. He pointed it right under his chin and smiled.

"Gun!" yelled one of the officers.

Everybody in the barn had their guns trained on Dunn who had his Glock ready to blow his own head off. No one knew what to do next.

"Go ahead and pull the trigger, Lindeman!" yelled Tate.

Steve Pelletti and Mayor Villanueva hopped off the helicopter and jogged all the way to the barn. Steve couldn't wait to see the look on Steward's face when they entered. Tate's plan had worked to perfection.

"What do we do?" asked a nervous officer.

"Do we shoot him?" yelled another officer.

"Stay engaged!" ordered Steward.

Pelletti kept the Mayor at the entrance of the barn to stay out of the crossfire. He didn't really care if the Mayor got shot or not, but he wanted to honor Tate's wishes.

"Pelletti?!" said Steward as he noticed him enter.

"Fuck you Chief," snapped Steve. "And fuck you too, Captain Dunn."

The whites of Dunn's eyes almost glowed against the crimson blood that completely covered his face. This was his grand finale, and he was honored to see all the players in his elaborate game.

"You've never lived until you've seen the life leave another human being," recited Dunn.

Dunn's eyes were wide open as he pulled the trigger.

The chaos had died down as the ambulance lights flickered and flashed red spotlights all over the property. Crime-scene techs scoured the barn area while uniformed officers finished outlining the perimeter with yellow crime scene tape. The coroner's van had just arrived when Tate was getting the wound on his forearm attended to by a paramedic. The Mayor, Chief Steward, Steve and Ramon were in a heated discussion next to the ambulance.

"I asked him to come," snapped the Mayor.

"He's suspended," shot back Steward. "You should have consulted me."

"He's here for a reason, Chief," confessed the Mayor.

"Chief Steward," announced Steve, "you're under arrest."

"What?" responded Steward. "What the hell's going on?"

"You knowingly broke your oath by withholding crucial evidence in one of the biggest cases in the city's history," continued Steve. "Evidence that could have helped capture The Eye years earlier."

"That's fuckin' awesome, bro," gushed Ramon.

"I thought we had a deal after the briefing!" Steward yelled at the Mayor.

"I'm sorry, Phil," said the Mayor.

"Your hands are filthy in this too, asshole," explained Steward. "You knew more than we did."

"Don't worry, I will take my own responsibility," assured the Mayor as he glanced at Tate.

Two uniformed officers walked the Chief to an awaiting black suburban. Every officer and crime-scene tech stopped what they were doing, and they reacted to the arrest of the city's highest-ranking police official.

Mayor Villanueva approached Tate and pulled him to the side.

"I'm really sorry Tate," offered the Mayor. "Thanks for honoring my request."

"I held up my end of the bargain," stated Tate. "Now you hold up yours."

The two men shook hands. The Mayor headed for his black Denali that had just arrived. Ramon and Steve stood next to Tate as the Mayor was ushered into the backseat.

"You went through some shit, bro," complimented Ramon. "The dumbwaiter shit was fresh."

"Not my choice," replied an exhausted Tate.

"You okay?" asked Steve.

"I need a few stitches," replied Tate, "but I'll be back in the water in a few days."

All the men turned and watched as The Eye's body was removed from the barn on a gurney. The yellow body bag had traces of Dunn's blood that had seeped through the lining. It was a surreal ending to a case that haunted each one of them in various ways, from finding the truth to hiding secrets.

Sheila Walker smiled at the guys and gave a little wave as she followed the gurney to the coroner's van.

"I'm sorry ... about everything, man," acknowledged Steve.

Ramon took the apology as a sign to give the former partners a little privacy.

"It's okay," replied Tate as he felt his ribs.

"No, I should've had your back," offered Steve.

"Thanks for taking the heat for my phone calls," acknowledged Tate. "It wouldn't have come to this if Dunn knew about the calls."

"I knew you were on to something," confessed Steve. "Things weren't adding up."

"It went high," informed Tate. "All the way to the Mayor. It was bigger than you."

There was an awkward silence between the two of them. It reminded Tate of a struggle between two men who didn't relish in showing emotions. Who was going to break first?

"Hey," called Steve as he gave Tate a strong handshake. "You did Jack proud."

Tate accepted his handshake and ultimately pulled him in for a hug. The men embraced with thoughts of Jack on their minds.

"Get a fuckin' room, bros," interrupted Ramon. "But he might charge you and shit. How much do you charge, bro?"

"Knock it off, Ramon," quipped Steve.

"But he's my hero and shit," explained Ramon.

Tate made a commitment to himself that he would always have Jack's back and do anything in his power to avenge his death. It took eight long years to finally find the truth, but he was ready to start living life again.

"How'd you pull this off?" asked Steve. "How'd you know Dunn would show up early?"

"I know everything," informed Tate. "Right down to the killer's identity and everyone's involvement, including yours, Mister Mayor."

"What do you want?" pleaded the Mayor. "How can I make this go away?"

"You're gonna call a briefing," ordered Tate. "Tell everyone you have a tip that I'm at the old cabin. Organize a raid at 10:00 p.m. Make sure Steve Pelletti is with you."

"Then what?" asked the Mayor.

"You let me handle it from there," responded Tate.

"What about me?" asked the Mayor.

"You resign," advised Tate. "Effective tomorrow. Call it personal reasons. Need to spend more time with the family. Whatever."

"You giving me up to the D.A.?" questioned the Mayor who rubbed his aching temples.

"No," conceded Tate. "You follow through with your end of the bargain and you stay out of jail. The guilt you've carried and the end of your political career will be your sentence."

"I'll call for a briefing," conceded the Mayor.

It had been nine days since the incident at the cabin, and this was the first day Tate started feeling like himself again. His wound felt pretty good and with the stitches getting removed earlier that morning, he'd be ready to hit the surf at sunrise. Rita had summoned him into the office for some important reason. He thought she was just trying to get him out of the house, but he intended to run some errands anyway so it wasn't an inconvenience to swing by.

Mayor Villanueva ultimately resigned and pulled out of the election. Chief Steward was relinquished of his duties but didn't go quietly. He blew the whistle on the Mayor and the police department's mishandling of The Eye case over the last eight years. The fact that he praised Tate and his efforts to re-open the case seven years earlier was the most amusing irony to everything. Really? Tate was enemy number one yet Steward used his knowledge of Tate's efforts to leverage his testimony against the Mayor. The district attorney's office was now investigating the timeline of what and when the Mayor knew anything. He would probably be brought up on charges. Tate held his promise that he wouldn't seek assistance or notify the D.A.'s office about Villanueva, but he couldn't speak for Steward — that was on him.

Steve Pelletti was the true winner in the scandal. His efforts to seek the truth above political and departmental pressure had him in line for a promotion to Captain. Tate felt he truly deserved the opportunity.

Unfortunately, Tate's personal life took a huge hit. He had hoped that Nicole would listen to his reasoning for making sure she was safe from any possible attack from The Eye. She barely took his phone calls, and he realized the entire incident was a lot to handle for a 27-year-old in a relatively new relationship. The word "exclusive" never came up in their courtship even though he knew that's what she expected. Even if she did get past it — he had the whole gigolo whopper to hit her with too.

Tate would respect her wishes to leave her alone and give her time. He realized at his age that was the kiss of death. Some things people just couldn't get past. He didn't know who was more upset about the breakup — Nicole or her Dad. Her Dad thanked Tate for keeping her safe and having her delivered to his home out of caution.

Rita met Tate in the parking lot with a grin as wide as Texas on her face. When he considered how much she risked and put on the line to make sure he proved his innocence — it made him appreciate her as a true friend and confidant. It also conjured up questions about her past, and how she was able to find out the information that ultimately assisted in his escape and his vengeance over The Eye. Maybe another day.

He hopped out of his Jeep and met her with a warm embrace.

"So great to have you back, sugar," cooed Rita.

"Good to be back," agreed Tate. "So, what's so important?"

Rita glanced at her watch and watched as a black custom Chevy Suburban pulled into the parking lot behind them.

"Y'all have perfect timing," stated Rita.

The Suburban pulled up next to them, and Jonathan Harper exited the vehicle. He was dressed in casual cotton slacks and a short-sleeved button-up — a far cry from the Italian suits he wore on a daily basis when he conducted business. There wasn't even the Bluetooth that was normally permanently attached to his ear.

"Tate," called out Harper. "I wanted to take this opportunity to thank you for finding out who killed my daughter."

"I'm really sorry for your loss, Mr. Harper," consoled Tate.

"Please call me Jonathan," requested Harper.

"What can I do for you?" asked Tate.

"You've already done it," stated Harper. "An agreement is an agreement — and I always keep my word."

Jonathan Harper handed Tate an envelope. Tate accepted it and glanced at Rita with a confused expression on his face.

"What's this?" asked Tate.

"You didn't tell him?" Harper asked Rita.

She shook her head while Tate opened the envelope. It was a cashier's check for $100,000.

"What the ... who the ... ?" rambled a speechless Tate.

"Thanks again," added Harper as he shook Tate's hand and drew him close for a man-hug. "I have to get to my jet. I'm looking to invest in a water purifying system in Sudan. It was one of Grace's passions. She bugged me every year."

Jonathan Harper couldn't finish his sentence and struggled to fight back tears. He excused himself and crawled back into the Suburban and was driven away.

"A hundred grand?" exclaimed Tate. "How in the world? What agreement, Rita?"

"Go ahead and do it," ordered Harper into the phone.

Rita pulled into a parking garage and killed her headlights as she drove to the 4th level and looked for spot 426. That was her instructions. She spotted the black 500 series Mercedes parked in the corner. She scanned the 4th floor and felt satisfied — no security cameras. The open parking space next to the 'Benz signified parking spot 427. She pulled into the spot but couldn't see through the windows of the Mercedes because the window tint was practically black. When she turned off her ignition, the back passenger door opened for her.

She slid into the backseat and found herself sitting next to Arthur Stein, Jonathan Harper's attorney.

"Mr. Harper is no longer comfortable with the 'investhigathion'," admitted Arthur in his severe lisp. "He 'feelsth' that the 'focusth' isn't on catching Grace's murderer but on protecting people's reputations and catching Mr. Holloway at any 'costh'."

"Cut to the cheese Mr. Stein," urged Rita. "I'm in the middle of aiding and abetting the most wanted fugitive in the country n'all."

"Mr. Harper would like to pay for Tate's 'servicesths'," offered Arthur. "If he finds the murderer, he will pay him $50,000."

"Let me get this straight, sugar pants," suggested Rita. "When Tate finds the real killer, you'll pay him $100,000?"

Arthur smirked at her sassiness and commitment to Tate.

"Yesth," he stated. One-hundred-thousand; but if the 'evidensth' points at Tate — we obviously have no deal."

Tate and Rita stood in the parking lot and watched Harper's Suburban pull out into traffic on his way to the airport. Tate was in a state of shock.

"I don't even know what to say," commented Tate.

"You can pay off your boat loan n'all and not have to crash with me, sugar," joked Rita.

"I wouldn't have been able to pay you rent," laughed Tate.

"Oh, I would have taken it out of your ass, sugar," laughed Rita.

Tate held up the envelope and looked into Rita's eyes.

"Thank you," said Tate with a genuineness that made Rita's eyes start to well up. "I will never forget this."

They embraced for a long minute before Rita broke the uneasiness. She wasn't a big fan of the emotional shit.

"Bonnie called," notified Rita. "Now that you're innocent n'all, the thought of you being a fugitive turned her on. She's willing to pay triple n'all if you dress in a prison jumpsuit. She wants to be the naughty prison warden."

"I have to make sure Nicole's stuff is boxed and ready for her friend to pick up," stated Tate. "Bonnie's the last thing on my mind right now."

"I'm sorry she won't see you, sugar," consoled Rita. "I know you cared for her n'all."

"Nothing says I love you like a fake abduction and the revelation that your boyfriend is a male prostitute," said Tate.

"You only went along with the abduction 'cause you wanted her safe n'all," reminded Rita. "Course the other thing, that's a tough one."

"You think?" joked Tate.

"Her dad understood," offered Rita.

"I wasn't dating her dad," responded Tate as he walked away from her and headed for his Jeep.

"Think about it! Triple your rate!" she yelled after him.

He stopped at his Jeep and turned back toward Rita and flashed one of his trademark smirks.

"Triple?" yelled Tate.

"Three grand!" she responded.

"Make it five and I'll put on the Batman suit underneath the prison orange," he hollered back.

Tate secured the surfboard on the roof of his Jeep and hopped inside. He smiled at Rita as he drove off to the marina.

Curt Munson stood at a makeshift laboratory he had constructed in his basement. He grabbed the small tube to the intravenous line that protruded from the embalming fluid dispenser. He blew into the tube to eliminate air bubbles and methodically attached it to a large glass container that was covered with a white sheet. He turned the switch to a motor and the liquid began filtering through the I.V. line and into the glass container. He was humming the Tyrone Davis classic, *"What Goes up, Must Come Down."*

He danced a two-step, twirled in a circle, and then turned the flow-valve to the embalming fluid to maximum.

"Daddy," called out a young girl from upstairs. "Time for dinner!"

"Okay, sweetie," answered Munson. "Be up in a few minutes."

His lab jacket snagged on the sheet that covered the glass container, and he unknowingly pulled it to the floor. He turned the light off and headed toward the stairwell that led to the garage. He stopped and noticed that the sheet had fallen to the ground.

He walked back over and picked up the sheet. He shook it out to eliminate the dust particles and folded it to the perfect size to cover the glass container. The glow from his computer screen revealed a human head floating in liquid.

He spread the sheet over the container and pushed the table that contained the head toward a thick iron door in the back of the basement. He pulled the locking mechanism and the sound of the door echoed as the air-seal was broken and it slid open. He wheeled the table inside the vault while still humming the Tyrone Davis classic. Over his shoulder, on a bulletin board, various photos of Nicole Stafford adorned the vault's walls.

VENGEANCE IS NOW

THE END

VENGEANCE IS NOW

THE TATE HOLLOWAY SERIES

SNEAK PEAK

"It had been an emotional eight-month rollercoaster for Nicole Stafford, 28, since her ex-boyfriend, Tate Holloway, was the most wanted fugitive in the country back in San Diego. It wasn't the fact that he was wrongly accused and successfully cleared his name; it was Tate's little secret that was revealed and became public knowledge. He was moonlighting as a male escort during the same time they were together. Not just emotionally together but physically together, and the thought of him crawling off one of his clients and then sliding into bed with her made her nauseous. It would make any woman nauseous.

Moving back to the Phoenix area with her Dad was the smartest and most therapeutic decision she could have made. Transferring hospitals was simple, and it allowed her to save money and reconnect with old friends. The St. Joseph's Hospital and Medical Center wasn't as large as Scripps Mercy in San Diego, but she loved the idea of helping people in her hometown. She also adored the emergency room staff she worked with. All pluses compared to the arrogant and phony physicians that she despised at Scripps.

She locked her car in the staff parking lot and headed for the hospital entrance when she heard her name being called.

"Nicole," hollered a man who approached her. He was in his mid-40's and wore navy blue slacks, a white dress shirt and gray tie. He was a decent enough looking man who had a leather attaché case slung over his shoulder.

"So nice to see you," said the out-of-breath man. "How have you been?"

"I'm so sorry," confessed Nicole, "but I'm drawing a blank."

"Curt Munson," he said a little surprised that she didn't remember him. "I was a pharmaceutical rep at Scripps."

She still couldn't place his face or name as she glanced at her watch to see if she was running late – and she was.

"I didn't deal with many reps, Kirk," she admitted. "Please forgive me."

"It's Curt," stated Munson with a forced smile on his face. "We had a conversation, and I just wanted to say hello."

"Well, hello again," offered Nicole as she headed for the hospital entrance. "I'm sorry but I'm running late."

Curt Munson was left alone on the front walkway as Nicole disappeared into the hospital. He looked irritated. His jaw was clinched so tightly, his jawbone protruded from his cheek. This was not the reunion he anticipated.

Her heart pounded after listening to the voicemail. She had left one of her private cell phones at the office all weekend and didn't realize it until 10 minutes ago. She tried to take a deep breath to relax and clear her head, but the thumping that emitted from her chest made her ears ring. It also made her dizzy.

He had been missing for almost 48 hours without as much as a phone call and no one had heard from him until now. She had made that assumption based on the repeated phone calls to her office that were intended for her nephew. She knew it was a bad idea to give him a summer internship, but she really wanted to help him out. It was her younger brother's kid after all. Why wouldn't she? Her office handled high-security clearance military contracts. Her clients appreciated her candor and sense of humor, but most importantly — her discretion. Rita Jones had taught her that.

Her job was not to judge or filter her clients' relationships with high-ranking military personnel or lobbyists who supported certain congressman's agendas. Her job was to ensure that the contracts between those corporations and entities were executed to the letter of the law. That her work stood up to any possible investigation or congressional hearing brought about by some hotshot politician who wanted a slap on the back from Chris Matthews on *Hardball*. She earned her salary based on her ability to make sure her clients didn't end up on a United States Department of Defense Fraud Report. That is what her clients expected. Nothing more, nothing less. War was great business for them.

Jesse was different. He was too much of a conspiracy theorist. She thought his blog was entertaining so she encouraged him to get an internship with *The Seattle Examiner*. He could better utilize their contacts if he truly wanted to pursue a career as an investigative journalist; but, he insisted on working with her.

"I can easily get you on at the *Examiner*," she promised. "Not a problem at all."

Jesse Moreno was head and shoulders brighter than most college seniors his age. He was tall, athletic, and his dark locks and big brown eyes made girl's knees buckle since he was in junior high school. She had witnessed it before. Her younger brother — Jesse's father — had the same effect on teenyboppers some 30 years ago.

"You negotiated Haliburton's contracts in Iraq, right?" questioned Jesse.

"Among others, yes," she agreed.

"There you go, why would I want to write obituaries or report on a missing cat when I could learn more from you?" he asked.

"This is a law firm," she warned him, "not The *Huffington Post*."

"I realize that," he said. "This will give me the chance to know if I want to go to law school or not."

Now she wished she would have pushed him in the other direction. He was reviewing some paperwork that dealt with a contractor who was hired to strengthen security at the United States Embassy in North Africa — specifically the Bamako-Mali Embassy. He was spending more time than usual on his review, but she never thought anything about it.

She decided to listen to the voice mail one more time, "Hey it's me. Um, I found something ... um, it's weird. You might want to check it out. Um, I'm going to come by your place now."

That was two days ago, and he never showed up. "What did he find?" she asked herself over and over. Due to the sensitivity of her clients and her dealings with clandestine and sensitive military information, she realized she had to make a call to a trusted friend before she could contact the local law enforcement agencies.

"Hi Rita, it's Bonnie," she said.

"Well hello there, sugar," answered Rita. "You comin' to town and all? Craving some naked Tate-ness?"

"I need to hire Tate as a private investigator," stated an anxious Bonnie. "I need him to help find my nephew."

VENGEANCE IS NOW

ABOUT THE AUTHOR

Photo by Brad Treadwell

Scott D. Roberts is the writer, producer, and co-director of the award-winning documentary, "Gas Hole," narrated by Peter Gallagher. He is also the executive producer, writer, and co-host of the monthly segment, "Gas Hole of the Month" which airs on FSTV. He wrote, produced, and/or directed two reality pilots in the last three years, "Giving, Celebrity Style," starring Melinda Clarke ("Nikita," "The O.C.") and "Ted & Jason: Building an Empire," featuring the hair stylist to the stars, Ted Gibson. He's written over 50 screenplays and TV shows during a career that spans over 20 years and has had his projects optioned and/or developed by New Line, Warner Brothers, Paramount, MGM, EUE/Screen Gems and Columbia. He is excited about his first novel, *Vengeance is Now,* and sharing his writing style with an entirely new audience.